DNA
The Alex Cave Series book 6

Written by
James M. Corkill.

Copyright 2017 James M. Corkill.
All rights reserved.

The characters and events in this book are fictitious. Any similarity to real persons, living or dead is coincidental and not intended by the author.

Chapter 1

SALT LAKE CITY, UTAH. DISCOVER NEW ANCESTORS FACILITY:

Zane Kinkaid was alone in his advanced genetics lab, studying the results from a DNA sample extracted from a twenty-five-thousand-year-old tooth found at a dig site in Colorado. When he saw the final results, he smiled to himself. "Well, Ms. Austin. Your discovery is going to change the scientific community's theory of our evolution."

He turned off his equipment and tossed the printed report into his briefcase, then grabbed the handle and his car keys as he headed out of the room. In the parking lot, he hesitated before climbing into his vehicle, wondering if he should call the archeologist to let her know he is on his way to her dig site. He grinned and climbed in. "I hope you like surprises, Mya."

***

SEATTLE, WASHINGTON:

His trip home had turned out to be the opposite of what he had expected, and ex-CIA operative turned geophysicist Alex Cave was reading a magazine in a business class seat on the aircraft, hoping to take his mind off recent events with his nephew, Derek. A rift had formed between them, and it was like a dagger through his heart. He looked up when a woman with short, dark hair sat down in the seat beside him. He gave her a courteous nod hello before returning to the article and moved his leg out of the way when she bent down to shove a small bag under the forward seat.

Mya Austin straightened up and looked over at the ruggedly handsome man with wavy black hair sitting beside her. "I'm sorry about that. They never give us enough room."

It was the first time he could study her features, and other than her soft hazel eyes, she had an unremarkable face and her tan skin was slightly weathered from being outdoors a lot. He guessed her age to be around forty. "I know what you mean."

He continued reading an article in the magazine. It was an interview with the owner of the Discover New Ancestors program, and the geneticist Zane Simon had made some incredible discoveries. Alex thought about his last mission, where he had become familiar with some aspects of genetics, and found the interview intriguing.

He hadn't heard the pilot welcoming them aboard or the safety instructions, but looked up when the plane began moving. Once it took off, he returned to the article until he noticed Mya trying to look out the window, which was even with his head. He set the magazine on his lap and leaned back so she could see.

She smiled at the man and then leaned over his lap. "I'm sorry again. I was just trying to see Mount Rainier."

He could not move back any further, and her face was only inches from his. "That's fine."

She turned her head and could see deep into the stranger's dark blue eyes. "Hi. I'm Mya Austin."

He noticed a few flakes of gold in Mya's hazel irises. "It's nice to meet you. I'm Alex Cave."

She turned her face back to the window. When the mountain disappeared from view, she leaned back in her seat. "Thanks."

He noticed the medallion hanging from a beaded leather necklace around Mya's neck. "Is that Sioux Indian?"

"Yes, I'm an archeologist for the Sioux Nation, and I'm currently working at a dig site near Fort Collins, Colorado."

"You're a long way from home. What brings you out this way?"

"A friend of mine at the university was helping me with some research."

Alex knew he couldn't tell Mya he worked at Area 51, but didn't want to lie. "I used to be a geophysics instructor at a small college in Montana, and now I'm a NASA consultant."

When she heard he worked for NASA, Mya wondered if this might be a fateful encounter. "I've just made a discovery in a cave on tribal land that will change the world."

He could see the excitement and sincerity in her eyes. "How is that?"

"If the local tribe is correct, what they call the vanishing stone should appear at the dig site any day now."

"I'm sorry. Did you say vanishing stone?"

"Yes, that's what they call it. Inside the cave is a drawing of a box-shaped object with two human figures standing beside it. According to the legend and cave drawings, the vanishing stone magically appeared above the cave twenty-five thousand years ago. The visitors left two new people with the tribe, and promised to return in exactly twenty-five thousand years then left in the vanishing stone. That's this year, Alex."

"How can you be so precise?"

"I've read about similar drawings in caves all over the world, and carbon dating of the various mediums used for the images indicate all the drawings were made twenty-five thousand years ago." Mya could tell she had his attention. "Since you work for NASA, is there any chance there might be a satellite taking pictures of that part of the United States?"

"That's not my area of expertise."

She wasn't about to give up. "All I need is an overhead view of the dig site."

"Well, a friend of mine might get you some pictures. Give me your contact information and I'll see what I can do."

She smiled, reached into her purse, and handed him a card. "You can have them sent to that email address. I'm usually at the dig site, so use the mobile phone number if you want to call me."

He was intrigued and decided to help her out. "All right, Miss Austin. I'll try to arrange for you to get some satellite images."

She smiled. "Thank you."

When Mya brought out an electronic tablet, Alex returned to reading the article, and during the rest of the flight, said little to her until they got off the plane in Las Vegas and he held out his hand. He hadn't realized how tall she was and estimated her to be about five-foot-nine. "It was nice meeting you, Mya. It shouldn't take long to get you those images."

She accepted his hand. "I appreciate it. Listen, since you're a geophysicist, would you like to come out to Colorado and see the cave? Maybe you can verify the age of the rock strata."

"No promises, but that might be interesting."

"I'll look for you." She indicated a walkway. "My flight home is down there."

"I'm afraid mine's the other way." He turned and headed along the concourse.

Mya stared after Alex until he disappeared around a corner, then turned and hurried toward her departure area. She stood in front of the large window and stared at the plane rolling across the tarmac, hoping her being seated next to Alex was a sign she was onto something big.

***

Alex left the air terminal and took a taxi to a remote hangar on the far end of the tarmac. He showed his identification to a guard at the gate who let him through to board a special plane. When he stepped into the cabin, he was the only passenger and set his luggage bag in a rack, then sat in a chair forward of the wing.

One of the pilots came out of the cockpit and pressed a button to bring up the stairs, then closed the door and gave him a nod before returning, and then the aircraft began moving. He stared out the window as the plane taxied past the terminal, and saw Mya outlined in the window frame, and for a moment, had a strange sensation she was staring at him as he moved along the tarmac. When she was out of sight, he returned to the article about the Discover New Ancestors article.

Chapter 2

GROOM LAKE, NEVADA:

The sun was dropping over the horizon when the private jet stopped in front of the small air terminal. Alex opened the side door, lowered the stairs, and then grabbed his tote bag as he headed down the stairs. At the bottom, a tall man with shaggy blond hair and dark green eyes stood grinning up at him. He and his best friend Okawna had shared several hair-raising adventures together and were bonded closer than brothers.

"Hey, Alex. Have a nice flight?"

Alex smiled back and slapped his friend on the back. "It was interesting. I guess you got a call as well?"

"Yeah, I got here about half an hour ago. Jadin is waiting for us inside the terminal. She was upset about something, but wouldn't tell me what's going on until you got here."

The two of them sauntered over to the security station, and once Alex cleared the checkpoint, he saw a petite, red-haired woman waiting for them on the other side of the room. He could tell by Jadin Avery's posture something was bothering her, and hurried over. "What's going on?"

"A woman named Holly Blake arrived earlier this morning and moved into one of the offices. She wants to meet with us right away, and David is already waiting for us in the conference room."

Alex walked out of the building with his team members, and then they climbed into a waiting golf cart. Okawna drove, so Alex turned in his seat to look over his shoulder at Jadin sitting in the back seat. "Do you have any idea who she is?"

Jadin leaned forward between Alex and Okawna. "No, but she had the right security clearance to get through the checkpoint."

"Did you come from the Jet Propulsion Lab in Pasadena?"

"Yes, it keeps me busy between missions."

Okawna drove around the corner of a building and glanced over his shoulder at Jadin. "Did she tell you what the meeting was about?"

"No, she wanted to talk to all of us at the same time."

Okawna parked in front of the main building for this area of the base, and then they all climbed out and entered through the front door. They continued along the hallway to the secure conference room, where Alex said hello to David while holding the door open for Jadin and Okawna to come in. When he started to close the door, a small woman pushed past him into the room. "I'm sorry. I didn't see you."

The woman stared up at the man with wavy black hair. "I know, Alex." She turned to Okawna, Jadin, and David. "I'm Holly Blake, and I'll be running your missions from now on."

Alex looked at his friends, who were staring at him with questioning expressions, and then he turned to Holly. "I thought someone here at the base would take over for Director Heinz."

"Director of National Security Martin Donner asked for my help."

Alex crossed his arms as he locked stares with Holly. "I don't know you, and Martin never mentioned it to me. When did this happen?"

"It became official two hours ago, but I was already on my way here." She sat down in one of the chairs and looked at the young man with short brown hair and brown eyes. "David? Let the Director know we're ready." She noticed David's hesitation to follow her orders as he stared up at Alex for approval. She knew this would happen, and it didn't bother her.

Alex thought Holly's demeanor was as curt as her attire. Just plain tan slacks and shirt. She had straight shoulder-length brown hair with a few strands of gray mixed in, and wide-set hazel eyes. He looked over at David, who was waiting for his okay. "See if Donner is available."

A moment later, Alex saw Donner's image appear on the screen. As usual, the Director was wearing a plain white shirt open at the collar with the sleeves rolled up past his elbows. "Hello, Director. I wish you would have told me about this earlier."

"I know, but Henry's death was rather sudden, and I had to move quickly on an urgent matter. I didn't want some desk jockey with no fieldwork experience in charge of your operations."

Alex wondered what type of fieldwork Holly had done, but decided to save the question for later. "Why the urgency, Martin?"

"Our new President doesn't know all the details about your missions, and I need some time before I tell him we have a working spaceship. Henry did a good job, but as you've already proven, things can change in a hurry. Sometimes I need plausible deniability, especially when I'm talking to the politicians, and Holly is the only person I can count on when things get bad. I'm sorry I can't talk longer, but I need to go. Believe me, Alex. You can trust Holly."

When Donner's image vanished, Alex looked at his new boss. "I guess we've gotten off to a rough start, Director Blake."

Holly grinned at Alex. "Understandable. I don't care for titles, so call me Holly." She reached into her pocket, brought out a small digital storage device, and then slid it across the table to David. "Bring this up on the monitor and you'll get a better idea of what we'll be dealing with."

Holly waited while David did as instructed, and a moment later, the monitor showed a hazy image of the moon. "You've probably heard of MUFON, the Mutual UFO Network. They claim it's a picture of your spacecraft approaching this base. We know it was only a reflection of light off the ship, but it was enough to go viral on social media. From this moment on, if the cloak is not working, the ship doesn't leave." Holly stood and looked at David. "I have a feeling we're going to need it soon, so get it working as soon as possible. The rest of you do whatever you like for the next few days until I contact you."

When Holly opened the door and stepped out of the room, Jadin leaned back in her chair. "Wow. That was intense. I wonder what she did for fieldwork."

Alex was thinking the same thing. "I guess we'll find out, eventually. By the way. If you have time, I need a favor." He explained the situation with Mya and gave her the business card he had received on the airplane. "Could you set it up to send her updated images whenever we have a camera in range?"

"I'm sure I can arrange something. Well, I don't see any reason to wait around here, so I'll head back to JPL. What are your plans, Alex?"

"I'm curious about something, and Mya invited me to her dig site. If I leave early tomorrow morning, I should be there by late afternoon."

Okawna was glad Alex was finally interested in a new relationship, especially since the breakup with his cousin two years ago had hurt him deeply. "I think I'll head home and see my family until Mike needs me back on the Mystic, or Holly needs us."

Alex stood. "I'd better call Mya and let her know I'm coming."

Jadin watched Alex leave the room, then grabbed Okawna's arm before he got up. "Did Alex tell you much about this mystery woman?"

"Enough to know he seems interested in something she found at her dig site. I guess she's a Native American archaeologist."

"Did he say if she was attractive?"

Okawna shrugged his shoulders. "Nope. Why are you so interested in what she looks like?"

"Just curious, is all. It's a woman thing, so I'm sure you wouldn't understand." She turned to David. "How is the work on the ship coming?"

"Well, I'm having an issue with the artificial intelligence. I guess I shouldn't have called it a circuit board. I think I need to do a little sucking up so I can find out what's wrong with the cloaking mechanism. If I didn't know better, I'd think I hurt its feelings. Not that I'm insensitive or anything."

She winked at him. "No, you're right. I'll bet you hurt its feelings. Bring it some flowers. I know it always helps with apologies."

David stared at her. "It's a spaceship, not a woman. Flowers won't mean anything to it."

When Jadin smiled and walked out the door, he hurried to catch up with her. "It's just a spaceship."

Chapter 3

THE DIG SITE. THIRTY-NINE MILES WEST OF FORT COLLINS, COLORADO:

Alex drove his rental SUV off the highway onto a two-lane road, where the aroma of dry grass and evergreens streamed in through the open windows as he drove through a sparse forest. He passed a nearly deserted campground just before the asphalt was replaced with gravel, then the road meandered back and forth up the side of the mountain. He slowed down as he drove past an opened steel gate and entered a narrow canyon filled with massive granite boulders, then the road made a sharp right turn, and he saw two vehicles parked near a large tent with screened windows.

He parked and climbed out, then strolled around the structure to find the door. When he reached the other side of the tent, there was a seventy foot wide oval-shaped meadow. He heard soft snoring and turned to see a Native American man sitting in a reclined chair, with a camera drone and controller on the ground beside him. From this vantage point, he had a beautiful view of the side of the mountain, and there appeared to be a flat area partway up, which was unusual for that type of rock formation.

Not wanting to disturb the man, he looked inside the tent through one of the windows and saw three tables with artifacts and some electronic equipment in the large room. He didn't see anyone inside and was about to walk over to wake the sleeping man when he heard a car door slam shut in the parking lot. A slender man studying a sheet of paper suddenly rushed past the corner of the tent, oblivious to his presence, and Alex cleared his throat to get the man's attention. When the man stopped and turned to look at him, he thought he looked vaguely familiar. "Excuse me. I'm looking for Mya Austin."

The man was cautious and didn't offer an introduction. "You came to the right place. What can I do for you?"

"I'm Alex Cave, a geophysicist from Montana. She asked for my help at this dig site."

"Oh, that's right. She told me you were on your way here. She made an amazing discovery. Let's go."

When Zane hurried away, Alex followed a few steps behind him, and after several turns through fractured rock formations, they entered a small clearing, about fifteen-feet below the flat area on the side of the mountain he had seen from the meadow. They wandered along a string-lined trail on the outer edges of a twenty-foot square excavation, where he saw Mya kneeling over something at the bottom of a five-foot deep pit. He saw she was wearing a tank-top shirt and shorts, and was engrossed with something at the bottom. When she looked up and waved, he saw swirls of dark hair growing from her armpits and wondered if she shaved her legs and waved at her before following Zane down into the excavated area.

Mya stood and reached out to shake Alex's hand. "Your timing is perfect. We may have discovered something that will change our understanding about the evolution of humans."

When Alex noticed the long hair on Mya's legs, he stifled a smirk and quickly looked down at the remains of a human skeleton protruding through one section of the dirt floor. It appeared to be wrapped in cloth, which seemed to be disintegrating around the bones. "What am I looking at?"

Mya had noticed Alex's reaction to her leg hair. "According to our estimation of when Homo Sapiens first arrived in North America, this woman is far more developed than normal evolution would have allowed. She was also seven inches taller than most humans were at the time." She saw the piece of paper in Zane's hand. "Well, Zane? What did you find out?"

Zane smiled at her. "The DNA from the tooth was viable. She has zero percentiles Neanderthal, European, Eurasian, or African DNA markers. That means not all of us are genetically connected back to Africa. Also, carbon dating indicates the body is close to twenty-five thousand-years-old."

The mention of DNA jogged Alex's memory. "You're that Zane? The geneticist?"

"That's correct. As you know, the Discover New Ancestors program I started several years ago has given me access to an enormous amount of genetic material. I've also been working with the GEN9 DNA Synthesis Lab in Cambridge, Massachusetts, and we were able to isolate what I named the GC117 gene. Only a small percentage of the samples sent to me from around the world had that genetic marker, and I found that same gene in this woman. By the way, the samples containing the GC117 gene came from some of the smartest people on Earth."

Mya stared down at the woman. "If this information is correct, a new lineage was brought here to North America twenty-five thousand years ago. It is as if she came out of the vanishing stone, just like the legend."

Alex remembered her talking about the drawings she had found when they first met on the plane. "Can I see the cave illustrations?"

"Yes, they're a short distance away. Follow me."

Alex followed Mya out of the pit and along a trail through a maze of large boulders to a fifteen-foot wide opening. He noticed the trail continued up the side of the mountain as he followed her into the cave.

Just inside the entrance, Mya stopped and grabbed two battery-powered headlamps and handed one to Alex before sliding the elastic strap of the other one over her head. "Out of respect to the native tribe's beliefs, I didn't run any electrical cords into the cave, so you'll need that to see what I'm about to show you."

Alex slipped the elastic band over his head, turned it on, and followed her further inside. They stopped when they reached a thirty-foot diameter room with a high ceiling and then continued across to a mural on the wall. He studied the illustrations, but didn't see the square object she had mentioned. "Is this the drawing?"

"No, those are less than a hundred-years-old. Follow me."

Together, they made their way to the back of the cave and an opening in the wall. As Alex stepped through a five-foot wide gap in the rock, he noticed the remains of a clay-like material attached to the stone surface. "Was there a wall here at one time?"

"Yes. The tribe thought it was just clay plastered on the surface, but a mild tremor six months ago caused it to crack open. They pulled the rest of it down, and after they saw what I'm about to show you, I was called in to research this new cave."

Alex followed Mya into an eight-foot wide room and looked at the paintings. On one side was a drawing of a square block with two human figures standing in front of it, and studied the symbols on the wall. "Do you know what these smaller pictures represent?"

"Yes, they tell the story of the vanishing stone magically appearing above this cave. According to stories passed down through generations of Native Americans living near this cave, the stone should appear sometime this year."

"On the plane, you said you found more of these drawings."

"That's right, but only in European countries. This is the first one found here in North America."

***

Zane remained in the pit when Mya and Alex left, then knelt close to study the jawbone and upper palate of the female skeleton. "You must have known about oral hygiene." He looked up when he heard a drone flying overhead, then climbed out of the pit and ran back to the meadow. The drone suddenly died and crashed, and when the man near the tent pointed up at the side of the mountain, he ran to the entrance of the cave and cupped his hands around his mouth to holler inside. "Mya! There's something going on above you!"

Zane jogged up a trail along the side of the rock and abruptly stopped in front of a massive twenty-foot square cube. He slowly reached out and placed his finger against the pewter-colored surface, and it was cool and smooth. He pressed his palm against the side and it felt solid, then he tapped his knuckles against it to confirm it was not hollow. He spun around when he heard footsteps and smiled at Mya and Alex. "Here's your vanishing stone."

Mya could not believe her eyes as she slowly moved over to the gray-colored block and turned to look at Alex. "Are you familiar with this type of stone?"

Alex recognized the swirled pewter color of the surface as he moved along the side and around the corner to the front, then looked up at the top. It was made from the same material as other ancient alien artifacts he had discovered, and then he turned to Mya and Zane. "It's not a stone. It's a metal alloy, and it's something you don't want to mess with." He looked at his wristwatch and the numbers were frozen at 5:27 PM. "We need to leave the area immediately."

Zane's mouth hung open for a moment as he stared at Alex. "You can't be serious. This is a monumental discovery, and you don't have the right to make us leave. We need to get a film crew up here to document everything."

"I'm sorry, but that's the way it needs to be."

Zane slapped his palm against the surface of the cube. "You see? There is nothing dangerous here. It appeared out of nowhere, and it has something to do with the GC117 gene. I'm sure of it."

Alex brought out his cellphone, but could not get a signal, and looked at Mya. "I thought you had reception up here."

"I do. Your phone should be working. Do you think it might have something to do with this cube?"

"Possibly. Let's go back down to your campsite and maybe we can call from there."

Zane wasn't about to let the cube out of his sight. "I'll stay here just in case anything changes. Don't forget to bring the video camera. I want to document everything."

Mya smiled at Zane. "I bet you didn't expect this to happen when you arrived."

"Not in my wildest dreams. But let's not allow people to know about this just yet. We don't want a mob of spectators showing up."

Mya pointed to the pickup truck racing out of the parking lot. "This is Indian land, and it won't be long until a lot more of them show up to see the stone. It is part of their history."

Alex looked at both of them. "The people I work with know how to keep a secret, and they are the only ones I trust to deal with this situation. Once I inform them, they'll close off the area."

Zane's hands clenched into fists at his sides. "You're not planning on cutting us out of this discovery, are you?"

Alex stared back at him. "Of course not, but I've learned the hard way an abundance of caution is necessary when dealing with unknown technology, and this certainly qualifies."

Zane let his fingers relax. "Of course."

When Mya gave Alex a nod she agreed with him, he led the way back down the trail. "Your colleague seems to be a little on the demanding side."

"He's not my colleague. I sent a tooth to a university in Utah for analysis and he just showed up."

"How come you're the only one working here?"

"This land belongs to the Native Americans and is sacred ground. I only got permission because I'm half Sioux, and I promised to be respectful of the site. That's one of the reasons the tribe members keep one person living up here at all times."

"To keep an eye on you?"

"Yes, that too, but the main reason is to be here when the stone arrives. That's how certain they were it will be this year, and they were right."

"I'm glad you told me. That will make things more complicated for my people, but we'll do the same. Once we know what we're dealing with, perhaps you can talk to the tribal leaders and get their approval, so we don't have to make a big issue out of this."

When they reached the tent, Alex looked up at the side of the mountain and saw Zane standing in front of the cube, then brought out his phone and looked at the screen. "I still can't get a signal."

Mya reached into her car and brought out a satellite phone. "This should work." She turned it on, but nothing happened. "The stone must be interfering with the reception."

"All right. I'll drive down the mountain until I can get a signal. I'll be back as soon as I can." He heard Zane holler something and looked up at the cube. "What was that?"

Zane cupped his hands around his mouth. "There is something happening up here!"

Alex ran up the path with Mya right behind him. When he reached the top of the trail, he saw Zane lying on his back on the ground. He knelt down beside him to feel for a pulse and check his breathing, and then relaxed and looked up at Mya. "He's just unconscious." He shook the man's shoulder. "Zane? Can you hear me?"

Zane slowly opened his eyes and saw Alex staring down at him. "How long have you been here?"

"We just got here. What happened?"

With Alex's help, Zane slowly sat up. "I have one hell of a headache. I, uh. I heard a voice and saw you looking down at me."

"I was trying to wake you up."

"No, it wasn't your voice. It was someone else. Help me stand up, will you?"

Alex grabbed Zane's hand and hauled him onto his feet, but didn't let go. "How do you feel?"

Zane felt wobbly for a moment, then let go of Alex's hand. "I'm fine."

When Alex looked over at Mya, her eyes suddenly went wide as she looked past him, so he spun around and saw a large opening in the side of the cube, then a man and a woman wearing black one-piece suits stepped out of the opening and stopped in front of him. This was not his first time meeting another race of humans, and when the woman held out her hand, a knot formed in his stomach.

When the stranger didn't accept her hand, the woman smiled. "Hello. You must be Zane's friend, Alex Cave. I'm Vesta." She indicated the man standing beside her. "And this is Paul. It's nice to meet you in person."

Vesta's speech had an odd, stilted accent that was disappearing even as she spoke. It was like she was practicing a new language.

Mya held her hand out to the woman. "Hello, I'm Mya Austin."

Vesta smiled and shook Mya's hand. "Yes, Zane's other friend. It's nice to meet you."

Mya realized this situation was happening just as described in the legend. "Are you the ones who came here twenty-five thousand years ago? Are you from another planet?"

"Yes. We came from another solar system to save some of your species from an extinction level event."

Chapter 4

THE DIG SITE:

Mya closed her mouth. "What do you mean, save our species from extinction?"

"A few minutes ago, Paul formed a mental bond with Zane. We know that you, Alex, are a representative of this nation's government, and we would like you to set up a meeting for us with this world's highest authorities. That's when we'll tell you the details."

Alex had a good idea why Zane had passed out. He was probably being scanned for information, and perhaps under some kind of mind control. Assuming these people had that capability, he could not let them meet the representatives in person. He also noticed the similarity in facial features between Vesta and Paul, wondering if they might be siblings. "That may be difficult because of security issues and time zones. It would be easier if we set up a video conference for a later date." When Vesta didn't answer and appeared to be concentrating on something, he looked at Paul, who had a blank stare as if in another world. "Is that going to be a problem?"

Vesta had her answer. "No, a video conference will be fine."

"All right. I'll set it up, but I'll need to leave this area to get reception. How did you learn to speak English?"

"From the audio and video signals you transmit to the orbiting satellites."

"Is this thing a spaceship?"

"No, our ship is on the far side of your moon. This is a transport module and cannot travel long distances in space."

"Well, your module seems to interfere with our electronic equipment."

"That cannot be helped while Paul is maintaining a mental connection with my crew on our spacecraft."

"So, I take it time is of the essence."

"That is a relative term, Alex, but yes. All we need to know is if your representatives will work with us. If they do not agree, we will leave right away."

"All right. I'll drive down the mountain to make some calls and set up a meeting at a secure location."

Vesta and Paul stared at each other without speaking, and then Vesta looked at Alex. "I'll go with you. Paul will come back and get me when I'm ready."

"All right, but it might take a day or two."

Vesta crossed her arms over her chest and gave Alex a stern expression. "I want to meet with them today. You have three hours to set it up."

Alex stared back evenly. "What's the hurry?"

"I don't think you fully grasp the urgency of your situation, so I'll explain it to you. In a few months, a rogue comet will hit your planet, and I'll explain the details to your leaders. Do you want my help or not?"

Alex stared into Vesta's eyes, and she appeared to be telling the truth, but he had a feeling she was holding something back. Everything about her seemed to rub him the wrong way, but he didn't understand why. He decided for the moment he would give her the benefit of the doubt. "All right. Let's go."

Mya grabbed Alex's arm. "I'm going with you."

"You don't have the proper security clearance for where I'm going. I think you should stay here with Zane."

Vesta got Alex's attention. "Zane must come with us to the meeting. That is why we came to this moment in time. We knew he would be here, and he is an important part of what needs to be done to save some of your people."

Alex felt the strange sensation he always got when something seemed out of place, especially since Zane was a geneticist. "You keep saying you'll save some of our people. Why not all of them?"

"There are concerns I need to discuss with your representatives. You'll find out then."

"All right. There's a place nearby with the facilities we need for the conference call, but with no need for a security clearance. I'm not sure who will join us on such short notice, but I'll set it up with my boss as soon as I get phone reception." He noticed Vesta was concentrating again, then Zane suddenly had a blank stare, and since he was worried about his new friend, he grabbed Zane's shoulder. "Zane? Are you okay?"

Zane blinked a few times and stared at Alex and Mya. "Uh, yeah. I'm okay. I'm ready to go when you are." Alex turned to Mya. "It looks like you're coming with us."

Mya didn't hesitate and stood on her toes to give Alex a quick kiss on his cheek and smiled up at him. "Thank you."

Everyone's attention was drawn to the high-pitched whine of an approaching drone, when suddenly the little craft became silent and fell from the sky. Alex hoped it had not transmitted a recording, but knew the odds were against him.

Vesta indicated for Paul to return to the ship and looked at the trio. "He'll follow us from orbit in the module."

Alex watched Paul enter the ship, then the opening disappeared, and the cube vanished. "That's a nice trick. Why don't you tell me what you were doing in Zane's head this time?"

"I had to be sure I could trust you and Mya. I'm here to help your people, so don't prove me wrong."

Alex remembered the last time he had dealt with a different species of human, but even though she had turned out to be okay, it left him wary. "I won't let anything happen to you. Can you connect with everyone?"

"Not me. Only Paul." She turned to Zane. "He likes you."

Zane wasn't sure if it was good or bad, but didn't like the idea Paul could read his mind at any time. "Tell him the feeling is not mutual, and to stay out of my head."

Vesta turned to Alex. "Your phone should work now."

Alex saw he had a signal, but didn't enter a number. "I need to be alone to make this call, so I'll meet you down in the parking lot."

When the others walked away, Alex pressed the speed dial number of his new main contact for whatever he was doing. "Hey, Holly. You're not going to believe what just happened."

***

FORT COLLINS, COLORADO:

Holly had made arrangements with the commander of the army base for the secure conference call, and Alex was sitting at a table in a room with Vesta, Mya, and Zane, all waiting for someone's image to appear on the large television. Alex heard a knock on the door, so stood to see who it was, and smiled at a young female army private. She entered with a tray of sandwiches and another thermos of coffee, and then set it on the table, and then he thanked her and closed the door behind her.

Vesta picked up a slice of ham and cheese sandwich, stared at it before sniffing it, and then set it back down.

Alex noticed Vesta's reaction. "Each one is different."

"Yes, I see that, but I'm not accustomed to eating this wasteful form of nutrition. We rely on liquid nourishment to reduce the amount of solid matter entering our digestive systems."

Alex grinned at her description. "I could ask them to bring you a protein drink."

"I don't know what it is. I'm fine for the moment."

Alex turned to look at the television when he heard Holly's voice and saw her image. The screen was divided into six sections, each one with a different person looking back at him, and one of them was Martin Donner. "Hello, Director. Who else is joining us for this meeting?"

"On such short notice, we only managed to get these four representatives. We'll record this meeting and show it to our new president and the rest of the world leaders when we're done. Holly will be speaking for the group."

Holly was surprised Donner was letting her run the meeting, and thought perhaps it was because she was the only person who wasn't a politician. She gave Vesta a quick appraisal, and she looked completely human, then the two strangers in the background. "We're ready for you to begin, Alex."

Alex introduced Mya and Zane and then indicated the woman in the black jumpsuit. "This is Vesta, the visitor I told you about."

When Alex indicated for her to proceed, Vesta studied the faces on the television screen. "A large comet is on a collision course with your planet and will impact in one hundred and forty of your days, and this will become a nearly lifeless world for several million years. We came here to offer our help in maintaining your species, and we will accept up to five hundred of your people to be taken to another planet to start a new colony for your race."

Holly already knew about the comet from her conversation with Alex. "Isn't there any way to change its course before it hits us?"

"I'm sorry, but you do not have the technology, and we cannot help you do it. We work with a group of time travelers who saw this coming, so twenty-five hundred years ago, several of our species were deposited here amongst the young societies on this planet. Their purpose was to help advance your technology enough you could stop the comet without our intervention. During what you call the Dark Ages, some of your religious beliefs considered science heresy, and it slowed your technological advancement significantly."

Alex was still curious about why Vesta kept saying just some people. "Why only five hundred of our species?"

"There will be restrictions on who we will accept. That is why we have arrived at this point in time. Zane Kinkaid has collected DNA samples through his program to trace the ancestry of those interested in knowing their background. Even though this is not done for most of the inhabitants, we are hopeful it will be enough to save those of you with the necessary genetic profiles."

Alex didn't like where this was leading. "We call that discrimination, and it's not tolerated on this planet."

"From what we learned from Zane, that's not true. Here is our offer. We are giving some of your species a chance to start a new civilization on a new planet, but there will be hardships to overcome. That is why we can only accept people with specific genetic traits to continue your race. We only have thirteen days before we must leave your planet, so we are not going to discuss this any further unless you unconditionally accept our terms."

Holly knew she was not what men considered attractive and was curious. "What about people with less than a perfect physical appearance?"

"We won't be looking for perfection."

Mya looked down at her tan skinned hands, then at Vesta. "Will heritage be an issue?"

Vesta stared at her for a moment. "What do you mean?"

"I mean a person's ethnic background."

"Of course not, but we can only take intelligent, healthy individuals."

Alex wondered about their space travel capability. "Where is the planet?"

"On the other side of the galaxy. The planet is like this one, but a particular type of radiation killed all the humans. It only attacked certain genes in the human immune system, and that planet still has a viable ecosystem of insects, animals, and consumable vegetation. There is an intact infrastructure, and your ingenuity can change it to suit your needs. I'm sure some of your engineers and technicians will meet the prerequisites to start a new society."

Alex sat with his arms crossed while listening to the prerequisites and realized for all he knew, there was no proof of an impending cataclysmic event. What if these beings are not who they claim to be and have ulterior motives? He noticed Holly was about to speak and held his palm up to her while he looked at Vesta. "You know, this is almost too unbelievable.

I think before we do anything, we verify you are who you claim to be, and you show us proof of this impending comet impact."

Vesta suddenly stood, glaring at Alex. "I can see we are wasting our time trying to save some of your civilization. Take me back to the landing site. We will leave immediately."

Holly agreed with Alex, but wished he had been a little more tactful with his demand. "Vesta, please excuse Alex's bluntness."

Alex stood and stared back at Vesta. "I don't think I'm making an unreasonable request. You want us to start a worldwide panic with no proof. Wouldn't you do the same if you were in our position?"

Vesta grabbed a small notepad and pen off the table, wrote some numbers, and held it out to Alex. "Here are the coordinates of the approaching comet. You have two days to discuss the requirements with your world leaders to decide if you want to proceed without our solution to your annihilation. If you agree to accept our help, you'll need to set up another meeting so I can explain the next steps in the procedure. If the answer is no, we will leave immediately. Now, take me back to the landing site."

Holly knew it was the end of the meeting, but didn't want it to end on a bad note. "Please don't think we don't appreciate everything you're trying to do for us, because we really do. It's just that you sprung this on us so unexpectedly. Alex will take you back to your ship as you requested, and we'll let him know as soon as possible."

Vesta crossed her arms and glared at Alex. "No, I want Zane to take me back." She turned back to Holly. "All communication will go through him until we move forward."

Zane stood and smiled at Vesta. "I would be happy to give you a ride. Let's go."

When Vesta and Zane headed toward the door, Alex moved closer to Mya so he could whisper in her ear. "Could you keep an eye on Zane for me? That Paul person seems to be taking over his mind."

"I was thinking the same thing. Do you really think they're frauds?"

"At this moment, I'm not sure what to think. I've learned not to take someone's word for the truth until they prove otherwise."

"All right. How are you going to find out if Vesta is telling the truth?"

"I have a friend in NASA who can verify her story."

"It looks like Zane and Vesta are ready to leave. I'd better get going."

When the room was empty, Alex looked at the television, where Holly's image was the only one on the screen. "What do you think about all this?"

"I agree with your idea about verifying who they are and where they come from. I want you to stay there with your new friends for now so you can keep us updated on any changes."

"Good. I'll call Jadin in Pasadena. She should be able to verify Vesta's story about an approaching comet, and I'll call you once I have a secure connection set up near the dig site."

When Holly's image vanished from the screen, Alex called Jadin and gave her the coordinates, then strolled out of the room and down the hallway to smile at the young girl who had brought the sandwiches and coffee. "Is there an RV rental nearby?"

***

Vesta remained quiet while the three of them were being driven off base to their vehicles in the visitor's parking lot. Once she and Zane were sitting inside his sedan, she put her hand on his arm when he inserted the key. When Mya's car drove away, she let go of his arm. "I don't need to go back to my ship right away. I told Paul what happened, and we decided you should take me to your research facility. I want you to begin the screening process right away. Start with the people you've already tested who have the GC117 gene and correlate the information from their social media postings. That will give us our first candidates for the new colony."

Zane gave her a wary stare. "I think we should wait and see if our representatives agree to your plan before I get started."

"Time is of the essence, and this will give us an advantage. If they don't agree, you can get rid of the information."

"You're sure putting a lot of trust in me, considering we've just met."

"Paul shared some information he gleaned from your mind with me."

"I hope it doesn't include mind control."

"No, he can only interpret your memories, and we know you can be trusted. It will take time to identify and convince the selectees to go with us, so we should get started right away."

"All right, but the logistics alone are staggering."

"Paul will bring you some new equipment when he picks me up after I'm done at your facility. It will make the DNA testing go much faster."

"I should let Mya and Alex know where we're going"

Vesta would rather he didn't, and aside from his belligerency, something about Alex's eyes bothered her, as if they pierced right through her soul. "I would prefer to keep Mister Cave out of the loop until your representatives agree to accept our help."

Zane thought about it and realized he didn't know anything about Cave's background except what Mya had told him. "All right. I'll wait until they reach a decision."

Vesta stared out the side window when Zane started the engine and drove out of the parking lot. When he drove onto an Interstate highway leading away from the landing site, she grinned.

<h1 style="text-align:center">Chapter 5</h1>

CAMPGROUND NEAR THE DIG SITE:

After borrowing some electronic equipment from the base supply department, Alex drove to UNCLE JIM'S RECREATIONAL VEHICLE REPAIR AND RENTAL, just off the highway leading back to the dig site. He rented a small motorhome with a satellite dish on top, and a trailer for his car. While he had made a quick stop at a grocery store, Uncle Jim had called ahead to reserve a spot for him at the only RV park near the dig site, and once the car was loaded onto the trailer, he headed for the campground.

Alex parked in front of the office to check in and noticed all the sites were now filled with tents and small trailers. When he stepped through the front door, a small crowd of people were staring up at the television, then saw a woman standing behind the counter and worked his way over to her. "You should have a reservation for Alex Cave."

The woman turned from the TV and slid a pen and registration form in front of Alex. "I sure do, and you're lucky Jim called when he did. I've turned away two television vans offering three times the normal fee for your spot. Everyone here is waiting for the miracle stone to reappear so they can go touch it, but the tribal sheriff has locked the gate."

"How long has it been on the news?"

"Just a few of hours. A couple of kids managed to get a video recording using a drone, but it crashed. Now the government has made the area a no-fly zone."

Alex slid the pen and paper back to her and pulled his wallet from his back pocket. "How much do I owe you?"

She slid a small map in front of him and circled a number. "Spot nine is a pull-thru next to the road up to the dig site like you asked for, and it's fifty-five a night."

Alex gave her one hundred and ten dollars. "Two nights will be fine."

After she handed him a receipt, Alex squeezed his way back through the crowd and drove to the campsite. He leveled the motorhome, hooked up the utilities, and then extended the slide out. There was a basic tool set in the motorhome and he carried it along with a small signal strength meter up onto the roof. He was adjusting the satellite dish when Mya parked in front of the motorhome. When she climbed out and looked up at him, he noticed her concerned expression. "What's going on?"

Mya shaded her eyes against the glare of the sun setting over the mountains behind Alex. "Zane and Vesta didn't come back."

"I'll be done in a minute. Help yourself to a beer from the ice chest while I finish making this adjustment."

Mya strolled over to the cooler on the ground next to the table and sat down while she grabbed a silver and gold colored can from inside. She leaned back and took a swallow, grimacing slightly at the bitter taste. She looked up at the top of the motorhome and saw Alex staring at a meter hanging from a TV cable below the satellite dish.

Alex made a few adjustments to the angle and elevation for the best reception, and then removed the meter and climbed down the ladder mounted to the rear of the motorhome, then set everything on the table and sat down across from Mya. "What happened?"

Mya reached into the cooler and grabbed a beer for Alex. "They were still in the parking lot when I left, so I don't know where they might have gone. I figured they would need to drive past this place on their way to the dig site, so I came back down to see if you had arrived."

Alex popped the tab on the can and took a swallow. "How far is it to Zane's research facility?"

"I have no idea. I was surprised when he called this morning, wanting to tell me something in person."

Alex grabbed the smart phone from his pocket and searched for Zane's facility. "He's in Salt Lake City, Utah. That makes sense, since the Mormons keep meticulous records of family histories. I know, because I have a few relatives living there."

"Zane didn't even bother to call me."

"He may not even know what he's doing. I believe Vesta and Paul are influencing his decisions."

"I agree. I can't imagine what it's like having someone else's consciousness inside my mind."

Alex heard a soft beeping sound coming from inside the motorhome and stood from the table. "That's the secure satellite connection. Come inside and we'll find out who is contacting me."

Alex climbed the steps into the motorhome and sat down at the small table in the slide-out area then entered his code into the computer and a familiar face appeared on the screen. "Hey, Jadin. I'm with a friend."

Jadin could not see Mya's image on her own monitor. "No offense, but some of our work is highly classified, and I don't believe they have the right security clearance to listen to our conversation."

Alex knew Jadin was right. "Just give us the information about the comet."

"All right. I found the comet at the coordinates you gave me, and Vesta is correct about it heading straight for us. It isn't close enough to the sun to have a tail, so we never would have seen it if we didn't know where to look."

Alex heaved a deep sigh of frustration. "I was hoping she was lying to us. Is she right about the time frame?"

"We don't have any telescopes out far enough to triangulate its speed. When I couldn't reach you, I told Holly."

"All right. I'll talk to you later."

Mya studied Alex's profile while he typed in another code. "Jadin is a nice-looking girl."

Alex didn't look up as he continued typing. "Yes, and she is very competent. I'm lucky to have her on my team."

"You never mentioned you have a team. Too bad I don't have the right security clearance, because my curiosity about what you really do for a living is driving me crazy."

Alex looked over at Mya. "We're just a few people who get together to work on unusual problems."

Mya's eyes went wide. "Are you telling me this happens a lot?"

"No, this is *way* more unusual than what we normally work on." He turned to the screen when he heard a familiar voice. "Hi, Holly. Jadin just told me Vesta is telling the truth."

Holly could see part of a woman's short brown hair next to Alex's image. "I see you have company."

Alex moved to the side so Mya could move into range of the camera. "You remember Mya."

"Yes, nice to see you again."

"Hello, Ms. Blake"

Alex moved back in front of the camera. "Have you notified the rest of the representatives?"

"Yes, and they've decided to accept Vesta's offer. They don't want to cause a mass panic, so they'll keep the coming apocalypse a secret while selecting candidates."

Mya nudged Alex out of the way so Holly could see her. "You should not keep it a secret. People need notification so they can be with their families when it happens."

Alex turned to look at Mya. "This is the type of situation my team deals with, and it won't turn out the way you think it will. For their own good, the public can never know about this situation."

Mya abruptly leaned back and crossed her arms. "It's not right."

Alex saw the bitterness in Mya's eyes. "I agree, but we have no choice."

When Mya turned away, he knew she might create problems. "Please promise me you won't tell anyone else about this."

Mya knew he was partially correct and slowly turned her head to look at him. "With protest, I agree to keep my mouth shut."

Alex gave Mya a soft smile of appreciation. "Thanks." He turned to Holly. "I guess all we can do is wait to hear the rest of Vesta's plan."

"I'll call Zane so he can tell Vesta we accept her terms. I'll keep in touch with you as things develop."

When Holly's image vanished, Mya looked at Alex. "Is there anyone in particular you want to be with at the end?"

He grinned at her. "How do you know I'm not going with them?"

"Because you pissed off the one person you need to convince. You must have some Neanderthal DNA in you, or you wouldn't be so argumentative with Vesta."

"Then I have an excuse for coming on too aggressively with her."

Mya smirked at him. "So far, you're doing all right."

Alex stood. "I bought a large microwaveable lasagna and garlic bread. You're welcome to stay for dinner."

"Sure, I like Italian."

"What about you? Anyone special you want to be with if you don't go with Vesta?"

"Not anymore. My parents and brother were killed in a car crash. A sixteen-year-old girl hit them while she was texting. The irony is she survived with only minor injuries."

"I'm sorry for your loss."

Alex opened the small freezer and grabbed the frozen lasagna. "I suppose I'll spend some time with my dad and niece if it's really going to hit us."

"You don't think Vesta is telling the truth?"

"Let's just say, even if she's right, I believe there are always other options."

Mya found Alex's attitude appealing. "I try not to give up hope, but after everything I've been through and the bad news delivered by an alien, it's hard for me to stay positive."

"I'll do anything to save my family. If I can save the rest of humanity while I'm at it, I'll do that, too."

***

When Alex heard his phone ringing, he opened his eyes and looked at the clock on his phone, which showed 7:36 AM, and answered while wiping the sleep from his eyes. "Hey, Okawna. Are you at the base?"

"No, Holly called and asked me to drive down to the base from my place in Wyoming to join you. Is Mya with you?"

Alex looked at the unruffled pillow on the bed. During their conversation last evening, he knew Mya's intentions, but with all the bad things that had happened to the women he had liked, he didn't want to get into another romantic relationship with someone who wasn't even his type. "No, she's staying someplace else." He noticed a flashing icon in the corner of the computer monitor. "I've got an incoming call on the satellite. I'll see you when you get here." He entered his code, and Blake's image appeared. "Good morning, Holly."

"Let's get right down to business. I contacted Vesta at Zane's facility, and she's agreed to meet virtually with the world representatives to discuss how to implement the procedure. She says they have done this before and know how best to proceed."

"When's the meeting?"

"The video conference will start in six hours, but there's a problem. You're not invited."

"Why not?"

"Vesta doesn't like you."

"Then she must be hiding something from us. I'm not letting this drop, Holly."

"I know, and that's fine with Donner and me. What do you have in mind?"

"Okawna's headed south from Wyoming, like you asked. I'll meet up with him and we'll check out Zane's facility."

"Get started, but wait for my okay before you barge in on him. I'll know more once I hear the details of Vesta's plan."

Alex noticed Mya's car pull up near the picnic table outside. "All right. Call me on my phone." When Holly's image vanished, he turned off the computer and stood to put his pants on as Mya climbed out of her car, then opened the door and invited her inside. "Good morning." He expected a smile, but received a frown. "What's wrong?"

"I tried calling Zane, but he doesn't answer."

"We were right. He's in Salt Lake City with Vesta, and she'll be doing a video conference call from his facility in a few hours to explain the details of her evacuation plan."

"Can we watch it from your computer?"

"No, you were right about me pissing Vesta off. I'm not invited."

"So, I guess you'll be leaving."

"Yes. I'll drop this motorhome off on my way to Fort Collins and be on my way."

"Will I see you again?"

"I can't say for sure while all this is going on. What's next for you?"

"The tribe will watch over the dig site, and there isn't much sense in continuing my excavation, so I'm not sure what I'll do." Her phone rang, and she pulled it from her pocket, and then looked at Alex. "It's Zane."

"Don't tell him I'm with you."

Mya gave him an affirmative nod, turned on the speaker, and answered. "Hey, Zane. I was wondering what happened to you."

"I need for you to come to my facility in Salt Lake City right away."

"What's so urgent?"

"You meet all of Vesta's requirements, so you can be one of the first volunteers."

"What if I don't want to go?"

"That's up to you, but could you at least come to my facility? There is something very important I need to tell you about your DNA." She noticed Alex's vigorous nods to accept. "All right. I'll see you this afternoon." When she hung up, Alex was smiling at her. "I'm not going with them."

"I know, but Okawna and I are going with you to Zane's place. You're our excuse to get inside his facility."

"What are you up to?"

Alex smirked at her. "I don't trust them."

"Okay. I'll follow you to the RV rental. Are we taking two cars, or one?"

"That will depend on Okawna."

"I'm ready when you are."

Chapter 6

THIRTY MILES EAST OF SALT LAKE CITY, UTAH:
Okawna always insisted on driving, which Alex didn't mind since it gave him time to think about Vesta and Paul's connection to Zane. They would be more believable if he could see their spacecraft, that way, he would know if it could hold five hundred people. He looked over his shoulder to the back seat and saw Mya staring out through the side window. "Are you excited to see Zane's DNA chop shop?"

She turned to face him. "Not really. I hadn't considered volunteering until Zane told me I met all the prerequisites. Now I'm out of a job, so it's something to consider. It's just I feel like a coward for thinking about running away."

Alex thought about the coming apocalypse and felt as if the weight of the world was on his shoulders. If he couldn't come up with a plan, in four months, the entire surface would become a desolate wasteland, killing over eight billion people and every living thing on the planet. He noticed the sunlight reflecting off a tear running down her cheek. "We don't have enough information about the comet, so don't give up hope for a different outcome."

"I guess I still have plenty of time to think about it. I wonder why Zane is so excited about my DNA? He made it sound so urgent."

"Are you related to that local tribe?"

"No, I'm half Sioux, but from a different tribe."

Alex's phone rang, and he recognized Holly's number. "I didn't expect to hear from you until after the meeting."

"We're just about ready to get started. Do you have any new information for me?"

"No, we haven't reached the facility yet."

"All right. Let me speak to Okawna."

Alex turned on the speaker. "He's listening."

Okawna leaned closer to the phone. "Hey, Holly."

"How soon will you be in range?"

Okawna checked his GPS location. "A couple of minutes."

"That's about all the time you have before the meeting starts."

Okawna eased the gas pedal closer to the floor. "I'll be ready. I just need to find a place to pull over. What's the code for tapping into his satellite signal?"

"GC117. It was Zane's idea."

"Got it. We'll be listening."

"I want both of you to listen to me carefully. Under no circumstances are you to speak during the meeting. That's an order. Do you understand?"

Okawna was about to tell Holly about Mya being with them until Alex gave him a signal he should not. "We understand, Boss. We'll keep our mouths shut until after the smart people figure this out for us. Bye."

Alex turned off the speaker and held the phone to his ear. "I'll talk to you later, Holly. This should be interesting."

***

THE MEETING:

Vesta sat at a small table next to Zane in one of his offices, studying the eight images of men and women representing various nations on the large wall monitor, then stared directly at the woman she recognized. "Hello again, Holly."

Holly could see the images of the other representatives on her own monitor. "Hi, Vesta. Since we already know each other, I've been asked to speak for everyone at this meeting. We have a few questions. First, social media has been flooded with images of your ship, so we'd like to know what to tell the public about your arrival."

Vesta leaned back in her chair. "I'll explain how this must happen and you will do exactly what I tell you to do. Start by telling them the truth about the impending impact, but tell them you should be able to change the comet's course."

"I thought you said we don't have the technology to make it miss us."

"That is true, but if humans know they cannot overcome their own demise, they lose hope and civilizations crumble. We've seen it happen on other worlds."

"What's our time frame?"

"If all of you agree to our terms, we will depart in thirteen days with as many of your kind as possible."

The image of a man with Great Brittan written on the screen below his face raised his hand. "Wait a minute. You didn't say anything about terms. What do you want in return?"

"Just your cooperation with the way this must be handled. We've done this many times before, and our way is the only option that works."

Holly knew any objections would only piss Vesta off, so she spoke to the other representatives. "I'm sure all of us are still getting used to the fact we're meeting people from another world, but please save your questions until she's finished. Please continue, Vesta."

"All right. Here's how it will be done. Volunteers will submit DNA samples to Zane Kinkaid's ancestry program, along with filling out a questionnaire about jobs, interests, and hobbies to be added to the test kits. You can work with Zane on that issue. Screening will accept anyone with the GC117 genetic marker, since those people have a predisposition for good health, longevity, and higher intelligence. For your own benefit, the people we accept need to be of significant generational distancing as to prevent diluting the new gene pool." She noticed the Englishman had his hand u again. "Do you have another question?"

"No, it's not a question. Our governments will need to set up agencies to monitor the tests. I'm sure you understand our need to make sure there are no biases in the selection process."

"That would take too long, but Zane could use your help with other issues as they arise. Transportation will be one of them." She noticed the Brit's image expand on the screen, as if he had leaned closer to his camera. "Is that a problem?"

"That's unacceptable. We don't know Zane Kinkaid well enough to know if he has any bias issues with our varied societies."

Vesta stared at him. "I don't think you fully comprehend your situation. I'm not asking you to agree with us. You do as we ask or we will leave you to your own demise."

Vesta's statement caused Holly to think of Alex's comment about ulterior motives, but for the moment, she needed to keep Vesta thinking she is on her side and would keep the idea to herself. "I'm sure Zane knows what he's doing, but once we make the news announcement about what's going on and the relocation program, he might be overwhelmed by people sending in samples."

"He will, and he'll also need to tighten security around his facility. Some humans have a tendency to act on their fears with violence, and the ones we accept will be despised by the ones who are not."

Holly wanted to make sure she would stay in contact with Vesta. "I'll take care of security and whatever else he'll need. Just contact me."

"That's fine. Any volunteer without the GC117 marker will automatically be eliminated. In addition, no one with a trace of Neanderthal DNA will be accepted. That genetic trait causes aggressive behavior, and we cannot allow that in the new colony. I suggest you leave out any mention of those two requirements, because those issues will cause your citizens to riot. We've seen it happen before, and from what we know about your societal structure, the unaccepted will revolt." She heard a familiar accented voice scoff at her and looked at the image of the man with the smirk. "If you disagree, this meeting is over."

"I'm sorry, and don't get me wrong, it's a good idea, but it's in our nature to be aggressive."

"That is not true. We have evidence to prove otherwise. It's all about the DNA."

Holly had never met England's representative before, and stifled a grin, thinking he must have a lot of Neanderthal DNA in his ancestry. "At least let us help by doing background checks on the volunteers."

Vesta knew those issues would be identified during her second screening, but decided to let the representatives think they were contributing to the selection process. "Yes, that would be helpful."

A woman with gray hair raised her hand. "What will be the age range?"

"We have learned a maximum age of forty-five and a minimum of fourteen are optimal."

A man with thick eyeglasses and a gray beard raised his hand, but didn't wait to be acknowledged. "I'm an astrophysicist from MIT, and I'm curious how many kinds of humans are out there?"

"Not as many as you would think. Out of all the planets in your galaxy, only one hundred and thirty-seven are naturally capable of supporting a human species, but most of those societies do not evolve far enough technologically, and cannot leave their planet before they are destroyed by natural forces. That is why we try to save as many as we can."

The astrophysicist gave Vesta a wry grin. "I guess we're one of those species."

"Unfortunately, yes, you are. That's why we came here."

"Can you tell me about your means of transportation and how you travel such vast distances?"

"No."

Holly remembered how adamant Vesta had been about Zane being the contact person and wondered if that was still the case. "Will we be dealing directly with you from now on?"

"No, Zane will keep you informed on our progress and the qualified volunteers. Your governments will be responsible for notifying the ones who are accepted during the primary selection process. Members of my crew will meet them at randomly selected locations around your planet for verification and final evaluation. They are what you would call qualified linguists, so you will not need to supply translators. Only security personnel."

"The logistics are going to be mindboggling. I don't think it can be done in just thirteen days."

"Yes, it can. That is all the time you have, because we don't need five hundred people to start a new civilization. We will leave with whatever number of qualified volunteers we have on the ship at the end of the thirteen-day period. I suggest you notify your citizens as soon as possible."

When Vesta stood up, Holly knew the meeting was over. "Thank you, Vesta. I'm sure all of us appreciate this opportunity to save some of our civilization."

Vesta stared at the Brit's image. "Not all of you."

Zane turned off the monitor and stood up from the table. "I guess the meeting went well."

When she didn't reply, he noticed she appeared to be deep in thought. He looked around, expecting to see Paul suddenly appear, but he did not, then noticed she was suddenly out of her trance. "Are you okay?"

"Yes. I've contacted Paul and told him they've agreed to our terms so he can start making preparations. He will meet me out back and you can unload your new equipment for the tests."

Zane strolled beside her as they left through the rear entry of the building and into a wide area of grass with trees along the border. "Are you going to show me how to use it?"

"Of course. Paul will send you the information through your mental connection. It's much faster that way."

"I'm not sure how I feel about him getting inside my head."

"Paul likes you."

"That's not very reassuring. When are you coming back?"

"In two days to check on your progress. We have another mission to take care of while we're waiting."

When Vesta suddenly stopped walking, Zane stopped next to her, staring at an open area of lawn between the tree line and the building. The air shimmered for an instant before the cube magically appeared, then he followed her to the entrance. "That's incredible. Judging from its size, you won't be able to take very many people at a time up to the other ship. Don't you worry about power consumption?"

"No, we collect all the power we need from various types of suns." She stepped inside and indicated for Zane to remove the test equipment. "These will make the screening process much faster."

Zane grabbed the handles of two silver cases just inside the opening and then stepped back from the entrance. "I'd rather have the instruction manuals."

Vesta smiled at him. "I'll see you in two days."

When Vest entered the cube, Zane stepped back as the entrance vanished and the cube shimmered, then it was gone. He stood there for a moment, realizing this was really happening, and life as he knew it would never be the same.

***

Okawna stared out through the front window of the SUV, parked at a pull off area next to the highway. "Well, it's not the first time we've been in a shitty situation. We'll figure something out."

Alex looked into the back seat and noticed Mya staring out through the side window. "We knew this was coming."

Mya turned to Alex. "I know, and I appreciate you letting me listen to the meeting. I'm just wondering how people will react when they learn if they don't have the right DNA, they will probably die."

"You promised you wouldn't tell anyone."

"I know."

When Mya stared out the side window, Alex turned to the front and thought about the situation. He knew Mya was right about the hysteria the information would cause. At least when society had dealt with similar situations in the past, they had a definable and conquerable enemy on whom to vent their rage. In this situation, people are literally their own worst enemy. He just hoped he could figure out a way to change the trajectory of the comet before things got out of hand.

Okawna noticed the despondent expression on Alex's face and started the engine. "Let's go find out what Zane is cooking up in his genetics lab."

Chapter 7

SALT LAKE CITY, UTAH:
Zane heard his phone ring and recognized Mya's voice when he answered. "Hey, where are you?"

"I'm just pulling up to your facility."

"I'm glad you decided to stop by. Park in front of the office and I'll meet you there."

A few moments later, Zane hurried out through the front door and recognized the man standing with Mya, but not the tall blond man standing with them. "I'm glad you showed up, Alex. You're not going to believe what's going to happen."

"I heard Vesta was going to brief a bunch of representatives today. Can you tell me about it?"

"Of course. It's going to be known to the public soon, anyway. We can talk on the way to my testing area."

Alex indicated the blond man. "This is my best friend, Okawna. He's part of my group of advisors."

Zane shook hands. "It's nice to meet you. Follow me and I'll show you around my facility."

Alex listened to Zane talk about what they already knew as they moved past the deserted reception desk and along a short hallway. He was relieved when Zane didn't leave out any of the details.

Zane gave his visitors a conspiratorial expression. "Of course, we're not going to tell the public about the genetic requirements. People are going to panic about the comet anyway, so why add fuel to the fire, right?"

Mya clenched her fists at her side to keep from blurting out her feelings on the issue. "So why was it so urgent I come here?"

Zane spun around and smiled as he grabbed both her shoulders and looked into her eyes. "Because not only do you have the GC117 gene and zero Neanderthal, but also a gene I've never seen before, and I've done over sixty-thousand tests from around the world. I'm calling it the GC118 gene."

Mya wasn't sure what to think of this new development. "If the GC117 gene is good for health and longevity, what does the GC118 do?"

"I have no idea. I'm hoping my friends at the GEN9 DNA Synthesis Lab can figure it out."

Before today, Okawna had never considered having his DNA tested, but now he was curious. "Can you check mine while I'm here?"

"Of course. As long as you're here, Alex, we might as well do yours, too."

"Oh, I don't know. I'm not planning on leaving with Vesta and her friends, so there's no sense wasting your time."

Mya ginned up at Alex. "Now's the chance to prove me wrong about your Neanderthal percentage."

Alex smiled at her. "All right."

Zane led them to the end of the hallway, pushed open the doors, and then walked inside to a young woman sitting at the first test station. "Vickie, could you do a test on my friends for me?"

Vickie Madison stood and smiled up at the handsome blond man. "What's your name, cowboy?"

Okawna grinned down at the large, red-haired woman with dark-framed glasses. "Okawna. What do you want me to do?"

Vickie raised an eyebrow. "Oh, lots of things, big boy. Too bad I don't have time right now," She reached into a drawer and brought out two small plastic tubes, holding one out to Okawna. "But for now, just wipe the swab around the inside of your cheeks and put it in here."

When Okawna was done, Alex took the other tube and did the same before handing it back to Vickie. "How long does it take?"

"About fifteen minutes."

Zane indicated the doors to his friends. "Let's go to my office. She'll let us know when she has the results."

Zane led them into his office and indicated the sofa and chairs to his guests. "Vesta gave me some new equipment so I can do the initial test in less than a second. That is once I learn how to use it"

Alex sat on the sofa next to Mya. "Are you saying her cube was here?"

"Yes, it suddenly appeared in the back lot, she got in, and it vanished."

Alex studied the test equipment on a table and realized the technology was far more advanced than his spaceship. He suddenly wondered if Vesta's main ship had any type of weapons, and turned to Zane. "You've spent some time alone with her. Do you think she's sincere?"

"Yes, I do. The only thing I don't like about Vesta and Paul is his ability to read my mind. I'm not too keen on the idea of someone being inside my head."

"How did it affect you the first time?"

"It wasn't unpleasant, if that's what you mean."

Vickie was smiling as she entered Zane's office. "Here are the results of the tests. You're not going to believe it."

Zane took the small electronic tablet and studied the data while Vickie left the room. "Well, Okawna. You have the GC117 gene, and three percent Neanderthal DNA. You also have the HERC2/OCA2 gene, which gives you your green eyes." He flipped to the next screen and looked over at Alex. "I can't believe it. You have the GC117 and the GC118 gene, like Mya, but you also have an unknown genetic tag on your HERC2/OCA2 gene. I've never seen one like this before. Are you sure you were born here on earth?"

Alex chuckled. "Positive. The way I understand it, we all have unused DNA left over from our evolution into Homo Sapiens."

"That's correct, but Vesta told us they have brought other humans here in the past. There is no trace of Neanderthal in your sample, Alex, so maybe your genealogy leads back to one of them. That would make you unique from the rest of us."

Alex already knew that much from what he had learned during the Pandora incident. "You said Mya's GC118 was the only one out of sixty thousand people tested, but there are, what, over eight billion of us living on this little planet? I'm sure there are more people with that gene."

"I guess we'll find out by the time we're done."

"When will Vesta be back?"

"In two days."

"Do me a favor. Tell her I want to be taken to her ship."

Zane stared at Alex for a moment. "I doubt she'll agree. She doesn't like you."

Alex grinned. "The feeling is mutual."

"I don't understand what you have against her, Alex. She's just trying to help us."

"That's what the Trojans thought and look what happened to them. Just give her my message and let me know what she says."

"All right. Do you want to see the rest of my operation?"

"I thought all you did was test DNA."

"Oh, no. That is only the first stage. Follow me."

Alex walked beside Zane as they left the room and entered the hallway. A moment later, he followed him into a much larger room with dozens of people sitting in front of computer monitors, but no test equipment.

Zane indicated his employees. "This is where we search social media sites for information. Originally, I was doing this for the clandestine services around the world to track down terrorists. Three months ago, I invested a ton of money to upgrade my data storage capacity, and we began searching all the social media sites, using names submitted with the DNA samples for an ancestry background."

Alex stared at the rows of black computer cabinets with small flashing colored lights. "For what purpose?"

"My original intent was to offer my customers a fully formed family tree for an extra fee. Now we have lists of anyone remotely related to those people, but I haven't offered the service to any of them just yet. Under the current circumstances, I doubt anyone will want to know to whom they are related anymore, so it was all a waste cf money. I suppose it doesn't matter, since I won't be around to spend any of it, anyway. I meet all the prerequisites needed to join the new colony, and I'm going with them."

Mya strolled between the rows of people, looking at the images on their monitors. All of them showed pictures of individuals posing with family, friends, and pets. "This is why I don't post personal stuff on social media. It's like an invasion of privacy."

Zane had been following her. "I'm sure they know whatever they post will be seen by the public, so it's not a violation of privacy. If they don't want it known to everyone, they should not have posted it."

"I know, but it still doesn't seem right."

Alex had an interesting thought. "Who has access to all this information?"

"Just me and my employees, but it cannot be uploaded to individuals. The only information we share is related to suspected terrorists and their relatives, and only with the clandestine services. Why do you ask?"

"Will Vesta have access to it?"

"Yes, and she wants me to do it for all the volunteers as part of the vetting process. No close relatives, remember?"

"That's interesting."

Zane gave Alex a quizzical stare. "What do you mean?"

"Oh, nothing really. I suppose it's necessary. She wouldn't want a psychopath as part of the new colony."

"I agree. The governments want to do their own background checks for her, but that would take too long. We only have thirteen days."

"Is this your entire operation?"

"Yes, for the discovery program. My genetic research facility is at a different location."

"All right. Well, thank you for the tour, and I hope you'll keep me posted on your progress."

Zane smiled and held out his hand. "Vesta is the one who has a problem with you, not me. I like you, Alex." He reached out to the blond man. "And it was nice to meet you as well, Mister Okawna."

Okawna accepted the handshake. "It's just Okawna. Same here."

Zane strolled with his friends out to the parking lot and stopped to say goodbye to Mya. "I hope you're considering going with us to a new planet. I'm sure we could use an archeologist."

"I'll keep it in mind as an option. So long, Zane."

Zane returned to his office and was looking at the new equipment when suddenly an image appeared in his mind. He instantly knew how the seven pieces fit together, and when he was done, it was a miniature assembly line for testing DNA samples. There was also an adapter cord to connect it with a human-built computer, but he was still baffled by the other piece of equipment and the Y-shaped piece of something resembling plastic. He left the assembled unit on the table and put the other pieces back into a case, and then closed and locked the door behind him as he left the office.

***

Once they were driving out of the parking lot, Alex brought out his phone to call Holly, and then put it on speaker. "We had a nice visit with Zane. It seems Vesta and her ship will be gone for two days. What happened after the meeting?"

"It took a while for all the representatives to come to an agreement on how much to tell the public. Tonight on prime time, our President is going to make the announcement to the world. The visitors came here to warn us about an approaching comet, but we have the technology to possibly change its trajectory. He'll tell the world the visitors are also looking for volunteers to repopulate a distant planet. The information will include the part about needing a DNA test through Zane's program and a background check. All the details will be posted in newspapers and on social media."

Alex remembered hearing the British representative voice his objections during the meeting. "Are you sure none of the representatives will leak the truth about the specific genetic requirements on social media?"

"You know we can't be positive about it. That's why I hate politicians. They agree if we are going to save our species, we need to save the best people for the job. They brought up a valid point I agree with concerning Zane. I don't like the idea of just one person deciding on who goes and who stays. That's too much power for one man to have over an entire species."

Alex knew that wasn't the situation. "I'm not worried about Zane. He's just Vesta's puppet, but she gave him some advanced alien technology, and we all know how fast things can get out of control when it ends up in the wrong hands."

Mya could no longer restrain her frustration and leaned forward between the seats. "It's wrong telling people the lie about being able to stop the comet."

Alex winced and spun around to stare at Mya until she leaned back in her seat. "Really?"

"Is that Mya?"

Alex turned and stared out the front window. "Yes, she was our only way into Zane's facility. And yes, she listened to the meeting with us, but it's not an issue."

Mya leaned forward again. "I won't say anything, Holly. I gave Alex my word, but I just think people have the right to know about this."

"They will be told eventually, but for the moment, there isn't anything they can do about it, so why create a panic? We have four months to change its course, and if we fail, we'll tell everyone the bad news."

"But that's still not fair. There are many people who will not volunteer to join the colony because they don't know they may die if they stay here."

"That's not up to me, Mya."

Mya heaved a deep sigh of frustration. "I know, and I'm sorry for lashing out at you."

Alex turned off the speaker, brought the phone up to his ear, and indicated for Mya to lean back so he could talk in private. "Vesta won't be back for two days, but when she does, I'd like to use our ship to check out her main spacecraft."

Holly thought about it for a moment. "Let me talk to David about the cloaking system first. What are your plans until then?"

"I'll catch a ride back to the base, and I suppose Okawna will drive home."

"All right."

The connection ended, and Alex put the phone away. After fifteen minutes of uncomfortable silence, he turned on the stereo. Along the way, he thought about how big Vesta's spaceship would need to be to carry five hundred people and it would be immense. Of course, he had no idea how their technology worked. He added it to the list of questions for Vesta when she returned.

Two hours later, Okawna took the exit for Fort Collins. He drove into the visitor parking lot at the base, then let Mya and Alex climb out of his vehicle, and rolled down his window as his friends moved up beside him. "It was nice meeting you, Mya. Take care."

Mya leaned in and gave Okawna a quick hug. "You, too."

When Mya stepped back, Alex leaned in close. "I'll catch a military hop to Fallon, Nevada, to see a friend before I head back to Groom Lake and meet you there in two days. We're going for a ride."

"Got it. See you there."

When Okawna drove away, Mya indicated her car. "If I remember right, it's my turn to buy you dinner."

"Let me check in and see when the next flight is available before we leave. I'll be right back."

When Alex walked toward the security building, Mya leaned back against her car and stared after him, wondering what he really did for a living. "I think you're more than just a geologist, Alex Cave."

Chapter 8

FORT COLLINS, COLORADO:

Alex awoke to the sound of someone knocking on the motel room door. He rolled out of bed and slid into his jeans as he stood and looked out the window, where Mya was smiling at him, so he opened the door. "Good morning, Mya."

"Hi. What time did you say your flight would leave?"

"Not until 9:30."

"Would you like to come to my place so I can make you something to eat?"

"I'd love to, but I need a shower before my flight and I don't want to be late. I'll grab something on the way to the base."

"Do you mind if I stick around until you leave?"

Alex wondered if perhaps he should have skipped having dinner and drinks with Mya. "Sure. I'll be out in a minute."

When Alex disappeared into the bathroom, Mya turned on the television and flipped through the channels, looking for news broadcasts. She found one with an image of a comet in the background, and she sat down on the couch and turned up the volume.

"We have verified sources telling us there is a comet headed on a collision course with our planet, and it should arrive here in about four months. They also informed us the US, China, and Russia are joining forces, and together have the means to change its course, so no one is in any immediate danger."

A picture of the cube on the side of the mountain filled the background. *"That brings us to the next item on this morning's broadcast. We've all been curious about the strange square object that appeared in northern Colorado. According to a White House press release, we now know we are not alone in the universe. They are visitors from another galaxy."* A Picture of Vesta recorded during the first meeting appeared on the screen. *"They are looking for five hundred volunteers to repopulate another world similar to our own, but they have a few stipulations."*

Mya listened to the announcer explain the process and the type of people they want for the new colony, then held her frustration in check until Alex came out to join her. "They lied about stopping the impact."

Alex glanced at the television screen. "What about the restrictions on who would be accepted?"

"It's just like Holly told us. If they want to be considered, they need to send a DNA sample and questionnaire to Zane and agree to a background check. They specified they are looking for doctors, scientists, engineers, and artists, but nothing about the GC117 gene or being part Neanderthal."

Alex sat down beside her. "Where will you go from here?"

"I want to be at Zane's facility while all this is going on."

"Do you mind if I ask why?"

"I'm considering joining the new colony. At least, that's the story I'm telling Zane. I'm still trying to come to terms with the fact the Earth will be destroyed in four months."

Alex stood and reached into his wallet, then handed her one of his cards. "Those are my private numbers. Call me anytime."

Mya stood and followed Alex out of the room to his rental car and waited while he tossed his bag into the back seat. When he opened the driver's side door, she wrapped her arms around his neck to pull him close and gave him a warm kiss, then smiled as she let go and stepped back. "I hope to see you again soon."

"I'm sure we will. Consider what I said and don't trust Vesta." He climbed into his car and drove toward the street. When he stopped to wait for a break in the traffic, he looked into the rearview mirror and saw Mya staring after him.

***

Alex was sitting in the air terminal waiting to board the plane when his phone rang and an image of his father, Robert Cave, appeared on the screen, and he answered. "Hi, Dad."

"Is it true what they're saying about the comet?"

"I'm afraid so."

"What about the rockets? Will they be able to stop it from hitting us?"

Alex closed his eyes in frustration. He knew he couldn't tell Robert the truth, but hated having to lie to him. "That's the plan."

"You don't sound too confident. What's your gut telling you?" Alex's silence was his answer. "I see."

"Listen, Dad. We still have four months to change its course, so don't give up hope."

"That's not the only reason I called you. I know you and Derek aren't talking to each other anymore, so I decided to let you know what's going on. He wants to join the new colony, and I'm hoping you can talk some sense into him."

"How can I do that if he won't talk to me?"

"Hold on a second while I walk to his bedroom."

***

CAVE RESIDENCE. SPARROW VALLEY, WASHINGTON:

Derek pulled out his earbuds when Robert walked into his room. "What's going on, Grandpa?"

Robert turned on the phone speaker and held it out to Derek. "Go ahead, Alex."

Alex had a feeling anything he said would only make matters worse between them, but had to try. "Joining the colony is a bad idea, Derek. I know what I'm talking about."

Derek ignored his uncle and put the earbuds back in place. "Tell him to stop telling me what to do."

***

FORT COLLINS, COLORADO:

Alex heaved a deep sigh of resignation while he waited for Robert to come back on the line. He didn't feel like he was telling Derek how to run his life. Only things to consider for the long term.

Robert heard Alex sigh. "Thanks for trying, Son. Derek is just as stubborn as you were at nineteen. He thinks he knows everything."

"I know. My flight is boarding, so I need to go. Give Kristie a hug for me and tell her I love her."

"I will. I love you, Son. Stop by when you get the chance."

"I will. I love you too, Dad."

Alex put away the phone and grabbed his bag as he stood. He got in line with the other passengers and followed them out through the door to the waiting aircraft.

***

Mya's plan to leave for Zane's facility was put on hold when she received a call to return to the dig site. When she drove past the campground, it appeared to be overflowing with Native Americans wearing beads and paint. Her windows were down and she could hear people chanting, which faded away as she continued up the mountain. She stopped at the closed gate and looked out the window at a Native American man in a sheriff's uniform. "Hi, Roger. What's going on?"

"The elders decided the appearance of the vanishing stone is an omen, and you need to stop your excavation. You can go in and collect your equipment, but we'll take your tent down and return the area to its natural state."

Mya had a feeling this might happen. "All right. Please tell them I didn't mean any disrespect."

"They know that, Mya, so don't worry about it. They're the least of my problems right now. Some white fanatics have been sneaking through the forest to the area where the stone appeared. They all want to touch it, and I've had to deputize six men just to keep them out."

"I'm positive the stone won't be returning to this spot."

Roger grinned at her. "At least, not for another twenty-five thousand years."

When Roger opened the barrier, she drove through and parked near her tent. She climbed out and went inside, and noticed all the artifacts had already been removed, and her equipment was stacked neatly just inside, including the gear from the gravesite. A shadow moving across the floor caught her attention, and she turned to see a young Native American woman standing in the doorway. "Hi, Catori."

"I'm sorry you're leaving, Mya. It's been fun working with you."

"Yes, it's been exciting. I couldn't have interpreted the symbols without your help."

"I want to volunteer to go to a new planet, but my parents are against it."

Mya watched Catori's expression suddenly change into one of pure rage. "Why?"

"Because I'm their only child and they insist I accept my responsibility to the tribe!" She grabbed one of Mya's black notebooks and hurled it across the room, where it bounced off the side of the tent and dropped onto the dirt floor. "I don't want the responsibility! I never did!"

Mya flinched at Catori's outburst, but then the young woman's bitter expression suddenly vanished. "How long has your family lived in this area?"

Catori walked over and picked up the notebook, setting it into the storage container. "I'm sorry about that. One of my mother's distant relatives was here the first time the stone appeared. That's why my family has been in charge of documenting the tribe's history for the past twenty-five thousand years."

Mya wondered if Catori Onestar had the GC117 gene, and since Catori was the Sioux word for Earth, perhaps her parents chose that name for a reason. "You should send in your DNA sample, anyway."

"I suppose it couldn't hurt to see if I would be accepted. I am eighteen, after all, so I can do what I want, right?" When Mya didn't answer, she reached down and grabbed a large plastic case. "I'll help you load everything into your car."

Once the tent was empty, Mya went with Catori to the cave to get the rest of her gear, stopping just inside to put on a headlight. "I'm going in for one last look at the drawing if you'd like to go with me."

Catori slid the strap of a lamp over her head. "This might be the last time anyone can see it, since they plan to seal it closed again."

They entered the room and Mya knelt in front of the wall with the drawing of the large cube. "Did you ever manage to translate these two words below the figures?"

"Yes, I showed a picture of them to my grandfather. They are names. Vesta and Paul."

Mya's jaw dropped, and she stood and spun around to face Catori. "Are you positive?"

"Yes. My grandfather had to translate them from an ancient language, but that's what he said. I'm sure he is right, since he knows far more than anyone else in the tribe."

Mya looked around the room one more time. "Well, I guess there's nothing more for me to learn in here. I suppose I'd better look for another job."

Mya led the way back to the parking lot and loaded the box with the headgear into the trunk. After closing the lid, she turned to Catori. "Again, thanks for your help."

"Does that mean you'll be leaving Fort Collins?"

"I'll stick around until I decide what I want to do."

"I'm headed over to the excavation. They'll be performing a ceremony before filling in the hole if you want to stick around to watch it."

"Thanks, but I have a few things I need to take care of today."

When Mya climbed into her car and drove away, Catori called the number to order a DNA test kit. "It's time I determine my own destiny."

Mya looked in the rearview mirror as she drove out of the parking lot and saw Catori talking on a phone. When she reached the gate, the sheriff was holding the barrier open for an incoming vehicle before he waved her through. She stopped at her apartment long enough to unload the equipment and grab her suitcase, then headed for Salt Lake City.

Chapter 9

SALT LAKE CITY, UTAH:

Zane's curiosity about something Vesta had mentioned during the meeting was driving him crazy. He had spent most of the day in his private office comparing the DNA samples containing the GC117 gene with their owners on social media. According to Vesta, people with that gene supposedly were healthier and lived longer, so he needed to verify if it was true.

He suddenly leaned back in his chair when he saw the results on the monitor. Out of over sixty-thousand samples his company had processed over the past five years, there were only three hundred and seventy-four people with the GC117 gene, and only two hundred and eighty-nine of those people had posted pictures on social media. Each one appeared to be physically fit and of average height, with fourteen percent of those being over the age of eighty-seven. The jobs they had listed on social media required a higher education, and their nationalities were a mixture from all over the world.

Another thought occurred to him and he leaned forward to type in another search parameter of those on social media. When he saw the results, he shook his head in wonder. If the information was correct, none of them were lesbian, gay, bisexual, or transsexual.

***

Mya was sitting in her car in Zane's parking lot watching people in coveralls unloading several large cardboard boxes and hauling them on hand carts into the building. A short distance away, workers wearing orange utility vests and tool belts were climbing into an open utility hole near the building. Behind her, workers with forklifts were laying out heavy concrete barriers on either side of a new security checkpoint on the road leading into the facility. They hadn't stopped her when she arrived, but she knew that would change soon.

***

Zane's phone rang, and he saw it was Mya. "I didn't think I'd hear from you so soon."

"I'm outside your front door. I'm considering joining the colony, but I'd like to see more of the selection process. Would you mind if I come in?"

"I'll be right there."

As Zane hurried from the room, he thought about the implications of the screening process. If word got out about the discrimination factor, there would be protests and riots all over the world, so he decided not to tell anyone else about his discovery. He saw Mya standing just outside the glass door into the reception area, staring out away from the building, so he opened the door and stepped out to join her. "It's been a busy morning."

Mya waved her hand at the construction activity. "What's all this about?"

"After you and your friends left, Holly Blake called and asked what she could do to help me, so I told her I needed more hard lines to my facility. Also, I needed more computing hardware to handle the increased amount of DNA and social media information, which is needed for the selection process."

"Why the beefed up security?"

"That was Vesta's idea. She warned me some people who are rejected during the screening process may try to destroy my facilities."

"She's probably right. How did you get a sample of my DNA?"

Zane felt his face flush. "I took the empty water bottle you left next to the pit while you were showing Alex the cave drawings. I should have asked first, and I'm sorry."

She was annoyed by his deviousness, but knew not to make it an issue right now. "How does all this work? Do you have your own mailing service?"

"No, we don't send out the kits ourselves. The request from the sender is electronically sent to our manufacturer and distribution contractors. The return kits come directly to us here, and we do the testing and save the results in our computers. We notify the sender when it's done so the person can see the results and decide what they want to do with the file and sample. People can save or delete the information, and can ask that the DNA sample be destroyed."

"It didn't look like you had enough employees to handle the increasing workload."

"My people just need to open the kit, verify the name and number on the label of the capsule, and drop the sample into the machine. It is hands free from there, with all the data correlated in our computers. We have over one hundred selectees already by using my earlier DNA collections from the Discover program, and we've already sent them a notice and the questions to see if they want to volunteer to join the new colony."

"Who's handling the questionnaires? What are the questions?"

"Vesta gave me a list of just three questions, with multiple answers. Types of work are medical, science, engineering, clerical, or labor. There is a list for hobbies with ten choices, and one for special interests, like the arts, music, and literature. They can select more than one answer and the choices will be scanned, then the data is correlated with their DNA information in our computers."

"I thought the questions would be more detailed, like religious preferences, social status, weight, height, and age." She noticed a slight change in Zane's expression. "Why aren't those on the list?"

"We glean all that information from their social media postings, but according to Vesta, those are not an issue for being accepted." He could tell Mya didn't like his answer, so to change the subject, he pointed to the person climbing out of the utility hole. "They're installing more high-speed internet connections for the server room, and we'll be able to handle a lot more information from volunteers around the world."

"Did you figure out how to use the other machine Vesta gave you?"

"No, I don't have a clue. I guess I'll find out tomorrow when she returns. One more thing. I did some research about our technological development, and Vesta was telling the truth. About twenty-five thousand years ago, there was a sudden increase in scientific discoveries and inventions."

"Because of the new species brought to the planet?"

"It makes sense. If it weren't for the Dark Ages, we would be far more technologically advanced than we are right now. During that period, the people with the GC117 gene were scientists, and most of them were murdered by the Catholic Church for heresy."

Mya indicated the building. "You might as well show me what to do."

"Are you serious about working for me? Because I'll need you to fill out some forms first."

"No, I don't want to work for you. At least, not yet. I'll help you until I decide if I'm joining the colony or not."

"It's a long commute from Fort Collins. I have a guest bedroom at my home if you need a place to stay."

"Thanks for the offer, but I'll stay at a motel tonight until I get a feel for things around here. Where do you want me to start?"

Zane indicated the front door. "I'll let Vickie show you. I need to get back to my laboratory so I can figure out the function of the new genes I found in you and Alex Cave."

"Is that where Vesta will meet you tomorrow?"

"No, she's only interested in overseeing this aspect of the project. I'll be back here in the morning."

Zane led Mya into the testing room and over to a workstation. "Vickie, I'm sure you remember Mya Austin. She's offered to give us a hand, so why don't you show her what we do with the samples?"

Vickie stood up and lowered her facemask to show her smile. "Hey, sweetie. Did you bring those two hunks with you?"

Mya grinned at her. "No, they have their own agendas. So, where do we start?"

Zane put his hand on Vickie's shoulder. "I'll see you tomorrow morning."

When Zane left the room, Vickie indicated an empty chair in front of a keyboard and monitor. "Take a load off and I'll run you through the process." Once Mya was seated, Vickie showed her a list of names on the monitor. "These people still need to be processed. Start by searching for the donor's name on social media sites. Copy any images and pertinent data into their file then do a general search for family members to see if any of them might have already sent in a sample."

Mya looked up at Vickie. "Is there something else I could do instead?"

"What's wrong?"

"I feel like I'm invading their privacy."

"Listen, sweetie. They shared it with the entire world, so they've already given up their privacy. We usually send the names and identification numbers to the people at the search stations in the next room, but I wanted you to use this station in case you have questions."

"Is that all there is to it?"

"Pretty much. The computers will do the rest. When the software matches the name and information you entered with that sample, it does a keyword search, compiles all the data for that individual, and adds it to the DNA file."

"All right, but I'm still uncomfortable with this."

When Vickie returned to her own station, Mya concentrated on her task. Within seconds, the person's entire history was at her fingertips. "Good grief."

Vickie turned when she heard Mya. "Is there a problem?"

"No. I'm just a little shocked. I see your point about them giving up their privacy. I'm just glad I don't post my private information on the web."

"I know. I blame the internet for creating all the problems in the world right now. You know, instant messaging, instant video, and instant access to information about anyone and anything."

"I know what you mean. It seems like the world keeps getting smaller while the population keeps getting larger. I think that's part of the global warming problem. We're over populating the planet. Billions of people, all needing food, water, shelter, and transportation, not to mention all the methane being pumped into the atmosphere from human and animal waste. Add to that the amount of body heat and carbon dioxide we exhale, and it's no wonder our atmosphere is getting so bad. I think our rate of growth is unsustainable."

"I hear ya, sweetie, but it's a global problem, and there isn't anything you and I can do about it."

Mya didn't care what Zane and Vickie had said about internet privacy. She still felt uncomfortable digging through someone's personal history and stood up from the workstation. "It's been a long day. Do you know of any decently priced motels nearby?"

"Yeah, when you get back to the turnoff, go left. About five miles further, you'll see the Mountain View Motel. There's a decent restaurant further up the road when you get hungry."

"Thanks. I'll see you tomorrow."

***

Mya arrived early the next morning to make sure she didn't miss Vesta's arrival, and was stopped at the closed security gate and asked for identification. When the gate opened, she drove through and parked next to three cars and an unmarked travel bus, then turned off the engine and climbed out. When she entered through the front door, she realized two people in uniform now manned the reception area and a woman in uniform stood from a chair and approached her.

"How can I help you, Miss Austin?"

"I'm here to see Zane Kinkaid."

"Mister Kinkaid is busy right now."

The guard handed Mya a clip on security pass and indicated a set of padded chairs along the opposite wall. "Please sit down and I'll let him know you're here."

Mya sat down and noticed metal bars had been added to the outside of the windows. She studied the pass and attached it to her shirt, then looked around at the large images of DNA strands on the walls.

***

Zane stood next to Vesta in his office while she assembled the remaining pieces of equipment on the table. Once complete, it was a stand for getting your eyes examined by placing your forehead against the strange Y shaped object.

"What's this for?"

"We need retinal scans of those being considered for joining the colony. It's the fastest way to verify their identity before we take them up to the main ship. My people will operate it, but I wanted to explain it to you in person, in case anyone asks about it."

Zane thought about the strange new gene he had found in Mya's DNA. "Is the GC117 gene the only one you're looking for?"

Vesta stared at him. "What do you mean?"

"I've found a previously unknown gene in Mya's sample. It appears to be dormant, and I don't have a clue as to its original purpose."

"Is she one of the volunteers?"

"Not yet, but she's thinking about it."

"Tell her you need a fresh sample and I'll take it back to my ship for analysis."

"I don't know if she'll agree."

"If she has an unidentified gene, then others might have it as well."

"I don't think so. She's only the second sample with that gene out of over sixty thousand tests."

"If there are two, then undoubtedly there are more. We can't take the chance of having an unknown gene introduced into the colony without knowing more about its original purpose."

Zane thought about Alex's strange eye color gene, and he hadn't been able to determine its purpose, either. "I have another sample with a different unusual gene I can't figure out. Would you take that one with you and let me know what you learn about it?"

"Are they one of the volunteers?"

"No, but I would like to know what it does. It's a tag attached to the HERC2/OCA2 eye color gene." He noticed her concerned expression. "Is everything all right?"

Vesta thought about the strange sensation she felt when she looked into Alex Cave's eyes. She had never touched him, so she wondered why. She saw Zane staring at her and forced a smile. "Yes. I'll take it with me and let you know what I find out. Who does it belong to?"

Zane liked Alex and knew Vesta felt just the opposite. If he told her who it belonged to, she may not help him learn about the strange gene, so he decided to keep it a secret.

"I'm not sure. Also, Alex Cave would like you to show him your main spaceship."

"Tell him no." She snatched the DNA sample from his hand, then turned and walked out of the office, and stopped when she saw Mya waiting in the reception area. "Hello again, Mya. I understand you're thinking about volunteering."

Mya stood. "That's right."

"Zane told me about your special gene, and we would like to learn more about it. Would you mind giving me a fresh sample?"

Mya thought about it for a moment. She wasn't sure if she wanted to know what it meant, but Vesta seemed overly interested, so it might be a way for her to gain access to Vesta's ship. "Alex Cave would like to see your ship, and so would I. Let us see if what you say is true, and I'll give you a fresh sample."

Vesta knew the time would come when she would need to show someone her spacecraft. "All right, but not Cave."

Zane was not going to miss this opportunity. "What about me?"

"Yes, you both can see what I'm offering is real and let the rest of the world know. I'll come back tomorrow to pick you up here at this facility."

Mya followed Zane and Vesta out through a back entrance of the building and stood with them in the grassy field. She flinched when the cube suddenly appeared a few feet away, then Paul and a woman she didn't recognize stepped out. Realizing the cube was empty, Mya turned to face Vesta. "Why can't we go with you right now?"

"Paul has a time sensitive mission to accomplish that will need Zane's help, and Sharon needs to get started right away. I'll be back tomorrow afternoon."

When Zane escorted Paul and Sharon into the building, Mya remained behind and watched Vesta step into the cube. The opening closed, and then it vanished. When she headed back toward the building, her phone rang, but she didn't recognize the number. "Hello?"

"Hey, sweetie. It's me, Vickie. Stop by my workstation. There's something I need to show you."

"All right."

Mya hurried back into the building, and then continued along the corridor and into the testing room, where Vickie waved her over to the workstation. "What's going on?"

"After you left yesterday, I ran my own correlation program to search for violent activity shared on social media and news broadcasts. The news stations are so desperate to compete for everyone's attention, they mostly run stories about violent behavior, and are actually creating more of the same violence. It showed the average time the news stations run the same disturbing story is thirteen days, and all the copycat violence occurs during that same thirteen day period."

Mya thought about it for a moment. "Have you told anyone about your findings?"

"I posted it on social media sites this morning before I came to work."

"Let's hope someone takes notice and does something about it."

"Like what? You and I both know they won't stop blasting the violence. All they want are the ratings."

"I'm tempted to join the colony just to get away from all the hatred on this planet."

Vickie chuckled. "Not me. I like my creature comforts. Starting a new colony is going to be tough, and it will probably take years before you can get fast food to go."

Mya grinned. "That's true. What do you want me to do today?"

"The first group of volunteers arrived this morning, with more scheduled to arrive throughout the day. We won't be involved with that aspect of the selection process, but the people who pass the second part of the test can be taken up to the ship right away if they're ready to go. I guess Vesta doesn't want to wait until the last minute to get five hundred people up to her spaceship. The same thing is happening all over the world, so there really isn't anything for you to do right now."

"All right. I still have a lot of packing to do, so I guess I'll head home."

"Stop by anytime, sweetie. Think about bringing those hunks with you next time."

Vickie stared after Mya until she stepped through the doorway, then turned back to her computer monitor. Even though she knew the room was deserted, she looked around before entering the password she stole from Zane, and then accessed his files.

Chapter 10

SIERRA NEVADA MOUNTAINS:

Paul enjoyed the wonderful aroma of evergreens wafting in through open windows while he drove past the lush green forests lining Interstate 80. He had never driven a vehicle with a combustion engine, but the basic concept of a manual steering wheel was familiar, so he had no problem driving one of Zane's spare cars. He was beginning to like this planet, but that would soon change, and from experience, he knew in a few more days the occupants would riot. He'd seen it happen before to a certain degree, with humans more evolved than the ones on this planet, and he expected this society to collapse into chaos in far less time.

He glanced over at the heavy-duty brown briefcase sitting on the passenger seat. Several bundles of money now replaced the eight blocks of pure gold he had brought down from the spacecraft. Since he still had a connection with Zane, it was simple to acquire any information he needed from the geneticist, and he had learned about a form of currency called credit cards, which were used for large transactions. Zane had provided cash and three pieces of plastic currency in exchange for the gold, and with an automobile at his disposal, he could complete his part of the mission.

A green and white sign on the side of the road read DONNER'S PASS, just before the concrete sloped downhill. He looked at the screen in the dashboard and the GPS unit showed it would take him two more hours to reach Sacramento. If everything goes as planned, he would be done before the end of the day, and since the transport module would pick him up when he was done with his meetings, his lips formed into a slight grin as he thought about telling Zane he would need to go to California to retrieve his car. When he turned on the vehicle's sound system, his grin turned into a smile when a catchy tune blasted from the speakers.

Chapter 11

GROOM LAKE, NEVADA:
The unmarked jet taxied along the concrete tarmac and stopped in front of the security terminal. Alex stood and looked at Okawna and Jadin, who had met him in Las Vegas, Nevada, for the ride to the base. "I wonder if Vesta has returned to Zane's place yet."

Okawna waited until Jadin climbed out of her seat, then followed her forward and stopped next to Alex. "I'll bet she won't take you into her spaceship."

Jadin grabbed her bag from the storage locker near the door. "We haven't been able to see it with any of our equipment, so it's probably behind the moon, as she says. But why keep it a secret?"

Alex opened the exit door and pressed the button to lower the stairs. "Exactly my point. What is she hiding?"

Okawna stopped in the doorway before walking down the steps and turned to look at his friends. "The only thing I can think of is she's lying about its size. Something big enough to carry five hundred passengers would be enormous, so maybe she's only going to take half that many, or even less."

Alex indicated for Okawna to get going, and they all went down the stairs and over to the security checkpoint. They passed through with no problem and continued across the terminal and out the opposite doorway. Okawna climbed in behind the wheel of one of the golf carts parked outside the building, and he let Jadin climb into the back seat before he climbed in next to Okawna. When they headed toward the hangars, he turned to look back at Jadin. "I'll call Mya and see if she made it to Zane's facility."

Jadin heard her phone ring and saw it was Holly calling, and answered. "We made it."

"I know. I just got a call from security you arrived. Meet us at Hangar 5."

"Okay." She leaned forward over the front seat to speak to Okawna. "Holly is waiting for us at Alex's spaceship."

Alex put his phone away. "I got Mya's voice mail."

Jadin was still leaning forward and noticed a slight frown on Alex's lips. "What's she like?"

"Oh, you know how those academics are. All they talk about is work."

"You like her, don't you?"

He gave Jadin a solemn expression. "You know why I can't get involved in a close relationship."

Okawna turned to Alex. "What are you going to do, remain celibate for the rest of your life?"

"Of course not, but I'd prefer to do it with a professional. Strictly business, if you know what I mean."

Jadin exchanged a mischievous grin with Okawna. "I hope David has good news about the cloaking system on our ship. I'd love to go up and take a look at Vesta's spacecraft."

When Okawna parked in front of Hangar 5, Alex climbed out with his friends, and then slid his identification card into a slender slot next to the steel door. The electronic lock buzzed, then opened the door and went into a small room, and closed it behind him. He looked up into the security camera lens, and when the opposite door opened, he left the room and waited for the others to pass through security.

Once Jadin and Okawna were through, they continued along the short hallway to the small break room, expecting to see Holly and David inside, but the room was empty. They continued along the hallway and through the double doors into the hangar, and sitting in the middle of the concrete floor was his spaceship.

It looked like a forty-foot wide hockey puck with a twenty-four foot high mirrored surface. The eight-foot square airlock door was open at the bottom of the spacecraft, so they passed through into the cargo hold and engine compartment. Alex caught sight of Holly and David on the far side of the room, so they sauntered over to the exposed section of the engine to join them, and he looked over David's shoulder into the vertical tube-shaped engine compartment. "Any luck with the cloak?"

David leaned back from the glowing neon blue fiber optic cables just inside the open hatch. "Yes. At least, I think it's fixed."

Holly looked at Alex. "Have you heard from Zane?"

"No, and I don't think I will. For some reason, Vesta doesn't like me."

"I can't imagine why, other than you called her a liar in front of several important people." When he started to protest, she held up her palm to stop him. "I told you I agree. I just wish you would have let me handle it."

"I know I didn't give you the chance, but we had just met each other, and I didn't know what to expect from you."

David was listening to the conversation, and had spent more time with Holly than the rest of the team had. She wasn't as animated as Henry, his old boss had been, but seemed all right. He would just have to let the others get to know her a little better. He stepped back from the engine compartment to look at his team members. "I was just about to go upstairs and turn on the cloak."

Jadin headed toward the steps curving up along the inside wall of the spacecraft. "I'll take care of it." He hurried up the stairs and stopped at the first landing to look into the small living area. Four narrow sleeping pads were inside the recessed areas in the opposing walls, and a small table with four chairs was in the center of the room. Straight ahead was a small sink, next to a door leading into the toilet/shower room. She chuckled to herself as she stared at the only thing that was not part of the ship. Okawna's microwave oven. It took him an entire day to get the correct AC voltage from the ship's odd electrical system just to power his food warmer.

She thought about the first time Alex told her about finding the ship in a dormant volcano in the Aleutian Islands, and had found it hard to believe it had been buried in lava for millions of years. The mirrored surface was unscathed, but it took several weeks to figure out how the ancient craft worked.

She continued up the stairs to the control room and smiled when she saw the vase of nearly dead flowers on the floor in front of the control console. She opened a drawer to retrieve one of the small communication devices and inserted it into her ear before sitting down in front of the main control panel. She reached up and touched a small button on the side of the earpiece to turn it on, then held her hand poised over one of the illuminated touchpads on the console. "Are you ready, David?"

David heard Jadin's voice in his earpiece. "I'm on my way outside. Turn it on."

Alex followed David out through the airlock and turned to face the ship. An instant later, it disappeared, and he turned and smiled at the young man. "You did it, my friend."

David grinned as he spoke to Jadin. "It works. Turn it off and on a few times to make sure." When it vanished for the third time, David heaved a deep sigh of relief. "That's good, Jadin. You can leave it off now."

Alex followed David into the ship and over to Okawna and Holly as Jadin arrived, then he spoke to the group. "I'd like to take it up tonight and check out Vesta's ship. If it's big enough to carry five hundred people, we'll know she's sincere about her offer. I'm not saying I'll start trusting her. I've been burnt too many times by aliens posing as so-called friends, but I'll give her the benefit of the doubt for a while."

Holly saw the others agreed. "All right. Once we have verification Vesta has returned, you can take it to the dark side of the moon. Just make sure you're not detected. I don't want her knowing we have a spaceship of our own."

Alex had already planned to keep the ship a secret. "I'll keep trying to reach Mya. She was going to be working with Zane, so she should know if Vesta is back."

Holly looked at her wristwatch. "I'm due at a secure conference in twenty-six minutes, so you can contact me any time before then if you hear from Miss Austin."

When Holly turned and hurried out through the airlock, Okawna put his hand on David's shoulder. "I guess you and the artificial intelligence are on working terms again."

David hooked his thumbs over his belt and puffed out his chest. "His name is Melvin, and if I had any cigars, I'd pass them out."

Jadin grinned at David. "I saw the flowers. I guess they worked."

David relaxed. "Only after I explained their purpose and why I brought them to him. After that, we talked for a while and he told me what the problem was with the cloak."

Alex had been leaning against the side of the engine compartment and suddenly straightened up. "Are you saying it talks?"

"Yes, and Melvin has been listening to us since we found the ship. The first time I was trying to get the cloak working, I saw a button under the main control console and pressed it. Melvin's first words were, 'it's about time.' He told me it was a mute control for his voice, and we turned it on when we were trying to figure out how the ship worked. I guess there isn't a way for him to turn it back off by himself."

Alex's posture stiffened, since he and his team had just dealt with a female artificial intelligence that nearly killed everyone on Earth. "Is it anything like the one in the Pandora operation?"

David shook his head no. "He's nothing like that one. His only concern is our wellbeing."

Okawna tilted his head to one side as he stared at David. "And his name is Melvin?"

"Actually, his real name is just a series of numbers and no sexual orientation, so I asked it if I could name it and have it use a masculine voice."

Okawna put his hands on his hips. "And making it a male AI named Melvin was the best you could come up with? Why didn't you make it female with a cool name like Shania? You know. Something sexy."

David looked over at Alex. "Because of what happened with Pandora, I'm not comfortable with even a semblance of a female artificial intelligence. I'm sure you understand."

Alex indicated he did. "Can Melvin help us with the comet problem?"

David shrugged his shoulders and walked toward the stairs. "Let's go up and find out."

Alex followed David up into the control room, and through the transparent sides and ceiling of the spacecraft, he saw the walls and overhead lights of the hangar. He followed him over to one of the four new chairs installed in the control room, which were much more functional than the original chairs that came with the craft. Each of the new chairs had a four-point harness, including a lever alongside the armrest, that allowed the back of the seat to drop back flat so they could look through the transparent ceiling. He stood beside David when he sat down in front of the main control panel. "How does it work?"

David turned his head to look up at Alex. "You're going to love this. Hello, Melvin."

A red dot appeared on the elevated holographic screen. "Good afternoon, Dave."

David chuckled. "Just like in the movie." He stopped laughing when Alex frowned. "Don't you get it?"

Alex stared down at David. "That computer took over the spaceship."

"Oh, right. I forgot about that. Anyway, he's not like that. Melvin, can you detect a comet heading in our direction?"

"No, I cannot perform that task while on this planet."

"But you can do it from outer space?"

"Yes, Dave."

"All right. Tonight we'll go for a ride."

"Will your friends be joining us?"

"Yes. Standby."

David turned to his friends. "That puts him on hold until I want to talk to him again."

Alex turned to Jadin. "Have your friends at the Jet Propulsion Laboratory been able to determine the distance to the comet?"

"No, because we can't without a way to triangulate its trajectory. Once we're in space, we can track it from two separate locations, but we'll need to stay at each stop for a while in order to determine its speed and trajectory."

Alex looked at David. "If we find out Vesta is back, is there anything we need to do to get ready?"

"No, we're good to go."

Alex looked at his watch. "It's nearly 7:00 PM and I'm starving. I'm headed to the cafeteria to get something to eat. Anyone care to join me?"

Jadin smiled. "I'm in."

David stood up from the chair. "I could use something to eat."

Okawna turned and walked toward the stairs. "I'm driving."

***

Alex set his hamburger down on the plate when his phone rang and he recognized Mya's number, and turned on the speaker before setting it on the table. "I was hoping you'd call. Did Vesta show up?"

"Yes, but she said no to your request to be taken up to her ship. She is going to take Zane and me up to check it out tomorrow afternoon. Do you remember Vickie?"

"I do."

"Well, she told me the DNA test kit distributer is barely keeping up with the number of requests to join the colony. Oh, and the first group of volunteers are already doing the second phase of testing, and the ones that pass are being taken up to Vesta's ship immediately."

"That's fast. What's the second phase?"

"That's the odd part. Nobody knows, and one of Vesta's people is doing the test in a private room, so none of Zane's people will be involved in this phase. That's not all. Zane figured out how to use the new equipment Vesta gave him. It's an automatic assembly line for testing the DNA samples and correlating the data with the answers to the questionnaire. Once the genetic data is entered into a computer, a program searches the internet for that volunteer. It will copy photographs and any information about that person and their relatives."

"Vesta said volunteers could not be related. That must be part of the screening process. How are you getting along with Zane?"

"He's okay."

"Are you going to stay there?"

"No, I'm already home. They didn't need my help anymore, so I left. I'll start packing my belongings and drive back tomorrow afternoon for my ride to Vesta's ship."

"I appreciate you letting me know what's going on."

"You're welcome. I'll call you again tomorrow when I get back."

Alex turned off the phone. "Vesta isn't wasting any time gathering volunteers."

Jadin set her can of orange soda on the table. "She's down to eleven days."

"When we're finished eating, you all head back to the hangar and I'll go tell Holly Vesta has returned. When I join you, we'll go for a ride."

***

Alex sat in a chair on the other side of Holly's desk and told her what he had learned from Mya. "We'll leave as soon as I get back to the ship."

"I envy you, Alex."

"And why is that?"

"I miss the adventure. I was a good agent until I was shot in the left kidney. They had to remove it and gave me some time off to recover, but then they stuck me behind a desk at Langley."

"How did you end up here?"

"I ran a few operations from a room, but it was frustrating not being in the fight. Martin and I have been friends for years, and he understood how I felt. He told me about this job and it sounded exciting, even though I'll probably never go up in your ship."

"What makes you say that? I'll take you into space any time you'd like a ride."

"Thanks, but that's not the reason. I have a problem with heights. I even keep the shade down on airplanes so I can't see out the window."

Alex's eyebrow rose. "And you were an agent?"

"I worked it out with my teammates and stayed on the lowest levels. Don't get me wrong. I'll climb the tower in Dubai if necessary. It's just not something I would volunteer for."

Alex was glad Holly was finally opening up about her past, but he wanted to make sure they saw the visiting spacecraft while it was still dark here on Earth. "I'd better get going."

"Before you leave, there's something else you need to be aware of. How many people can your ship carry?"

"It's set up for four. Why do you ask?"

"The President wants to use your ship to save him, his family, and his top advisors from the impact."

Alex's hands clenched into fists at his sides as he stared at Holly. "I'm not spending what could be the rest of my life on a ship with a bunch of politicians."

"Vesta is proof there are other inhabited planets in our galaxy, and the President thinks you can fly him and his people to one of those."

"I have no idea where they are, and I know Vesta won't tell me. Even if I knew, I sure as hell wouldn't tell him and his cronies. Besides, we could never carry enough supplies for that many people."

"I see your point, but you may not have a choice in the matter."

"Listen, Holly. Once we learn more about the comet, we might be able to change its trajectory."

"Vesta told us she can't do anything to help us. What makes you think you can do it?"

"You've read about our previous missions, so you know my team and I are good at improvising."

Holly was impressed by what she had read about Alex and his team. But, according to her conversations with Donner, they got lucky. She heaved a deep sigh of resignation. "All right. Good luck and I'll see you when you get back."

Chapter 12

HANGAR 5. GROOM LAKE, NEVADA:

Alex set the timer on the control pad for the massive hangar doors to open in three minutes, and then he hurried over to the airlock into the ship. He stepped into the cargo hold and pressed the button to close the airlock doors before jogging up the stairs. When he entered the control room, Okawna and Jadin were staring out through the transparent outer walls of the ship while David sat behind the control panel. He hurried over to the window to join his friends just before the lights blinked off, and as his eyes adjusted to the darkness, he saw a widening gap of starlight as the hangar doors parted in the middle.

The interior of the control room was as dark as the hangar, and David had only the holographic display and the colored touch pads on the control panel for illumination. Through the open hangar doors, he could not see any lights leading to the runway, but he didn't need one as he eased the spacecraft out into a moonless sky, then looked over at his friends while he held his finger over the control panel. "All right. Buckle up, cause here we go."

Alex placed his hands on the transparent barrier to stare down at the outline of the main runway, now quickly shrinking away below him. When he turned around, starlight filled the room through the transparent walls and ceiling as he stared across the endless sea of sparkling dots. The Earth slowly slid out of sight beneath the floor, and then the moon appeared directly overhead. He wondered if Holly would have his back like Donner had in the past, since the last thing he needed right now was a bunch of politicians telling him what he could or could not do with his spaceship.

Jadin noticed Alex's troubled expression reflecting off the outside barrier and moved over beside him. "I never tire of this view."

Alex looked down at her and smiled. "I like the one when we're headed back, better." He looked up and saw the moon growing larger by the minute. "You know, it took each Apollo mission three days to reach the moon. It's hard to believe this ship can get there in four minutes at slow speed."

"I know what you mean. This is an incredible piece of technology. We won't be able to keep this ship a secret forever, but at least it's yours for now."

"I suppose so. At least until the President takes it for his own survival."

Okawna snapped his head around to look at him. "What the hell are you talking about?"

Alex told them about his conversation with Holly and saw the lightning bolts shooting from Okawna's eyes. "I won't let it happen."

Okawna hooked his thumbs over his belt. "You're damn right! Those chickenshits ain't going anywhere."

Alex turned to David. "Is Melvin detecting the other ship?"

David smiled when he heard Alex call the artificial intelligence by name. "Why don't you ask him yourself?"

Alex grinned. "All right. Melvin, can you detect the other ship?"

"Nothing yet, Alex. How do you want me to make the approach?"

"Stay on the light side, but keep us close to the surface and follow the terrain. No offense, but I'm sure her ship's technology is more advanced than you are. Stop when you first detect any part of Vesta's spacecraft. Let's make sure they can't detect us when we're cloaked before we fully expose ourselves."

"Understood, and no offense taken. We'll reach the surface in less than two minutes."

With Melvin in control, David swung his chair around to face Alex. "What if their ship is cloaked, too?"

"If they could, why hide it behind the moon?"

"That's true."

Jadin realized something had changed with the AI. "David? Did you do something different to Melvin's speech?"

"Yeah, it was too much like the movie. After a while, it started creeping me out."

Alex looked up as the surface of the moon slowly rolled across the ceiling. A moment later, the surface appeared to stop moving, and he heard Melvin's voice.

"Alex, I've detected an object on the horizon. Should I proceed?"

"Can you verify if our cloak is working?"

"Yes, all my systems are functioning."

"All right. Nice and slow."

Alex stared at the horizon, trying to locate the other ship. At first, he couldn't find it, but noticed an area of space with no stars. The dark area grew larger for a few moments before sunlight was reflecting off a large, oval-shaped object with a mirrored finish sitting on the surface of the moon. "Melvin, can you estimate the size of the other ship?"

"Yes, it is twenty-eight hundred feet long, by eighteen hundred feet wide, by two hundred feet in height."

Okawna thought about it for a moment. "That's about three football fields in length and two in width. At two hundred feet high, I'm sure they could fit five hundred people in that thing."

Alex turned to look at his friends. "All right. So far, Vesta has told the truth. Now it's time we concentrate on dealing with a comet. Jadin, you're the astrophysicist. What's next?"

"We need to determine its mass, exact trajectory, and speed."

"All right. Melvin, did you copy that?"

"Of course. I hear everything, and I've already determined the first location. I'm just waiting for someone to say go."

Jadin shook her head in amazement that Melvin seemed to have a personality. "All right. Go."

When the ship spun away from the moon, Alex had no idea where they were going, and sat in one of the chairs to enjoy the ride. He wondered why he couldn't shake the feeling Vesta was still hiding something, and a thought occurred to him. "Melvin, could you sense an artificial intelligence on the other ship?"

"I tried, but I could not detect any type of operating system."

"That's too bad. Vesta is up to something, and I'd like to know what it is."

"I'll let you know if I learn anything more about her ship, Alex. By the way. This is the first chance I've had to tell you how much I've enjoyed your adventures."

Alex exchanged looks with his team, and then turned to the monitor, even though it only showed their course and speed. "Melvin, I'm sorry we accidently turned you off."

"I was never off, only muted. We'll reach the first stop in three hours, and we will need to stay there for another two hours."

Alex hadn't realized how long it would take to gather the information, and turned to Okawna. "What's in that box you were so desperate to bring with us? I hope it's a deck of cards."

"Even better. My digital movie collection, and popcorn."

Alex chuckled while the others grinned. "I should have known."

Okawna stood and headed for the stairs. "I'll go unpack."

Jadin jumped out of her chair. "I want to see what movies you brought."

Alex looked over at David and could tell he wanted to join Jadin and Okawna. "There isn't much to do until we arrive. I'll stay here if you want to go below."

David got up from his chair. "Now that Melvin is back in control of the ship, you can go, too."

"I'm sure whatever you pick out will be fine."

David headed down the stairs, and when he reached the living area, he found Jadin and Okawna lying on the mattresses. "What's going on?"

Okawna squirmed out of the cramped space recessed into the wall just above the floor, then stood up. "It's like sleeping in a coffin."

Jadin was in the opening directly above Okawna and reached into her pocket to grab a small audio player with ear buds. "I think it's kind of cozy."

Okawna knelt down to study the underside of the bed. "Yeah, well, you're not as tall as me, either. I think I'll design a slide out for mine." He got up and looked at David. "What about you?"

"I'm okay with mine the way it is."

Okawna turned back to Jadin. "Would you like an upgrade while I'm at it?"

"No thanks, but make the offer to Alex, since he's nearly as tall as you are."

"Right." He grabbed his large screen laptop computer off the table. "Let's go up and watch a movie."

***

TWELVE HOURS LATER:

Alex stared forward at the beautiful blue planet rapidly growing in size. The bad news was the comet was definitely headed toward Earth, and was about the size of the state of Maine in the US. They could only guess at its composition, but whether it was mostly rock or ice, its impact would still have a devastating effect. This new information also verified Vesta's claim about having less than one hundred and eighty days before it arrives.

He looked around at his friends, each apparently lost in their own thoughts, as they headed home. He turned away and stared down at the Earth and heaved a deep sigh of resignation, knowing billions of people were going to die. When he thought about his family in Sparrow Valley, his vision blurred and a single tear rolled down his cheek. He wiped it away and straightened his shoulders. He wasn't about to resign himself to accepting the inevitable and give up hope. There had to be a way out of this situation, and he was determined to find it.

Chapter 13

SALT LAKE CITY, UTAH:

After seeing the interior of Vesta's spaceship and the hundreds of stasis chambers, Mya stepped out of the transport module with a sense of awe. When she turned around, Zane was smiling at her, but the craft had already vanished.

Zane reached out and gently grabbed Mya's hand. "Vesta's telling the truth about taking people to another planet."

Mya wasn't so sure. She had a nagging feeling in the back of her mind Vesta was holding back a key piece of information and pulled her hand from Zane's grasp. "Perhaps. I still have a lot of packing to do, so I'm going home."

Zane found it hard to believe Mya still had doubts about Vesta's sincerity. "I know you're good friends with Alex, but this just proves his suspicions are unfounded."

"Then why is she being so secretive about the second phase of testing?"

Zane didn't know the answer and made a mental note to ask Vesta about it. "She must have a good reason."

When Mya turned toward the back of the building, he indicated another route. "We don't need to go back inside. I'm headed to a meeting in town and I'll walk you to your car." He led Mya around the building to the parking lot and over to her SUV. "You're welcome to come back anytime."

"Thanks. It's definitely been interesting."

Zane climbed into his car, started the engine, and then noticed the time on the radio. He realized he was late for a meeting with his distributor, who wanted to renegotiate their contract because of the massive jump in DNA requests. He took one last look at Mya, who had gotten into her car and was sitting with her hands on the steering wheel, but was just staring out the front window. He backed out of the parking spot and headed toward the security gate.

Mya was about to turn the key to start the engine when she received a text message from Vickie asking her to come to her station before she leaves. She climbed out of the car and hurried into the building. When she saw the two guards, she thought they were going to stop her, but when they nodded, she realized she was still wearing the visitor badge. She continued along the hallway to the testing facility, and when she walked through the doors, she saw Vickie sitting in front of the computer terminal.

Vickie heard the door open and looked away from the monitor to wave Mya over. "Have a seat. You need to see this."

Mya grabbed an extra chair and slid it over beside Vickie, then sat down. "What's going on?"

"I've hacked into Zane's computer and found something interesting."

"How did you get his password?"

"That was easy, sweetie. I asked myself what password I would use if I were a geneticist, so I entered the word chromosome. I also found the bleed through on a piece of tablet paper in his office."

"What did you find?"

Vickie indicated the thirty images on the screen. "These are some people who passed the second phase of testing here yesterday and were accepted for the colony. There are hundreds more, just like these, who were tested at other locations around the world, but only eighty-seven were selected to join the colony."

Mya studied the pictures of people posing for photographs, which had been shared on social media. "They all look like they're having a good time."

"No, look closer. Not a single person is overweight, and they're all decent looking. I think they're discriminating against anyone that's not a perfect specimen."

Mya had given her word to Alex she wouldn't tell anyone about the genetic requirements, and wasn't about to break it. "Are you positive?"

"Damn straight, sweetie. The computers are using our own social media postings to choose who is good enough to join the colony. That means a big lady like me isn't getting off this rock, even if I wanted to go with them. Hell, that's discrimination."

"No, it's tribalism."

"It's what?"

"Humans have a genetic tribe mentality. If you're not one of us, then you could be dangerous. Sadly, it's been that way for all of human history."

Vickie stared into Mya's eyes. "Do I look dangerous to you?"

Mya saw the rage in her expression. "At this moment? Yes, you're scaring the hell out of me."

Vickie heaved a deep sigh of resignation and leaned back in her chair. "I guess you have a point, but that doesn't make what they're doing right. I've already sent emails to some friends who are large like me and want to join the colony, and this information means it ain't gonna happen."

Mya knew this was the last thing the world needed to know right now, but it was too late. "I'm sure there's a reason. They said it was going to be a struggle just to survive, so perhaps obesity would be a problem."

"Oh yeah? I did some digging around, and there are no mentions of the accepted volunteers being a lesbian, gay, bisexual, or transgender."

"What did your friends say about it?"

Vickie brought out her smart phone. A moment later, she showed Mya what was trending on social media. "They're pissed off."

Mya felt bad she couldn't tell Vickie the truth as she stood from the chair. "I've got a long drive home. It was nice to meet you, Vickie. Thanks for letting me know about what's going on."

Vickie got up and wrapped her arms around Mya for a hug. "I know you're just an observer, but could you let Okawna know what these bastards are doing?"

"Why him?"

"I have a feeling he's the rebellious type, and he seems to be someone important. Maybe he can help us somehow."

"If I see him, I'll let him know."

Vickie let go and stepped back. "Thank you."

Mya turned and left the room and headed for the exit. As she passed the desk in the lobby, the woman guard stood and held out her hand, palm up, and realized her visitor badge was still clipped to her lapel. "Oh, right. I forgot all about it."

The woman smiled and accepted the card. "Okay, Miss Austin. You look like you're in a bit of a daze."

"I just need a good night's sleep."

Mya continued out of the building and climbed into her car, started the engine, then drove out of the parking lot. When she looked in the rearview mirror, the heavy duty security gate was closing.

Chapter 14

SPARROW VALLEY VOLUNTEER FIRE STATION:
Derek Cave was sitting at the table with his captain, Julio, and three fellow fire fighters, discussing the training exercise he had set up for noon next Saturday. He felt his phone vibrate in his pocket, and brought it out to look at the screen, and recognize the number. A woman asked him to verify his name and then gave him instructions. When the call ended, he smiled at his friends. "Guess what? I've been selected to become a member of the new colony. They'll be doing the next test in Seattle in three days."

Julio stared across the table at Derek. "That's this Saturday, the day of our drill with the State Forest Service. Do you want to call them back and cancel the training session?"

Derek felt as if his soul was being ripped in half. He loved the adrenaline rush of fighting fires, but as a volunteer, they just didn't happen often enough, so he had plans to become a full-time Federal Firefighter. At least, until the visitors showed up. Part of him still wanted that career, but he was also a lot like his uncle Alex, who yearned for a great adventure. He wasn't sure if he would pass the second phase of testing, so he didn't want to miss this opportunity for more training. "No, I'll leave for Seattle early in the morning. It shouldn't take too long and I'll be back in time for the drill."

Julio leaned back in his chair as he stared at Derek. "What does your uncle have to say about what's going on? You know? What the news was saying about the comet."

"I don't know. We're not on speaking terms anymore."

"I thought you two were getting along just fine. What happened?"

"He thinks he can tell me what to do with my life. Besides, Alex is a geophysicist, not an astrophysicist. How is he supposed to know anything?"

"Everyone knows he works for the Federal Government. He must have some insight into whether it's going to hit us or you wouldn't be so anxious to leave."

"It has nothing to do with the comet or my uncle. It's something I want to do and I may never get the chance again."

Julio remembered when he was finally old enough to be in control of his own destiny. "Just keep in mind if you go with them, you'll never see your family again."

"I've already talked to them about it, but they don't understand." He indicated a spot on the map spread out on the table. "This is where we should stage our equipment when we start the drill."

***

SATURDAY. SEATTLE, WASHINGTON:

Derek entered the lobby of the hotel and continued to an elevator. When the door opened, he stepped inside and pressed the button for the second floor. When the doors opened again, he stepped out and continued down the hallway, looking for room number 227, and when he found it, stopped in front of a serious-looking man sitting in a chair next to the closed door of the room. "Hi. I was told to come here."

The man picked up a computer tablet. "What's your name?"

"Derek Cave."

"Can I see some identification, Derek?"

Derek reached into his back pocket, brought out his wallet, and then flipped it open to show his driver's license to the man.

"Please take it out for me."

Derek did as asked and watched the man compare the information on the card to what was on the clipboard. The man used a special scanner to verify the ID was real, then looked up and smiled as he gave the license back to him. "You can go inside, Derek."

Derek put his wallet back in order and shoved it into his pocket before opening the door and stepping inside. He saw four people standing in a row about ten feet back from another person sitting in a chair in front of a small desk. He moved over and stood behind a young woman with long black hair, and a moment later, she moved back and stepped on the toes of his left foot. He grimaced in pain, but when she turned around, he forgot all about it when he saw how beautiful she was.

Catori spun around when she realized someone was behind her, and couldn't believe her luck when she saw the handsome young man, as she looked up into his soft blue eyes. "Oh, I'm so sorry. Are you okay?"

Derek ignored the slight throbbing in his toes. "Yeah, I'm fine."

Catori turned her head to look at the desk. "I'm not sure if I really want to do this. I don't think I can do it on my own."

The man who had been sitting in front of the desk stood and moved past him on the way to the door. The line moved forward, and Derek stopped next to Catori. "Where are you from?"

"Northern Colorado."

"That's a long way to travel for someone who hasn't decided."

"I thought I had. My parents didn't want me to send in my DNA, so I'm doing this behind their backs. I really didn't think I'd get selected, and now that I'm here, I feel guilty about deceiving them."

"How did you get all the way out here?"

"At first, I didn't have the courage to do the next part of the test in Denver, and by the time I decided to do it, they had already finished the testing in Salt Lake City and San Francisco. I have a friend who knows Mister Kinkaid personally, and she got me a round-trip plane ticket to come here."

"What's your name?"

"Catori Onestar."

He held out his hand. "I'm Derek Cave. It's nice to meet you."

Catori shook his hand. "I've heard about a man with that same last name. He was at a dig site I was working on. I didn't get to meet him, but my friend really liked him."

The line moved forward, and Derek stopped beside her. "Maybe I'm related. What's his first name?"

"Alex. He's a geophysicist from someplace in Nevada."

Derek looked down at her. "That's my uncle. He thinks he can tell me what to do with my life, just like your parents." He noticed Catori's posture stiffen. "You're still thinking about them, aren't you?"

"My family has been responsible for saving the history and stories of my people for many generations, and I'm tired of it. I want to live my life the way I want to, not because of some tradition."

"Listen, if there's one thing I learned from Alex, it's pursuing my dream no matter what anyone else says, which is ironic, considering he keeps trying to interfere with my plans. That's why I'm joining the new colony. I want to go on a great adventure."

"I know, and I think it's exciting, but my main reason is to get off this planet so my parents won't hound me about my responsibility. They say it over and over, and I'm sick of the word."

The woman in front of Catori stood from in front of the desk, and as she moved away, Derek noticed she looked upset. He realized Catori had also seen the woman's expression, and smiled as he indicated the vacant chair. "It looks like it's your turn."

Catori reached over and gave Derek's hand a gentle squeeze as she looked up at him. "Thanks for talking with me." She let go, stepped forward, and sat down facing a man sitting on the other side of what looked like a retinal scanner. When the man smiled at her, she felt at ease. "Hello. I'm Catori Onestar."

"Hello, Catori. I'm Paul, one of the people in charge of determining who will be accepted for the new colony. This machine will scan your retinas and fingerprints to be used for verification if we take you to our ship. Just place your hand on the reader, your chin against the bottom pad, and lean your forehead against the top pads to make sure you are in alignment with the scanner."

Catori did as instructed, and then Paul told her to look straight ahead at a small black screen. A blue light flashed, and she heard Paul tell her she was done, so she leaned back and stood up from her chair. "How long before I know if I'm accepted or not?"

"Right now. Welcome to the colony. You'll be contacted again with instructions on where to be picked up and taken to the ship."

Catori turned and hurried back to Derek. "I've passed the test, but I don't want to go alone. I'll go with them, but only if you're going, too."

Derek smiled. "I'll meet you in the hallway when I'm done."

Catori reached out and squeezed Derek's hand again. "Good luck."

Derek stared after Catori until she stepped out of the room, then moved over to the chair and sat down. "I'm Derek Cave."

"Yes, you're Alex's nephew. I'm Paul. I was glad to see your name on the list."

Derek grinned. "Yeah, me too. What do you want me to do?"

"I'm not asking questions, only gathering information for later verification."

Derek followed Paul's instructions, and the light flashed, but unlike the others, he had a vision, where he is five years old with his Father, Tom Cave, both looking scared as they ran along a sandy beach. Two gunmen were shooting at them, and Alex was in the background, gun in hand, running to catch up. Tom was hit and collapses, and he was staring down at him as the gunmen slow down. A gunman was aiming his gun at him, ready to shoot, and then was shot in the back of the head. Another gunman brought his gun up, looking around as a bullet entered his forehead and he dropped to the ground. He felt Alex wept him up into his arms, and he stared back over Alex's shoulder at the bodies, his tears flowed onto Alex's cheek. Alex set him down, took his hand, and they continue along the beach. His tears were dirty as he looked back once, and then up at Alex, who gave him a sorry expression.

Derek heard a voice telling him he is done and snapped out of it, then looked across at Paul. "Was I supposed to have a dream while doing the test?"

Paul tried to hide his concern, wondering why Derek would have a dream, since this had never happened before. "No, you're the first one to mention it." He noticed the curious look in Derek's eyes. "I'm sure it's nothing to worry about. The good news is you're now part of the colony."

Derek had noticed the pause between sentences, and could sense Paul's demeanor had changed, and continued to look at him as he stood. "So I'm good to go?"

"Yes, you'll be contacted again with instructions on where to be picked up and taken to the ship."

Derek turned and strolled past six more people standing in line before he stepped out of the room. He was getting a strange feeling in his gut, and it was like an itch he couldn't scratch. He stepped out of the room and found Catori waiting for him with a questioning expression on her face. "Yeah, we're going together."

Catori felt both relieved and sad at the same time. She was excited about having Derek with her as she started a new life, then tears blurred her vision when she realized how disappointed her parents would be when she told them what she had done. She desperately needed a hug for reassurance, but was afraid to be brazen with someone she had just met.

Derek noticed the tears forming in Catori's eyes and held his palms out at his sides as a sign he was here for her. She suddenly reached up and wrapped her arms around his neck, holding him close to her, and felt her relax before she stepped back. "I hope those are tears of joy."

Catori wiped the tears from her cheeks with the back of her hand. "Yes, and no, but the yes is for you going with me. If I hadn't met you, I probably would have walked away."

"So, Catori Onestar. What are you doing until you're taken to the spaceship?"

"I hadn't really thought about it." She looked down the hallway at the elevator door. "My flight home doesn't leave until tomorrow morning, and I have a room here on the 8th floor. What is there to do in Seattle to pass the time?"

"Would you like for me to give you the grand tour?"

"That would be great."

Derek strolled beside her toward the elevator. "Why did your parents name you Catori?"

"In the Sioux language, it means Earth."

"Well, Earth Onestar, it's a beautiful name for a beautiful woman."

Catori looked up at Derek and smiled as she grabbed his hand. "Thank you."

Chapter 15

SUNDAY 6:00 AM. SPARROW VALLEY, WASHINGTON:
Derek lay on the worn couch in his living room, thinking about his friends in the fire department. He was dreading having to explain why he had forgotten about the drill because of a wonderful woman, then a trace of a smile formed on his lips when he thought about the only female volunteer in the fire department. She would probably just smile at him and start asking questions, and he could hardly wait to tell her it was love at first sight, and all about his magical night in Seattle, but also knew the rest of the crew would be disappointed with him. The thing was, now that he knew for sure he was accepted for the new colony, their feelings didn't seem as important as making the journey with the most beautiful woman he had ever met.

He was staring at the television, not listening to a word the news announcer was saying, until the image of a crowd of protesters appeared and the camera zoomed in on a young man holding a sign that read, LGBTQ have a right to join the colony. He grabbed the remote control and turned the volume up a little more and the image shifted to show another protest, only it was stating large people have the right to go with the volunteers. Some people held up signs stating the visitors are insensitive to minorities, and others thought the protesters are putting the discrimination issue ahead of saving our species from extinction.

The announcer was talking about a government source stating the visitors will only help us if we agree to their terms, because people starting a new society need to be physically fit if they are going to survive. Evidently, his source didn't comment on the LGBTQs, because the image changed to a picture of a glowing comet. The announcer talked about what the impact would do if it hit, and what would happen to the climate.

A new video in the background showed six separate rockets roaring off launch pads as the announcer talked about the plan to blow up the comet, and that they should impact the comet in three days.

He turned the television off and stared up at the ceiling. He wasn't too worried about the comet. He hadn't thought about it while he was in line with Catori, but thinking back now, none of the people he saw were overweight. Even the upset woman appeared to be in decent physical shape, so there must have been another reason she was rejected. He wondered if maybe her fingerprints connected her to a crime.

The image of Catori's unbridled exuberance while they strolled around Pike Place Market played through his mind. After they took the tour through the underground city, they had dinner in a restaurant on the pier as the sun was setting over the horizon, then had walked along the waterfront, stopping in all the curiosity shops. When they reached her hotel room door, he gave her a kiss before telling her he would see her again, and remembered whistling all the way back to his car.

He remembered after he and Catori had left the testing room, she had not mentioned being accepted to join the colony, and he understood why. Now he was facing a similar, although much less complicated, situation with his own family. In a few more days, he was going to have to say goodbye. His eyelids slowly closed as his thoughts turned back to the day with Catori.

Chapter 16

DENVER, COLORADO:

It was late afternoon when Catori stepped out of the air terminal and climbed into the shuttle bus to the parking area. The heated air rippled above the black asphalt as she climbed out and hurried over to her car. When she opened the door, a wave of hot air rushed across her face and she pressed the buttons to roll down all the windows.

While she waited for the interior to cool down, her lips formed into a soft smile as she thought about Derek. Last night was more romantic than she could have imagined. He was the perfect gentleman when appropriate, and a playful rascal the rest of the time. She was immensely grateful he didn't need to talk about going with the visitors on his new adventure. He had stroked her cheek before giving her a soft kiss good night, and when he walked away, she thought it was the perfect ending to the beginning of a closer relationship.

She climbed into her car, started the engine, and then drove out of the lot. She took a shortcut to bypass Denver and met up with the Interstate highway for the drive to Fort Collins. She thought listening to an audio book would distract her from thinking about her parents, but it did not work. She knew her mother would not take the news too well and was dreading having to argue with her. Hopefully, her father would understand and be supportive of her decision to leave.

***

Darkness hid the forest when Catori drove into the parking space across from her rustic old home. She climbed out and stared across at the window, where her parents were in the living room watching the television. She left her small backpack on the backseat and slowly approached the front door, hesitant to grab the brass handle. The door suddenly opened, and her father was smiling at her. "Hi, Dad."

Michael Onestar stepped back to let his little girl in, closed the door, and then followed her into the living room. "Your mother and I were getting a little worried. This is the first time you have stayed the night at the sacred site."

"I know I should have called, but I never made it to the site. I spent the night in Seattle."

Dove Onestar leapt out of her chair and stared at her daughter. "You did what?"

"I was given a free round-trip airline ticket from Denver to Seattle, and I couldn't pass up the opportunity. I didn't want you to worry about me, so I didn't call you."

Dove crossed her arms and stared at Catori. "What were you doing in Seattle?"

Catori smiled. "A young man named Derek Cave showed me around the city, and it was magical." She stopped smiling when her father's mouth dropped open. "He was a perfect gentleman, Dad. Well, most of the time, but he did not do anything inappropriate."

Michael closed his mouth. "Did you sleep with him?"

"I'm eighteen, Daddy. Stop thinking of me as your little girl. And no, I didn't sleep with him. Like I said. He was a gentleman."

Dove uncrossed her arms. "I'm glad nothing happened to you, but you should have let us know you were leaving. How old is Derek?"

"He's nineteen."

The corners of Dove's lips formed into a sly grin when she saw the sparkle in Catori's eyes. "Is he good looking?"

"No, he's handsome, in a rugged sort of way. His uncle was helping Mya at the dig site."

Dove frowned. "Tell me this had nothing to do with the visitors."

Her joy at sharing the news about Derek instantly fell away, and the moment she had been dreading had finally arrived. "I can't. That's how I got the free ticket. I went there to take the test to see if I would be accepted for the volunteer program."

Dove crossed her arms again when Catori didn't continue. "Well?"

Catori took a deep breath and released it to build up her courage before answering. "I'll be joining the new colony."

Dove waved her arms into the air in frustration and turned away from her daughter to gather her thoughts. When she turned back around, she had her anger under control and put her hands on her hips as she stared at Catori. "So, that's it? You're just going to walk away from your responsibility. You've been training for this your entire life."

"That was your dream, Mom, not mine. I never wanted any part of this family tradition. I'm going to live my life the way I want to, not because of some ancient ritual. That's why you make recordings. You need to start living in the 21st century, Mom."

"And who's going to record our history after I'm gone? No, young lady. You are not joining that ridiculous colony. You're going to stay here and fulfill your obligation to the tribe. It's your responsibility."

"I'm sick and tired of your backward traditions! I'm leaving, and if you don't like it, you can go to hell"

Dove slapped Catori's face. "Don't you ever talk to me like that again! Go to your room until you accept your responsibility."

Catori put her hand on her throbbing cheek and daggers flew from her eyes as she glared at her mother. She turned and stomped down the hallway into a room filled with folders and ledgers containing thousands of years of tribal history. She dragged them off the shelves onto the floor, kicking the piles of paper and leather-bound books against the walls. When her frustration was spent, she turned and saw her father restraining her wailing mother from entering the room.

When her daughter stopped, tears streamed down Dove's cheeks as she stared at the carnage on the floor. She squirmed out of her husband's grasp and glared at her daughter. "Get out of my house and never come back!"

Catori shoved Dove out of the way and stomped along the hallway to her bedroom. She snatched up a few personal items and then hurried along the hallway. When she reached the living room, she turned back to her mother. "I hope the comet hits and you die a slow and painful death!" She turned and stomped out through the front door, slamming it closed behind her.

She hurried over to her car, climbed in, and then drove back onto the asphalt road. She had planned to stay at home until she was taken up to the spaceship, but now she didn't know what to do. She thought other volunteers were in a similar situation, and wondered if there was some place where they could meet and talk about their issues. She realized she didn't even have a phone number to call to find out and slammed her fist against the dashboard in frustration.

Her mood softened when she recognized the song she and Derek had heard at the marketplace. The only issue she had with Derek was his hatred of his uncle, but now she was feeling the same way about her mother. Suddenly, she knew where she needed to go.

***

Catori parked her car in the parking lot of the apartment complex and stared across at a light behind a curtain on the other side of the window. She grabbed her phone and selected a contact and waited.

Mya heard her phone ring and recognized Catori's image. "Did you make it back from Seattle?"

"Yes, several hours ago. Am I disturbing you?"

"No."

"Good. I'm in the parking lot."

"All right. I'll meet you at the door."

Catori grabbed her backpack from the back seat before locking the doors and hurrying across to Mya's first-floor apartment. She saw her looking out through the center window just before the door opened. "Sorry to bother you, Mya."

From her body language and tone of voice, Mya knew something was bothering her friend. She closed the door and walked toward the kitchen. "You might as well stay the night."

Catori laid her pack on the floor near the hallway, and then sat down in one of the padded chairs, where she could see into the kitchen. "That's the best offer I've had since I landed."

Mya opened the refrigerator door and looked inside. "Would you like something to drink? I know you like orange soda, but all I have is a mixed citrus drink, a couple of beers, and a box of wine."

Catori grinned. "I wonder what the drinking age will be in the new colony."

Mya straightened up and turned to her guest. "You've been selected?"

"I have, and my mom is furious. That's why I drove over here. I had to get out of there."

Mya reached into the refrigerator, grabbed two bottles of beer, then went into the living room and held one out to Catori. "I think the drinking age for the new colony should be eighteen for beer and wine." When Catori accepted, Mya sat down across from her on one end of the sofa and then twisted the cap off her bottle. "I guess congratulations are in order."

Catori noticed a sense of disappointment in Mya's voice and figured it was because she was out of a job. She opened her bottle and held it out to touch its twin. The bottles tinkled, and she took a sip, then her lips puckered at the bitter taste and the bubbles tickled her throat as she swallowed. "Uh! I always hate the first sip."

Mya grinned. "I feel the same way. So, tell me about your trip to Seattle."

Catori smiled and flopped back into the chair. "It was fantastic. You'll never guess who I met in the testing room. Alex Cave's nephew, Derek."

Mya noticed the sparkle in Catori's eyes. "Is he as handsome as his uncle?"

"He is handsome, but I've never met his uncle. You like Alex, don't you?"

Mya leaned back on the sofa and curled her legs beneath her. "Yeah, we get along all right, but we're just friends."

"I can see myself with Derek. He took me on a whirlwind tour of Seattle and we had a great time. He was accepted too, so we'll be seeing a lot of each other on the new colony." She noticed a change in Mya's expression. "What's wrong?"

"Don't tell anyone you've been accepted, other than your immediate family. Have you listened to the news lately?"

"No, I haven't had time. What's happening?"

"People are protesting the visitor's selection process, claiming discrimination against LGBTQs and overweight people. They were peaceful until late this afternoon, when some degenerates in the crowd beat up anyone who said they were selected to join the colony."

"Is it true about the discrimination?"

"I believe it is, but I don't hold it against the visitors. They're trying to help us save our species, and it makes sense to take only healthy people."

"Are you going to volunteer?"

"They offered to let me take the next test, but I haven't decided if I want to go with them or not. What happens with the second test?"

"It's easy. They do a retinal scan and take your palm print for identification. They don't even ask questions."

Mya thought about the pieces of equipment Zane had received from Vesta. Retinal scanners were becoming less expensive, so why would the visitors want to bring their own? She thought it was also odd they did not ask questions. She remembered Paul had made mind contact with Zane and wondered if the new scanners might read people's minds. It would eliminate the need for questions. But what if it could invade your deepest thoughts, even ones hidden from yourself? The idea only increased her suspicion Vesta was holding back important information.

Catori could tell Mya was deep in thought. "Is there something else I should know about?"

Mya looked across at her friend. "Did anything happen when they scanned your eyes?"

Catori gave her a quizzical stare. "No. It was just a flash of light, and then it was over."

"Okay. What are you going to do about your family? Do you plan on seeing them before you leave?"

"No, I hate them. That's one of the reasons I came here. Since you're involved in all this, do you know of a place where people like me can hide until we leave?"

"I'm not that involved, but I know someone I can ask about it."

"Would that be Alex?"

"Yes. I'll make the call first thing in the morning. Now, tell me more about your date with Derek."

Chapter 17

GROOM LAKE:
Holly still shared Alex's skepticism, as she discussed the background checks over a secure video connection with Vesta. "Our people are barely keeping up with the number of checks you're asking for. Most of the people have minor criminal records, but there are a few smart ones who were arrested as leaders of small crime rings."

"Any criminal record is unacceptable, Holly. They may be descendants with the GC117 gene, but everyone is influenced by their environment as they grow up, and we can't allow that kind of mindset to influence a new colony."

"I find it odd almost every name you send us has a criminal background."

Vesta knew it wasn't necessary, but didn't want to make Holly or Alex even more suspicious about the selection process. "Zane is in charge of that part of the program. I'm sure he has his reasons."

"All right. I'll send him the names of people with a clean record, but there are not very many of them. Have you seen what's trending on social media lately? You're being called insensitive to minorities."

"I didn't tell the people of your planet we are only accepting people with certain traits. I specifically stated that point to you during the meeting. One of your representatives has betrayed you."

"I'll check into it. Are you going to reach your goal of five hundred colonists within the next five days?"

"Probably not, but I believe there will be enough diversity for a new colony."

"I believe you're truly committed to saving our species, Vesta, but I get a strange feeling you're holding something back. What is it?"

Vesta ignored the question. "Your society is prone to violent behavior, and jealousy is one of the driving forces. The selectees will become targets, and you need to warn them."

"You really have done this before, haven't you?"

"Did you doubt me?"

"No, that's not what I meant, Vesta. This all seems so surreal to me, and I'm impressed by how you know exactly what needs to be done and when to do it. How many species have you saved?" She noticed a moment of sadness in Vesta's eyes. "I'm sorry if I upset you."

"I've managed to save three."

"You don't sound too happy about your great accomplishments."

"I've helped relocate seven, but the first four were failures."

"What happened?"

"What always happens with un-evolved humans? Two strong-willed people can't get along and draw a line in the sand. Their new society dissolves into chaos, and with small settlements, the survivors can't make it on their own, so the species dies out."

"Now I understand why you're so selective. Do you think our people will survive?"

"From what I've learned from the selectees, I believe they will do just fine."

"All right. I'd better get back to work. It was nice talking with you."

The call ended and Holly felt a sense of relief and a moment of pride, knowing she was helping to save her species. However, it was quickly dampened by knowing she and billions of people had less than four months to live.

Chapter 18

GROOM LAKE:

With the ship now safely tucked inside the hangar, Alex and his team were in the control room reviewing the data from the tracking expedition. For the moment, they still didn't have a definitive plan to change the comet's trajectory.

Jadin had an idea. "What about the artificial gravity device we discovered in Iceland? If the people at JPL and I can find a way to build another one, we might have more success changing its course."

Okawna yanked on the handle to bring the back of his chair up and stared at Jadin. "You can't be serious. The damn thing nearly killed me when we tried to move that asteroid."

Alex thought about that mission. "We didn't have enough power to change its trajectory, but we managed to slow it down."

Jadin knew Alex was right. "I remember, but that time we were trying to move an enormous chunk of solid gold. The mass was against us, but this is an ordinary comet. Its mass is far less than that asteroid, so we should be able to move it off course with just the power of the engine."

Okawna suddenly had an idea. "Melvin, do you still have the records of that mission?"

"Of course. What would you like to know about it?"

"Compare the drag effect you had on that asteroid to what we could do against the comet and calculate if we could change its trajectory."

It only took a fraction of a second for Melvin to answer. "Jadin is correct and I will move it much easier this time, but since I don't know the exact composition of the comet, I cannot give you the exact numbers."

"Just ballpark it for me."

"I don't understand that statement."

"Just give me a rough estimate of what it would take to move the bastard."

"Thank you for the clarification. Using the comet's distance from Earth right now, a ballpark estimate would be two hours at maximum reverse thrust. That would redirect it safely past the planet. However, that is only if we were already at the comet."

Okawna scratched the stubble of beard on his chin. "So, add in the time it will take us to get there, and what does that do in our attempt to make it miss the Earth?"

"It will take three days to reach the comet, but each passing hour before we leave changes the algorithm. If we delay too long, I won't be able to change the trajectory enough to make a difference."

"All right. Let's leave now to increase our odds of success."

Alex was in one of the chairs and abruptly stood up, then hurried to the side of the ship when he saw movement in the hangar. "What the hell?"

A dozen armed soldiers had surrounded the ship, and were guarding the controls for the hangar doors. Alex recognized the person giving orders to the soldiers and turned to his friends who had moved up beside him. "Wait here while I go down and find out what's happening."

Alex hurried down the stairs and found the man in charge entering the cargo hold. "What's going on, Lieutenant?"

"I'm under orders to keep this spaceship from leaving the base."

"On whose authority?"

"My commanding officer, Colonel Bishop."

Alex knew Bishop worked out of the Pentagon. "I thought Holly Blake was in charge of base security."

"Not anymore. The President has commandeered this ship for reasons of national security."

Alex fought to keep his anger under control. "We'll see about that."

Alex ran up the stairs to the control room. "The President has commandeered our ship and won't let us leave."

Jadin watched the knuckles on Alex's clenched fists turned white with anger. "My Uncle Jerry always said it's better to ask forgiveness than to miss an opportunity to do something good."

Alex let his hands relax. "Perhaps, but Uncle Jerry doesn't work for the US Government at a top secret facility."

Jadin stared up at Alex. "I say we steal him."

Okawna gave Jadin a serious stare. "We are not stealing him, Jadin."

Jadin's jaw dropped. "That's the last thing I would have expected from you, Okawna. You can't be serious."

Okawna gave her a smirk. "Legally, Melvin belongs to Alex, so I say, why wait? Let's get going."

Alex held his palms up. "Just hold on a minute. Melvin, how long until it's too late to change the comet's trajectory?"

"Seventy-six hours."

Okawna stared down at the men in the hangar. "Let's close the airlock and bust out through the doors. I'm sure it won't do any damage to the ship."

Alex knew Okawna was right about Melvin, but also knew some soldiers might be killed in the process, and they were just following orders. "Listen, I'm as frustrated as you are, but we still have time to make a difference, and I don't want to get our new boss in trouble. At least, not yet. I'm hoping Holly will convince Donner to tell the President to go to hell and send us on our way."

Okawna flopped down onto one of the chairs. "Fine. What are we supposed to do in the meantime?"

"I've thought of something. Melvin, since I rescued you from a dormant volcano, I believe that makes us friends, correct?"

"I'm glad you feel that way. Yes, it does. I know your friends believe I belong to you, but I don't belong to anyone. I do as you ask because we are a team."

"Will you take my direction, whether I am on board or not?"

"Yes, Alex, I agree with that position. However, I will need instructions that prevent any attempts to bypass your request."

"Fine. In seventy-two hours, if I'm onboard or not, you are to proceed to the comet and change its trajectory to save our planet. After achieving the change in trajectory, return here. This order cannot be rescinded by anyone but me."

"Order accepted. You will need to close up the ship so I can lock out entry to anyone but you."

"Excellent. Now that we have a backup plan in place in case something goes wrong, I'll go tell Holly about our idea and time constraints. Perhaps she'll take matters into her own hands and let us get on with our mission." He turned to Okawna. "Don't go anywhere without closing up the ship."

***

Holly saw Alex standing on the other side of her office window and indicated for him to wait one minute. When she finished her call, she waved him inside. "Have a seat, Alex."

Alex sat in front of her desk. "I've just learned the President has commandeered my ship."

"It wasn't my call, Alex."

He filled her in on the details of their plan. "We're under a time schedule, so the sooner we leave, the better our chances of success, but we can't go anywhere with those soldiers standing guard in the hangar."

"I agree with you, but have you been watching the news lately? People are already panicking and the President is considering moving his family and himself here to the base, so he's ready if he needs to leave in the spaceship. I'm sure some of his special staff members will stay here, too." When she saw his jaw muscles flexing, she held up her hand before he could speak. "I feel exactly as you do, Alex. Do you really think you can pull it off?"

"I do, but not if we don't get out of here before it's too late."

"This is still my operation. Just give me a chance to explain the situation to Director Donner. If that doesn't work, it won't be the first time I've taken heat for stepping out of line. Believe me when I say you'll leave before the deadline."

"Let's hope so."

"Until then, all of you can take some time off to be with your families. I'll call you if anything changes."

***

When Alex returned to the spaceship, the lieutenant was standing outside the airlock. He gave him a cursory nod of greeting before entering and jogging up into the control room, where his friends sat up in the chairs and stared up at him. "The President thinks this ship is at his disposal, but Holly is going to try to change his mind. She promised we would leave before the deadline, and will let us know if we can leave any sooner. Until then, we're on our own. Let's seal up the ship as we leave. If we can't use it to save the world, the President and his cronies won't be able to save their own butts, either."

David indicated the walls of the ship. "Are you one hundred percent ready, Melvin?"

"I'm good to go."

"All right. I think I'll head home until it's time to leave."

Jadin stood. "I want to visit my family in Oregon. I haven't seen them in a while, and I want to see Christa and her new family while I have the chance."

Alex was glad Jadin's sister had found happiness. They had met on his first mission as a civilian during the Dead Energy operation, where he had broken her heart and nearly gotten her killed. "I guess that's about it. I'll see you then."

Jadin could tell by their expressions and lack of enthusiasm about leaving, they were just as disappointed as she was. "I'll tell you what. You can all join me at my uncle's marina in Oregon. It's great weather this time of year, and we can chill for a day or two and maybe go fishing. We might even see some whales. What do you think?"

Okawna stood. "Count me in. I love being on the water."

David thought about it for a moment. "Thanks for the offer, but I want to spend some time with my family and friends before we leave."

Jadin saw Alex was about to refuse her invitation. "Why don't you ask Mya to join us? I'm sure she'd like to spend some time on the Pacific Coast."

Alex thought about it for a moment. Even though he did not want a romantic relationship with Mya, she was a nice woman and helped him with information about Vesta and her plans. And going home to face Derek would probably end on a sour note. "All right. It sounds like fun. I'll find out if she can make it. How are we getting there?"

Okawna answered. "We're flying, of course. A friend of mine in Las Vegas has a plane we can borrow. It's an eight seater with twin jet engines and plenty of room."

Alex stared at his friend. "And he is just going to let you borrow it?"

"Actually, I won it off her in a poker game in Las Vegas a year ago, but she was so drunk I told her to keep it, as long as I can borrow it once in a while. We just need to pay for the fuel. I'll call her once we leave the ship."

"What if she's using it?"

"She bought a newer model this year, and doesn't use mine unless her new one is down for service. She still keeps mine in her private hangar, which works out great for me, since I don't want to park it in the open at my ranch. Let's get out of here."

Alex followed Okawna down the stairs of the spaceship and out into the hangar, strolling beside him, with Jadin and David following them. "Who is this woman?"

"Kathy Bateman."

"The actress?"

"No, that's Kathy Bates. Her husband owned a big software company in Seattle and died a few years ago. No kids, so she got everything, and we had a great time that weekend."

"You never cease to amaze me. You always manage to find a woman."

"That's why I'm never going to be monogamous. I like variety."

Alex glanced over his shoulder before stepping through the double doors. His lips formed into a sly grin when he saw the opening into the ship had vanished.

Chapter 19

FORT COLLINS, COLORADO:
Mya grabbed her phone and called Alex, but he didn't answer, so she left a message to call her back and looked at Catori. "You're welcome to stay here for a couple of days until I'm done packing."

"Are you moving out of town?"

"Yeah, with the dig site closed, there's no reason for me to stay here."

Mya turned from dragging boxes off the shelf in the closet when her phone rang. When she saw who was calling, she stepped out of the room. "Hey, Alex."

"Are you busy?"

"Not really. Just packing some of my things."

"Oh, that's right. They closed the dig site. What can I do for you?"

"The reason I called you is a friend of mine was accepted to join the colony, but with all the protests, I was wondering if Holly had a safe place for her and the other colonists to hide until they're taken to Vesta's spaceship."

"I'm afraid not. I called for another reason. You remember Jadin Avery. Well, her uncle owns a nice marina on the Oregon coast and she invited us to stay there for a few days. I was wondering if you'd like to join us."

"That sounds great, Alex. I need a break from the mountains. What are the plans?"

"How does a ride in a private jet sound? We can pick you up at the Fort Collins airport in a few hours."

Out of the corner of her eye, Mya saw Catori standing slightly behind her. "Hang on a moment." She covered the microphone and turned around to Catori. "I'll be leaving sooner than I thought. Evidently, there isn't any place for you to hide, but you're still welcome to stay here."

"That's Alex Cave, isn't it?"

"That's right. He's invited me on a trip."

Catori smirked at Mya. "A hot date?"

"We're flying with some friends of his to a marina on the Oregon coast for a few days."

"Did he say if Derek was going with them?"

"He didn't mention him, but I doubt it. They're picking me up here this afternoon in a private plane."

"Can I go with you?"

"I'm a guest, so I can't ask to bring someone else." She saw the pleading look in Catori's eyes, heaved a deep sigh of resignation, and brought the phone up to her ear. "Alex, I know it's not my place to ask this of you, but would you have room for one more person? She's in love with your nephew, Derek, and wants to meet you in person."

"How does she know Derek?"

"They spent a night together in Seattle after they were both selected to join the colony."

Alex was surprised Derek had been accepted, but not that he volunteered, despite his warning. "Hang on a second while I check to see if it's all right."

Mya looked at Catori. "He's checking."

"Okay, Mya. Jadin says she can come with us. We'll call when we're on our way."

Mya put the phone away and looked at Catori. "You're invited, and they'll pick us up in a few hours."

Catori smiled and brought out her phone. "I'll call Derek and let him know I'll be joining his uncle in Oregon. Maybe he can talk Alex into picking him up, too."

Mya's jaw dropped. "Now wait a minute. We're already taking advantage of Jadin's hospitality, and that's not fair to Alex."

"You mean it's not fair to you?"

Mya gave her a wary stare. "What do you mean? It has nothing to do with me."

"I think it's because you want a chance to form a romantic relationship with Alex and I'm interfering with your plans."

"Well, you're wrong. It's just supposed to be him, his three teammates, and me. You weren't invited in the first place, and now you're taking advantage of our friendship."

Catori crossed her arms and glared at Mya. "Really? Well, I don't see it that way. I'm leaving this planet in a few more days, so I don't care about the ramifications. If you hate me for wanting to enjoy myself before I leave, that's too bad."

Mya was stunned and didn't know how to respond to the selfish comment. She put one hand on her hip and pointed toward the door with the other. "Get out. I'll call and let you know what time to be at the airport." When Catori didn't move, she reached out and grabbed her arm. "NOW!"

Catori flinched at the harsh tone of voice, but didn't move. "I'm sorry, all right?"

Mya let go of Catori's arm. "I'll see you at the airport."

Mya turned and stomped back into the bedroom. A moment later, she heard the front door slam shut. She stepped into the bathroom and dug through one drawer until she found a disposable razor, then reached into the cabinet for shaving cream before turning on the water to fill the bathtub.

***

SPARROW VALLEY, WASHINGTON:

Derek heard someone rustling around in the kitchen and opened his eyes, and when he saw his twelve–year-old sister, Kristie, he sat up on the couch as she approached him. "Good morning."

"I see you never made it to bed. How did it go?"

Derek leaned back and smiled. "I met the most wonderful woman in the world."

Kristie grinned and grabbed his hand, urging him off the couch. "Come into the kitchen and tell me all about her."

Derek stood and followed her into the kitchen, then sat on a chair facing the counter. "What are you making?"

"Just cereal. Is she pretty?"

"She's beautiful. I met her while I was in line to get tested." He filled her in on the details and smiled as he showed her the pictures on his phone. "It was the best date I've ever been on."

"What about the test? What was that like?"

"Nothing to it. They just do a retinal scan, and it's over." Derek suddenly remembered the dream he had when his eyes were scanned. Then remembered Paul had said no one mentioned dreaming before him.

Kristie noticed the faraway look in her brother's troubled expression. "Are you okay?"

"What? Oh, I'm fine."

"Well? Did you pass?"

"Yeah, I'm accepted."

"You don't sound too excited about it."

"It's nothing. The good news is Catori and I are both going to a new planet. What are the chances we would meet up in Seattle? I think it was fate, and we're meant to be together."

Kristie smirked at him. "What about all the other ladies in the new colony? I thought you didn't want to be monogamous."

"Well, I still don't know what the rules will be in the new society. Maybe men can have more than one wife."

Kristie gave Derek a smirk. "Or maybe a woman can have more than one husband. Men shouldn't be the only ones who can have a harem."

"All right, smarty pants." He expected a smile, but Kristie took on a troubled expression. "Did I say something wrong?"

"No, it's just now you'll be leaving soon and the rest of us will be here waiting to see what happens with the missiles. What if they don't work?"

Derek gave her his most confident expression. "The smartest people in the world say they can stop it from hitting us."

"All right. I'm going to miss you."

"Hey, I'm not gone yet. I can always change my mind."

Kristie grinned. "No, you won't. Not as long as Catori is going. It's like the last days while we waited for grandma to pass away. I knew it was going to happen, but it was hard to get used to the idea. Once you leave, I'll never see you again."

Derek's phone rang and he checked to see who it was, then grinned at Kristie. "It's Catori." He stood and went out onto the back porch before answering. "Hi."

"I had a wonderful time in Seattle, and I'd really like to spend some time with you before we leave."

"Yeah, me too, but you're halfway across the States from me, Catori."

"Well, your uncle just invited me to a getaway in Oregon. He's even picking Mya and me up in a private plane."

"I thought you had never met him."

"I haven't, but he called to invite Mya to join him, and I was invited too. If he has a private plane, maybe he can pick you up so you can be with me."

"You know I'm not talking to him. If I call for a favor, it's like admitting he was right."

"No, it's not. You're still joining the colony, so you win. I want you, Derek, more than any man I've ever met. Couldn't you swallow your pride just this one time for me?"

Derek felt his heart rate increase at the thought of being with Catori. "I suppose I could put up with him for a few days."

"Great. I hope to see you soon. Bye."

Derek entered Alex's number and had to leave a message, and noticed a cloud of dust rushing up the road. A moment later, a beefed up, camouflaged colored Humvee entered the driveway. He hurried down the steps as the vehicle stopped and the engine roared twice before it went silent. When the window went down, he recognized the young man sitting behind the steering wheel and sauntered over. "Hey, Smitty. Where did you find this gas guzzling beast?"

"It was my dad's. He bought a new one and let me have this one. Get in and I'll take you for a ride."

Derek walked around and opened the passenger door, but just looked at the interior without climbing in. "Kind of sparse, isn't it? I expected to see lots of stereo equipment."

"This was my dad's survival truck, so no amenities. Aren't you going to get in?"

"Not now, but I'd like a ride when I get back. I'm expecting a phone call, and I might need to leave right away."

"How did it go with your test?"

Derek thought about the news broadcast and decided not to let anyone but his immediate family know he had been selected. "I haven't decided yet."

"My dad says only cowards want to leave, so I'm not volunteering."

Derek heard his phone ringing. "Listen, I've got to go. I'll take you up on your offer some other time."

Derek closed the door and hurried around the vehicle. When he reached the porch, he recognized Alex's ID on his phone. When Brian's truck engine roared to life, he couldn't hear anything else and dashed into the kitchen, closing the door behind him. "Are you still there, Alex?"

"I'm here. I was surprised you called me. Listen, I'm sorry for our misunderstanding."

Derek held his frustration in check. *You think it's just a misunderstanding?* An image of Catori formed in his mind, so he calmed down. "I just heard you're having a party in Oregon and you invited my new girlfriend. We're joining the colony together."

"I know how much you want to go."

"Yeah, I guess."

Alex could tell something was bothering Derek. "What's going on?"

"I don't really know. Anyway, I was wondering if I could join you."

Alex's lips formed into a soft smile, knowing this was a great chance for him to spend some time repairing his relationship with his nephew. "I have a plane at my disposal, so I'll call you when we're an hour out from the Mount Vernon airport."

"I'll see you soon." He saw Kristie standing in the doorway to the living room. "I guess you heard everything."

"You were talking so loud I couldn't help it. So, you're hooking up with Catori sooner than you thought you would. That's great. How long will you be away?"

"I'm not sure. I'd better call Frank down at the hardware store and let him know I need a few days off work."

Kristie was jealous she wasn't invited, but understood why they wouldn't want a twelve-year-old girl hanging around. "Tell Uncle Alex I said hi."

"I'm not leaving yet. He'll call before he gets to the airport. We can watch a movie while I'm waiting, but I need to pack some clothes first. I'll be back in a moment."

Chapter 20

HUMPBACK HARBOR, OREGON:

Alex was sitting in the copilot's seat of the jet, staring out the window at the Pacific Ocean stretching away to the horizon as he thought about their stop in Fort Collins. When Mya had asked him to let Catori join them, he had thought they were good friends, but they hadn't said a word to each other since he had picked them up. Once they had gotten Derek in Mount Vernon, Catori had given him her full attention.

When he had boarded the jet, Derek had been courteous to his uncle and was glad he didn't have to converse with him during the flight to Oregon. Now he would spend all his time with Catori, no matter how apologetic Alex was to him.

The plane swung around toward the coast on final approach into North Bend, Oregon, and Alex stared out the front window at what appeared to be the crescent rim of a small volcano on the shoreline. There was also a long mound of gray boulders forming a breakwater protecting the harbor.

The plane made a quick descent onto the asphalt surface and taxied over to the parking area for transient private planes. Alex climbed out of his seat, opened the side door for the passengers, and then stepped out of the way as they disembarked. A moment later, a white passenger van drove up and parked near the bottom of the steps.

Jadin smiled when she recognized her brother driving the marina's bus, and when he climbed out, she wrapped her arms around his neck and gave him a warm hug. "Look at you, Aaron. All grown up and as handsome as ever."

"Hey, Sis. This is a nice surprise."

Jadin turned and introduced everyone to her brother. "He works at the marina with my uncle, Jerry."

Aaron finished shaking hands and indicated the rear end of the van. "I'll put your luggage in the back, so go ahead and climb in."

Alex helped remove the luggage from the storage compartment behind the wing and carried it over to join Aaron outside the van. "Jadin told us about what you did to save your uncle's marina. I'm looking forward to seeing it."

"It wasn't just me, Mister Cave. It was a community effort. I just got things started for them."

"You can call me Alex. Derek is a year older than you are, and just as modest about his accomplishments."

"His girlfriend is nice looking. Is she from one of our local Native American tribes?"

"No, she's Sioux, from Fort Collins, Colorado."

"Oh, wow. Did she see the spaceship?"

"No, I'm afraid not."

"Jadin didn't say how many rooms you needed, so I reserved five at the new motel. It's within walking distance of the marina."

"That's great. Thanks."

Alex went to the side door of the van and climbed in back with Derek, Okawna, and the two women, while Jadin sat up front with Aaron. During the drive to Humpback Harbor, the tension between Mya and Catori seemed palpable, and Derek was trying to ignore him. He had enough on his mind already, so he hoped it would ease up once they arrived at the marina.

***

When Aaron stopped in front of the motel and they climbed out, everyone paused to admire the view. The sun was just over the horizon, creating a pastel tapestry across the sky and reflecting off the water in the marina.

Jadin waited with Aaron while he unloaded the suitcases. "Is there a vehicle I can borrow while I'm here?"

"Yeah, I'll get my car on the way home so you can use this van in the morning to pick up your friends. I'm glad you're staying at the house. We've all been talking about what's happening with the visitors and the comet, so I'm happy we get to spend some time with you."

"Yeah, me too."

Jadin walked back to her friends and indicated the restaurant a short distance up the street. "Let's all meet there for breakfast in the morning and I'll take you on a tour of the marina. I'd better get going. Good night, everyone. I'll see you all in the morning."

When Jadin and Aaron climbed into the van, Alex went with Mya into the office. Once they had their key cards, they went back outside while the others checked in. Derek filled out a registration form and noticed Catori had slid hers out of the way without writing anything on it. "Don't you want your own room?"

Catori smiled and wrapped her arm around Derek's waist. "Why do we need two rooms?"

Derek felt his heart rate increase. "I just thought since we've only known each other for two days, it was too soon to take it to the next level."

"I'm a free spirit now, and I don't want to live by anyone else's rules."

Derek grinned and slid the registration form and his debit card to the woman behind the counter. Once he had a key card, he and Catori went outside while Okawna checked in.

Okawna slid his keycard into his shirt pocket as he walked out of the office and joined his friends. "The clerk said there's an old nautical bar about four blocks up the street. Does anyone want to join me for a drink after we're settled into our rooms?"

Alex looked down at Mya. "I'm in. Care to join us?"

"Sure, I'll meet you guys there when I'm done."

Derek looked at Okawna. "What's the drinking age in Oregon?"

Catori grabbed Derek's arm before Okawna answered. "I don't want to go sit in some stinky bar. Let's go for a walk around the marina."

Derek shrugged his shoulders at Okawna. "Never mind."

Alex felt his heart break when Derek directed his question to Okawna. He just hoped somehow he and Derek could mend things between them tomorrow.

***

The aroma of stale beer wafted out from the tavern when Alex opened the door and stepped into a scene from an old movie. The plaque hanging on the wall just inside the doorway proclaimed the Fast Harpoon Tavern was a historical landmark, established in 1843. The thick floorboards creaked under his feet as he and Okawna went over to the bar and sat down on nautical style stools.

A bald man with a handlebar mustache walked up and smiled at the two strangers. "What can I get for you?"

Okawna studied the names on the beer tap handles. "Olympia for me."

"I'll have the same."

Okawna took a better look around and saw all the nautical memorabilia hanging on the walls and ceilings. There were no booths, just tables and chairs, and six other occupants, three of them women. He also noticed the wooden wedges supporting two of the pool table legs and turned back to the man behind the counter, pouring the beer. "This is my kind of place. Is it yours?"

"Yep. Been in my family for three generations."

"I'm Okawna, and this is Alex. We're here with our friend Jadin Avery."

The man held out his hand and smiled. "I'm Sam Adams, named after a distant relative. Nice to meet ya. How do you know Jadin?"

"She's a member of our team."

"Oh. So you work for NASA. Is it true the rockets will destroy the comet?"

"Well, that's not really my department."

Alex could tell Sam was going to ask more questions, so he turned to Okawna. "Do you want to shoot a game of pool?"

Okawna smirked. "A dollar a ball?"

"You're on."

Alex walked over and selected a cue stick, inserted fifty-cents, and racked the balls. Okawna flipped a coin and won the first shot.

Mya stepped into the tavern and wrinkled her nose at the smell of stale alcohol. She saw Okawna shooting pool, and Alex leaning his back against the bar with a cue stick in his hand, and continued over and sat on a stool beside him. "Who's winning?"

Alex indicated Okawna. "The hustler. He usually runs the table if he gets the chance."

Mya ordered a glass of wine and watched Okawna miss a shot. "It looks like it's your lucky day."

Okawna turned to Alex with his palms up. "The table is out of adjustment."

Alex grinned and walked over. "Which way?"

"It dips toward the far left corner."

Alex lined up his shot, allowed for the slope, and then got three balls into the pockets before he missed.

Okawna went back to the pool table, and after sinking two balls, he took a break when a man who was sitting at a table with two young women stood and came over to him.

"Mind if I play the winner?"

"Sure. I'm Okawna."

"I'm Steve."

Okawna waited while Steve slid fifty cents under the cushion and went back to the table. He watched Steve sit close to a woman who appeared to be his girlfriend and noticed the other lady was grinning as she checked him out. He smiled at her, then made his next shot and smirked at Alex. "I've got it figured out."

Alex turned his attention back to Mya. "That's it for me. He'll run the table now."

A few minutes later, Okawna grinned at Alex as he sauntered up to the bar, then took a drink from his mug of beer and indicated Steve, who was racking the balls for the new game. "I'm hoping he'll introduce me to his lovely friends."

When Okawna walked away, Alex smiled at Mya. "We won't be seeing much of him for the rest of the night."

"Is he always so aggressive with women?"

"I'm afraid so."

Mya stared at her nearly empty glass of wine as she slowly rotated the stem. "I hope Jadin isn't to upset with me. I didn't know Catori was going to invite Derek."

Alex had noticed how well Mya and Jadin had gotten along during the plane ride, and knew that wasn't the real issue. "Is that why you haven't spoken to Catori since we picked you up in Fort Collins?"

"Can we talk outside?"

"Sure. It's a nice night for a walk."

Alex followed Mya out of the tavern, and then they walked along the street towards the motel. "Actually, I'm glad Derek could join us. We haven't been on the best of terms lately. He seems in love with Catori."

Mya looped her arm around Alex's elbow. "She's not as sweet as she appears." She told Alex what had happened between Catori and her parents and how she had acted after he had ended the call. "She's manipulative and doesn't care who she uses to get what she wants."

"Do you think she is using Derek?"

"No, I think she really does like him, but you should warn him she'll turn on him if it suits her needs."

"He won't listen to me. Is that what's keeping you from joining the colony?"

"No. In fact, I decided to go before she came over to my apartment."

"What changed your mind?"

"Vickie. The woman who took your saliva. She made me realize just how crowded it's getting here on Earth, and it will be nice to start over and create a better society." When Alex didn't say anything, she looked up at him. "You never told me why you're not joining the colony."

Alex couldn't tell Mya about his spaceship or that he had his own plan to stop the comet, but knew he had to answer the question. "I don't trust Vesta."

"Why not? I've seen the inside of her ship and she has plenty of room. I think she's sincere about wanting to save some of us."

"I can't place my finger on the exact reason. It's just a gut feeling she's not telling us everything."

Alex and Mya strolled past a few small stores in comfortable silence, each lost in their own thoughts. They stopped to look down into the harbor, where lampposts illuminated the boats.

Alex turned from the view to look at Mya. "Have you ever gone on a boat ride on the Pacific Ocean?"

"No, only on lakes."

"I'd love to take you out on the water tomorrow."

"I'd like that."

She saw Catori and Derek walking along the docks, so she pulled on Alex's arm to guide him away before they saw them. "I'm getting tired. Would you mind walking me back to my room?"

"Not at all."

Alex walked her to the motel and waited while she opened the door. "I should go back to the tavern and check on Okawna. I'll see you in the morning."

When Alex turned to leave, Mya stared after him, wondering if he had ever been married. She didn't think he was the type to settle down.

Chapter 21

9:15 AM. DANNY'S RESTAURANT:
The sun was climbing into a cloudless sky and Alex was sitting with his friends, enjoying the aroma of sausage, bacon, and coffee as he stared out the window of the restaurant. He recognized Jadin driving the van parking in front of the window and looked at Mya. "Do you still want to go for a boat ride?"

"Of course. I've been looking forward to it all morning."

***

When Jadin stopped the van in front of the restaurant, she could see her friends and new acquaintances sitting at a table on the other side of the window, and then turned to look at her Uncle Jerry. "The dark-haired man is Alex Cave, my team leader I told you about, and the blond man is Okawna, another member of the team."

Jerry Avery indicated the people on the other side of the glass. "Your friends sure have good taste in women."

Jadin grinned at her uncle. "The younger man is Alex's nephew, Derek, and sitting beside him is Catori Onestar, a Native American of the Sioux Nation. The other woman is Alex's new friend, Mya Austin. She's an archeologist he met at a dig site in Colorado."

"I thought Alex was a geophysicist."

"He is, but she needed his advice."

Jerry opened the car door and climbed out, then walked around to join his niece. "Your friend Okawna. What's his last name?"

"That is his last name, so don't ask him about it."

"That's a little strange, but all right. Anyway, you said he's a mechanical engineer, so I can see you working with him and that physicist you mentioned, David. But I can't figure out how Alex fits into your team working for NASA."

Jadin hated to lie to her uncle, but knew she couldn't tell him the truth. "He's an advisor. Let's go inside and I'll introduce you to them."

Jadin led Jerry through the door into the restaurant and over to the table and did the introductions while Okawna dragged another table and two chairs over to butt against the others. The aroma of sausage, toast, and coffee permeated the air around the partially empty plates of food in front of her friends. She remained standing until Jerry and Okawna were seated, then reached into her handbag to grab two photos and held them out to Okawna. "These are the before pictures of the marina, so you can see the difference when we go down there, and it's all because of Jerry." She sat down and smiled at her uncle as she reached over and gave his hand a light squeeze. "I'm so proud of you."

Alex was second in line for the photographs and could see a dilapidated seafood processing plant, and several run down eateries and taverns along the shoreline of the marina. Another picture showed a makeshift system of piers and floating docks cluttering the harbor. He passed them to Mya and looked over at Jerry. "How long have they occupied this cove?"

"Forever. The Native tribe leased it to the fishing boats coming north from Mexico around 1800 and then sold the rights to the city in 1937. Commercial salmon fishing took off and supported the town back then. They kept adding docking space using whatever was available. That's why everything became a jumbled mess of mismatched parts."

"I'm eager to see what Jadin has been bragging about."

When the server arrived, Jadin and Jerry ordered while they talked about various subjects, then Jerry took advantage of the break in the conversations when their food arrived to look down the table at Mya. "Jadin told me you got to meet the visitors in person. What were they like?"

"Well, they're basically the same as us, except much more civilized than we are."

Jerry took a sip of coffee to wash down some toast. "Oh, I don't know. I've found most people are civilized at heart, but sometimes their circumstances make them act like assholes."

Mya chuckled. "That is so true. I just hope the rest of the people joining the colony can get along under their new circumstances. I would imagine we have some hard times ahead of us."

Derek smiled as he grabbed Catori's hand. "We've been accepted to join them, and I'm sure everything will work out just fine."

Jerry indicated a man sitting alone at the counter. "When Frank's boy was accepted, a few people treated him like he had the plague. Some younger people called him a coward for leaving, but I think they're just afraid of what will happen if the rockets don't blow up the comet. I guess we'll find out in four months, but I'm not going to lose any sleep worrying about it." He noticed everyone was finished eating and slid his plate forward as he stood. "Well, enough talk about all that. I'm headed down to my shop. Stop by when you finish your tour."

Jadin stared after her uncle as he left the restaurant. She felt bad she couldn't tell him the truth, and could only hope they could stop the comet from hitting the Earth. When everyone else stood, she grabbed the bill for her and Jerry, but Alex indicated he would take care of it, so she gave it to him, then strolled outside and stood next to the van with Catori and Derek. "Are you looking forward to seeing the marina?"

Catori shook her head no. "Not me. We saw it last night."

Derek grinned. "I am. It will look a lot different in the daylight. I'm hoping we can rent a boat and go for a ride. Maybe do a little fishing." He felt Catori pull on his arm, and when he looked at her, she gave him a stern expression. "What's the matter?"

Catori was about to answer when Alex, Mya, and Okawna came out from the restaurant, so she pulled Derek off to one side. "I don't want to be stuck on a boat trying to catch a stupid fish. Last night, you said we would walk along the shoreline today."

"We don't have to do any fishing. We can just cruise along the shoreline and admire the view."

Catori crossed her arms and gave Derek a cold stare. "Fine. I'll go by myself."

Alex watched Catori stomp away from Derek, so he moved over to him. "What was that about?"

"Oh, nothing." He hurried to catch up with her.

Mya had been watching the exchange between Derek and Catori, and when Derek hurried to catch up with her, she noticed Alex staring after them and moved beside him. "She's mad because she didn't get her way. Wait for it."

When Derek caught up with Catori, she wrapped her arm around his and smiled up at him, but he didn't return her smile and pulled his arm free. "What's the matter with you? We spent the entire evening and night together, and now I want to spend some time on the water before we leave."

Catori crossed her arms and glared at Derek. "I invited you along to spend time with me, not everyone else."

"Our lives are about to change and you're acting like a spoiled brat."

Catori forced her lips into a pout. "I thought you loved me. Why won't you do what I want to do?"

"I said I like you a lot, but when you act this way, it makes me wonder if I might be wrong."

Catori thought she had Derek wrapped around her finger, like the boys she grew up with in high school. She was sure he would not be the only handsome young man in the colony, but now she wondered if they would be like Derek and not cater to her whims. She realized if she backed off a little, she could still get him to do what she wanted.

"I'm sorry. I'll go for a boat ride with you as long as we don't do any fishing."

Derek smiled and grabbed her hand, then led her back to the group. "Sure."

Jadin indicated the van. "Who needs a ride?"

Alex let Derek and Catori climb into the second bench seat, but before he climbed into the first seat with Mya, he noticed Okawna standing next to the open passenger door, looking around the area. "What's going on?"

"My new friend and the women I met last night are supposed to meet me here this morning. There are a lot of boats for sale and we're supposed to take Steve's speed boat out for a test drive."

Derek leaned forward to talk to Okawna. "I noticed all the for sale signs last night while we were walking around the marina. Did he say why?"

"Yeah, they all think if the comet hits, there won't be any marinas left standing, so they're trying to get rid of their boats."

Catori gave Okawna a sarcastic laugh. "If the comet hits, everyone is going to die, anyway."

Okawna knew that might not happen if they altered the comet's course, but couldn't tell her. "Well, as long as they're thinking that way, I plan to take advantage of it and go for a free test drive."

Jadin had climbed in behind the steering wheel and looked over at Okawna. "Did you exchange phone numbers?"

"No, but his name is Steve Curtis."

"I know him. I'll call for you."

Okawna turned to look at the four people in the back. "What are your plans for the day?"

Alex looked over at Mya for a second, then back to his friend. "We're going to rent a boat and go for a ride along the coast."

After the incident a moment ago with Catori, Derek realized he was acting just as badly toward his uncle. He had said it himself. Everything is about to change, and this was probably the last time he would see Alex, and they had been close at one time. He decided it wasn't worth throwing all that away when it didn't make any difference now, so he reached forward and placed his hand on Alex's shoulder. "Do you mind some company?"

Alex had been wondering how to repair their friendship, and smiled as he turned in his seat to look at Derek. "That would be great."

When Derek smiled and leaned back, Alex noticed Catori had a perturbed expression. He wondered if this might give Mya and Catori a chance to work things out if they were forced to spend time together. He suddenly realized he had not checked with Mya to see what she thought and turned to look at her. "Is that all right with you?"

Mya knew Alex was looking forward to spending time with Derek, so she reluctantly gave him a nod of approval. She had a feeling this day would not be as pleasant as she had hoped.

Okawna smirked at Alex. "You can probably test drive one for free."

"No, I don't want to be under any time constraint or have the owner go with us."

Jadin ended her call. "Steve said he'll meet you down at the marina office in an hour." She looked back over her shoulder at Alex. "You can borrow Jerry's boat. It will seat four people."

"Is it open or enclosed?"

"It's open, but it has a canvas top you can put up if you want to."

"Are you sure he won't mind?"

"He rarely uses it anymore, so I'm sure he'll let you borrow it for the day."

Okawna climbed into the passenger seat, closed the door, and then looked over at Jadin. "Ready when you are."

***

It was just after noon when Alex drove Jerry's boat into a small cove along the shoreline. He and Derek helped the women over the side, and then he tied the bow rope to a large rock. "The tide will come in fast, so I don't want any of you walking too far from this spot."

Catori grabbed Derek's hand and indicated the shoreline. "Let's go this way."

Derek let go of Catori's hand. "You go ahead. I need to talk to Alex first, but I'll catch up to you in a few minutes."

Catori spun around in the sand and stomped away from the group. "Fine!"

Alex noticed Derek staring after Catori. "Are you two going to be okay?"

Derek turned to look at Mya. "I know you don't like each other, but could you keep an eye on her for me until I catch up with you?"

When she didn't reply, he gave her a nod of understanding. "I doubt she'll get lost, but she's never been on the ocean before."

Mya knew Derek was right. Catori probably didn't have any idea how dangerous an incoming tide could be. If she wasn't careful, she could be cut off from the boat.

"All right. Just don't take too long."

Derek waited until Mya strolled away before looking at Alex. "Do you have any idea how bossy you are?"

The statement took Alex by surprise. "What do you mean?"

"Like just now, when you ordered everyone not to go too far from the boat."

"It wasn't an order. It was a suggestion."

"Well, you sure made it sound like an order. Just like the way you tell me what to do with my life."

"Listen, Derek, I'm sorry if that's the way you took my suggestions. I wasn't trying to tell you what to do. It's just that I've made a lot of mistakes in my life, and I was just trying to make sure you don't make the same ones I did."

"Your life is completely different from mine. I'm a man now, Alex. If joining the colony turns out to be a mistake, at least it will be mine, and I can live with it. I know what I'm doing, so just let me live my life my way. You're not my father, so don't you dare think you can take his place just because you got him killed."

Alex realized Derek had not fully forgiven him for getting his parents killed four years ago. It had been a revenge killing from his days working for the CIA. "You're right, Derek. It is your life, and I hope it turns out to be a great one."

Derek thought he heard a condescending tone in Alex's voice and turned to look out across the water. "You think you're always right, don't you?"

Alex saw Mya running in their direction and got Derek's attention. "I guess that didn't go too well."

Mya stopped in front of the men and tried to catch her breath. "I walked all the way to the river, but couldn't find her. She must have crossed while the tide was lower, because I couldn't get across it."

Alex grabbed Derek's shoulder to keep him from running to find Catori. "We can find her faster in the boat."

Derek spun around, ran to the rock, and then untied the bow rope. "Come on! Let's go!"

Alex climbed in and helped Mya over the side, and waited while Derek shoved them away from shore and leapt onto the bow. Once Derek was in the boat, he started the engine and steered along the shoreline. When they reached the area on the other side of the small river, they saw Catori waving at them. He eased the boat into shallow water and waited while she waded out to meet them, and Derek hauled her in over the side of the boat. "Are you okay?"

"I am now. I tried to get back, but the water was too deep and too fast for me to cross the river. I was so scared you'd leave without me."

"Why would you say something like that? We would never leave without you."

Catori sat on the bench seat and grabbed Derek's hand, pulling him down beside her. "When you didn't want to go for a walk with me, I thought you didn't like me anymore."

Alex looked over at Mya, who rolled her eyes at him as confirmation Catori was a spoiled brat. He smirked at her to show he agreed, and then backed the boat away from shore before heading back to the marina.

***

Two hours later, Mya was admiring Alex's boating skill as he eased the boat against the fuel dock in Humpback Harbor. Her phone rang as she was getting out of the boat, and once on the dock, she read the text message before looking at Alex. "I just heard from Zane. I need a ride to the airport right away. The government is sending a plane to pick me up and take me to a departure point for a ride up to the spaceship."

Derek had climbed out to tie the lines from the boat to the dock cleats when his phone rang, and when he heard Catori's phone ring at the same time, he looked at the message. "I just got a text to go to the North Bend airport as soon as possible. I thought we had another two days until the deadline."

Catori shrugged her shoulders. "I'm sure they were not planning to wait until the last minute to get five hundred people up to the ship."

Derek reached into the boat and grabbed Catori's hand to help her out, then noticed her broad smile. "I guess you got the same message."

Catori stepped out onto the dock and wrapped her arms around Derek's neck. "This is so exciting. We finally get to see the spaceship."

When Catori let go to follow Mya up the ramp, Derek turned and gave Alex a somber look. "Are you going to the airport with us?"

"Of course."

"Well, don't do it just for me."

Alex felt the knife through his heart again. It seemed no matter how hard he tried, Derek remained mad at him.

Derek checked to make sure the boat was secure and then followed Alex up to the pier. "I'll go find out about our ride."

Jadin was sitting on the bench seat in front of Jerry's shop and jumped up when she saw Alex walking in her direction, but stopped him just before he reached the rest of the group. "Did you talk to Holly?"

Alex instinctively felt the front of his pocket for his phone, but remembered he had decided not to take it out in the boat and had left it in his motel room. "No. What did she say?"

"Donner has been ordered to send a special security detail to take control of your spaceship. Apparently, he's been stalling for two days, but he's out of excuses. Holly said they will arrive later today, so we need to get back to the base right away."

"Where's Okawna?"

Jadin indicated the fuel dock. "He just got back from his boat ride. I called him and told him to hurry."

Okawna thanked Steve for the boat ride and saw his disappointed expression, then jogged up the ramp to join his friends. "What's up with the 911 text, Jadin?"

"The President is coming to take Alex's ship, so we need to get back right away."

"That's fine by me. Steve isn't too happy I'm not going to buy his boat, so let's get out of here."

Jadin looked over at the man sitting on a bench. "I'll meet you at the van. I want to say goodbye to Jerry." She went over to her uncle, but didn't sit down. "We need to leave right away."

Jerry stood and held his arms out. "I kind of figured as much."

Jadin wrapped her arms around Jerry's neck and held him close. "Take care of yourself."

Jerry let go and stared into Jadin's eyes. "I know you have secrets you can't tell me, but that's okay. Just come back and see me before the comet hits us, okay?"

"I'll try."

Aaron was waiting by the van when Jadin came over. "Alex told me you're all going with the rest of the group. I'll take all of you back to the motel, then to the airport as soon as you're ready."

***

Aaron drove the group to the airport and parked the van at the departure terminal, and once the luggage had been removed, he wrapped his arms around his sister. "Take care of yourself."

"You, too, and take care of Jerry."

"I will."

When the van drove away, Jadin grabbed her bag, entered the terminal, and then saw a man and a woman standing with her friends. "What's going on?"

Mya grabbed Jadin's hand. "They're here to verify our identities and escort us out to the jet. I told them we wouldn't go until we saw you before we leave. It was a pleasure meeting you, Jadin. Thank you for your hospitality."

Mya wrapped her arms around Alex's neck, pulled him close, and gave him a gentle kiss on the lips before letting go. "I hate saying goodbye."

Alex saw the tears forming in Mya's eyes. "It was nice knowing you. Take care of yourself in the new colony."

Derek saw the expectant look in Alex's eyes, but didn't walk over to say goodbye. Instead, he turned and stared out through the window at the waiting jet.

The man indicated the exit. "Let's go."

Alex waited until Derek walked outside without looking back, and then turned to Okawna. "Is our jet ready to go?"

"Yeah, I called while we were packing and told them to prep it and top off the tanks."

"All right. Let's get out of here before we lose our ship."

Chapter 22

DAY 13. THE MOON:

Vesta took the last load of passengers up to the ship and let her team direct them to the stasis chambers. She was disappointed they didn't get the full five hundred people, but it would be enough. One person appeared to be disappointed and remained behind, and she put her hand on his arm. "Thanks for all your help, Zane. You should go with the others."

"You know what, Vesta? Until this moment, I kept hoping this was all just a bad dream, but now I think of it as a nightmare. The way some people reacted when they learned about the comet was bad enough, but the way they reacted against the people who were selected makes you realize just how savagely self-centered humans can be. I feel sorry for the good people being left behind just because of their ancestry. A lot of them will be murdered before the comet even comes close to hitting the Earth."

"I know, Zane, we've seen it before. That's why we rushed things along to get the right people off the planet before your society crumbles. I'll see you again when you come out of stasis. Sleep well."

Once Zane was gone, Vesta strolled along a narrow hallway and entered the control room on the first floor of the enormous spaceship. She saw Belinda waving her over to the DNA laboratory and went over to join her. "What's going on?"

Belinda brought an image up on the monitor, showing two strands of DNA. "What do you know about the backgrounds of these two samples you gave me?"

"One is from a woman with only Native American markers. She's a descendant of one of the original pair of humans brought here twenty-five thousand years ago." She suddenly realized she didn't know the owner of the other one. "I have no idea where the other sample came from."

"It's definitely a male sample, but there's a strange tag on the eye color marker. Is he one of the volunteers?"

"I don't think so. Why do you ask?"

"Under the right conditions, his eyes will actually sparkle, and some of his other markers are not found in our database. I think this person is a descendant of a completely different race of humans. He should be saved with the others."

"I'll find out who the owner is while we still have time."

Vesta hurried out of the room and along the hallway to the entrance into the stasis chambers and found Paul. "Is Zane in full stasis yet?"

"No, I was just getting ready to slide him into the tube and seal his hatch. He's right over there. Level two, row three, number one-forty-eight."

Vesta stepped onto a large square platform and entered the number on a control pad. It moved and stopped in front of a narrow table extending from a thirty-inch opening in the wall and went over and stared down at Zane. "Are you comfortable?"

"I'm a little cold, but not too bad. I didn't expect to see you so soon."

"I forgot to tell you about the second DNA sample you wanted analyzed. We can't identify the genetic tag. Who did it belong to?"

"Alex Cave." He noticed the sudden look of concern in Vesta's eyes. "Why? Is something wrong?"

"There could be." She slipped a set of narrow sunglasses over Zane's head. "I'll see you again when you wake up."

She thought about Alex's upcoming attempt to change the course of the comet, and with this new information about his eyes, she decided to tell him the truth and went back to Paul. "Zane's ready. I need to make one last trip to the planet, but I shouldn't be gone too long."

She hurried back to the transport module and set a course for Groom Lake, Nevada. When the cube began moving away from the moon, she hoped it wasn't too late to find Cave.

***

GROOM LAKE:

It was late evening when Alex and his team landed at the base, and Alex was loading some supplies into the storage compartments inside the cargo hold of the spaceship. He tried not to make eye contact with the armed secret service agent standing a short distance away near the airlock, and to keep the four agents from getting suspicious, he had told them he was getting the ship ready for the president.

David went down the stairs from the control room into the cargo hold and stopped when he had Alex's attention. "I'm having a problem with the guidance system. Can you come up here and give me a hand?"

"Sure."

Alex followed David up the stairs, and when he stepped into the control room, he saw an image of Vesta on the holographic monitor. "This is a surprise."

"I've known about your spacecraft since your visit to the moon. It's an antique model and the odds are against you moving the comet, but I'm willing to help."

"Hold on a second. Why did you tell us you couldn't help us move the comet?"

"At that time, I didn't know you had a spacecraft at your disposal. I want to help."

"I'm still not sure if I can trust you."

"Time is of the essence, Alex. The only way you will succeed is with my help. You must meet me on the far side of the moon in less than one hour, because without me, you'll fail."

The image vanished, and Alex gave David a questioning stare. "Are we ready?"

"We can leave at any time. I have four extra power crystals just to make sure we aren't stranded on some planet or moon. Okawna and Jadin are in the break room."

"All right. I'll go get them."

Alex went down the stairs and out through the airlock, past the secret service agents, then casually strolled across the hangar to the hallway. When he entered the small break room, he saw Jadin sitting across from Okawna, who had his foot on the table, a cup of coffee in one hand, and was swinging his other arm above his head.

Okawna lowered his arm when he noticed Alex walk in. "I was just telling Jadin about your lousy aim when falling at high speed." He noticed Alex's concerned expression and took his foot off the table. "What's going on?"

Alex told them about Vesta's visit. "We have less than an hour to join her on the dark side of the moon."

Okawna stood and stared at Alex. "Do you believe her?"

"We were planning to leave anyway, so I might as well find out what she can do to help us."

"What else do you need to do to get ready?"

"Nothing. David says Melvin is ready. I'll go first, so give me time to get inside and take out the agent."

When Alex went out the doorway, Okawna peered around the corner and waited until he entered the ship, then walked down the hallway with

Jadin. He didn't make eye contact with the agents, who ignored them as he and Jadin entered the ship. At least until they tossed the unconscious agent out and closed the airlock door.

Alex was staring out at the agents as Okawna and Jadin approached the ship, then the agents drew their guns, aiming them at the spacecraft as if they could stop him from leaving. "They're in, Melvin. Cloak the ship and bust through the doors."

Alex stared at the stunned expressions of the agents when the ship appeared to vanish and then watched them all jump out of the way as the massive hangar doors collapsed out onto the tarmac. An instant later, Alex stared down at the shrinking base as the ship gained altitude.

Alex watched through the side of the ship as Melvin stopped a short distance from the side of Vesta's craft and hovered above the moon's surface, and he was still impressed by the size. He wondered how he was supposed to contact her and had an idea. "Melvin, try to contact the other ship." He was surprised when Vesta's image appeared on Melvin's holographic screen.

"Hello, Alex. I'm glad you decided to join me."

David had a sinking feeling in his stomach. "Are you still with us, Melvin?" When he didn't reply, David glared at Vesta's image. "What did you do to him?"

"He's still there, but hidden in the background. We're in control of your ship."

Okawna moved to the control panel. "The hell you are." He tried different combinations on the touch pads, but the ship didn't move.

Alex crossed his arms and stared at Vesta's image. "What's going on?"

"The comet hitting the Earth story was to give us a chance to gather as many of your species as we could in a limited amount of time. The comet is still coming in your direction, but it will miss the Earth by twelve-hundred miles without outside interference."

Okawna slammed his fist down on the console. "You lying bitch! You'd better run, because if I meet you again, I'll choke the life out of you!"

"I had to lie to you, Okawna, because in fifteen minutes, your planet will be hit by a blast of an exotic type of radiation. It only affects a certain marker in human genes, causing the immune system to shut down, similar to your AIDs virus. Every human on your world will slowly get sick and die."

Alex lowered his arms and his hands clasped into fists at his side as he glared at the image. "Damnit, Vesta! Why didn't you tell us this from the beginning?"

"Your primitive society would have collapsed, and your infrastructure would have been destroyed before we could complete our project. This way, as people slowly get sick, they turn off their appliances, creating less demand for electricity. As more people die, they shut down power plants, public transit, and businesses, leaving the infrastructure in reasonably good shape so the new colony can start over on your planet. Hopefully, they will choose a wiser path for the development of their new society."

Alex wasn't sure how to respond as he realized the people in stasis would actually go home. "Why are you telling me this now?"

"Because you and your crew need to decide. I know you've suspected me since I first met you, but I have never lied to you, Alex."

Alex thought about it for a moment. "You know, you're right, but you left out some very important details."

"Your people are far enough along the evolutionary path that in a few hundred years, they'll be able to leave your planet on their own. Believe me when I tell you this was the best and only scenario to save your species."

"I still don't understand. What are we supposed to do about it?"

"We all wait in stasis and in one year, your society will have buried most of the dead, and the few remaining survivors will die and decay where they lay. In three years, the new colony will establish itself near a solar energy facility and branch out from there."

Alex thought about Robert and Kristie. "If you would have told us sooner, we could have saved a lot of people by moving them underground."

"It would not have been enough protection. This form of radiation is similar to neutrinos and can penetrate thirty miles of earth before the energy is spent."

"Don't we need to get going so we won't be affected?"

Vesta indicated their surroundings. "No, we're protected by our ships."

"How is that possible?"

"The mirrored exterior will reflect the radiation the same way it reflects certain photons of light. The radiation will continue bombarding your planet for approximately twenty-seven hours, after which the sun will form a natural barrier for three months. By the time your planet emerges, the radiation will have left this area of the galaxy. People in poor health will get sick in approximately three days, and your entire race will be long dead by the time we return."

Alex was having difficulty accepting the idea there was nothing he could do to save the rest of the people on the planet. "You said my crew and I would need to make a choice. What is it?"

"Your choices are these. Number one. You sit in your ship for the next twenty-seven hours, either here or on the planet, watch everyone die horrible deaths, and help bury the dead. If you manage to avoid being murdered by the survivalists before they die, we'll meet up with you when we take the colonists back down to the surface in three years."

"That would be close to a living hell. What's number two?"

"You go into stasis on your ship until any trace of biological contamination from decaying corpses is over. We know from experience three years from the time of the bombardment will be sufficient. When you wake up, you can help transport our passengers down to the surface."

David studied the control console and then looked up at Vesta's image. "I've always thought we should have that type of equipment, but I couldn't find anything about this ship having stasis capability."

Alex turned to look at his friends for their opinions. "What do you think we should do?"

Okawna was the first to answer. "I almost lost my dad once, and it was painful. I don't think I could stand watching him and my mom die a slow death. I'm in favor of stasis."

"I feel the same way," Jadin told them. "I don't want to watch my family die, knowing I'm going to live. It's stasis for me, too."

Alex looked over at David, who gave him a solemn nod, he agreed, so he turned to Vesta's image. "What will happen to our ship?"

"It will remain here on the moon's surface with ours."

Okawna had a thought. "Hold on a second. I'd like to see the inside of your ship, so we know you're telling the truth about having our people in stasis. For all we know, you might have hundreds of your own people in stasis already, and are just waiting for our race to die so you can take over our planet."

"All right. I'll show you."

Okawna stood up. "Great. How do we get into your ship? Can you beam us aboard?"

"What do you mean?"

"You know. Teleport us over to your ship so we can look around before we go to sleep."

"I'm afraid that takes too much computer storage capacity. I'll align your ship's airlock with an entry into my ship, and you can walk inside."

The ship started moving across the gray surface and Alex stared up at the stars against an indigo background. He felt a soft thud through the floor as the ship settled onto the moon's surface and looked over at his distorted reflection on the surface of the other spacecraft. He turned from the window when he heard Vesta's voice.

"The connection with your ship is secure, Alex. You can open the airlock and finally get to see the inside of my ship."

When Vesta's image vanished, David watched Alex hurry down to the cargo hold to open the airlock doors, but he was still upset about losing Melvin and remained seated while the others walked out of the room. When he saw the blank monitor, something occurred to him. "Melvin? Can you hear me?"

When Melvin didn't answer, he hurried over and opened the small door of a cabinet built into the wall. He grabbed a small box containing four new power crystals, rushed back to the control console, and replaced the partially used ones with the fully charged ones. "Melvin? If you can hear me, these new crystals need to last us at least three years while we're in the stasis chambers, so please try to conserve enough power to keep us alive."

He waited and hoped for a response, but when he did not get one, he hurried down the stairs and found his friends waiting for him. He stopped at his locker and tossed the box with the used crystals inside, then went over to join his friends standing near the airlock. "I'm ready."

Alex saw the mirrored side of the other craft and stepped inside his airlock, and then an opening into the other ship appeared to match their own. He saw Vesta standing in a short hallway and walked through to join her.

Jadin followed Alex over to Vesta. "Thank you for letting us see the inside of your ship."

"Since you already have one of your own, I don't see why not."

Vesta sealed the opening in her ship with a focused thought. "Follow me and I'll show you around, but there's not much to see. Ninety-five percent of the ship is for stasis chambers."

Jadin had not been included in the meetings with Vesta, and something suddenly occurred to her. "How many times have you done this for other humans?"

"My race has been doing this for many generations. It started when they met the time travelers who wanted our help to save other intelligent species."

Alex had received help from a time traveler named Paladin and wondered if the ones Vesta's people had met were the same race. He was about to ask her about it when they entered the ship's control room.

David noticed there were no buttons or touch pads in front of a holographic monitor, and no one else in the room. "Does your artificial intelligence control all the functions on this ship?"

"We don't use an AI. Even the simplest units eventually develop their own personalities. Most are unpredictable, so we don't rely on them to take over our systems when there are so many lives at stake. I'm surprised Melvin hasn't taken over your ship for its own purposes."

David gave her a conspiratorial grin. "We have an agreement. It's Melvin's ship, and he lets us use it occasionally. He enjoys a good adventure as much as we do, and he likes us. Although I think he might have an issue with you when you release him." He returned to his original thought. "If you don't use an AI, how do you control your ship?"

"We connect with the main computer through a type of telepathy, and the ship is always under our control. The computer keeps things running, but it can't make any major decisions on its own and wakes one of us if necessary."

Vesta turned and led them down a short hallway and into a small laboratory. "This is our genetics lab, although we don't do experiments, only research. All the genetic material we have sampled over hundreds of generations has been uploaded into our data storage unit, and we keep adding data with each new human species we encounter. Your species was fortunate to have Zane working with the De Code Genetics lab in Iceland. That made it much easier for the selection process."

Alex noticed there was no one working in this room, either. "Where is the rest of your crew?"

Vesta indicated a blank wall which suddenly vanished by her thought, exposing twelve stasis chambers with clear lids spaced evenly across the floor. "This is my crew."

Alex moved closer to look down inside and saw eleven people sleeping on their backs, then turned to Vesta. "Six men and six women. This ship is a regular Noah's Ark."

She gave him a puzzled expression. "What is a Noah's Ark?"

"It's a story about a ship that saves two of every animal on our planet from extinction."

Vesta stared at him. "We do not save animals so this cannot be a Noah's Ark."

"Never mind."

Vesta turned to look at Jadin. "Like I told you, there isn't much more to see except for the stasis chambers."

Jadin panicked. "No, wait! I want to see the engine room, air handling system, and your computers."

Vesta held her palm up to stop Jadin from continuing. "They're sealed systems, and can only be accessed while in a repair facility."

Okawna felt a slight sense of anxiety. "How often does it break down?"

"Never. Everything is serviced before each trip."

Alex needed to verify one more thing before he would be satisfied with Vesta's true intentions. "Would you mind showing us the stasis chambers containing the colonists? Show us someone we know so we can be sure it's not your people."

"Not at all." She reached into a drawer, brought out four sets of sunglasses, and held them out to the visitors. "You'll need these later. Follow me."

Alex followed Vesta back the way they had come, but they continued past the entrance to his ship. She led them into a massive room with hundreds of thirty inch round hatches lining the walls from the floor to the twenty-foot high ceiling. "How many did you manage to save?"

"Not as many as we had hoped for. More than half never made it to the departure locations."

Now Alex understood how they could accommodate so many people and stared at several transparent hatches. Most of them were too dark inside for him to make out any discernable features, but occasionally the angle of the light in the walkway would allow him to see a head and face. He also noticed they were all wearing the strange-looking sunglasses Vesta gave them. "If the chambers are dark, why the need for sunglasses?"

"They're for when they wake up. After being in stasis for three years, your eyes will be extremely sensitive to the smallest amount of light. It usually takes fifteen minutes for them to get used to it, and it's painful without them." She touched one of the closed covers and a light inside illuminated a familiar face.

Okawna leaned close to the cover. "Hey, that's Zane."

Vesta studied Cave and saw he was convinced. "It's almost time for the radiation to hit us. Let's get back to your ship and I'll tuck you in."

Alex and his team followed Vesta back to the now exposed airlock of his ship, and everyone continued through into the cargo hold. When Vesta stopped beside him, Alex indicated the room. "If there are stasis chambers in here, I don't see them."

"Yours are older versions and are built into your sleeping chambers. I'll show you."

Vesta led them up the stairs to the living area and indicated their beds. "I'll open them for you, but just one at a time because of the limited space in this room."

A light came on inside one of the lower chambers. When the mattress slid out, Vesta indicated for Okawna to climb onto the bed. "Let me show you how it works."

Okawna stared at her. "I thought you were not going to allow anyone into the colony that has Neanderthal DNA."

"We accept a small amount of Neanderthal DNA in volunteers who are integral to the welfare of a new society. Those are usually good candidates for law enforcement officials. Both you and David are within the accepted parameters."

Okawna dropped to his knees and crawled onto his bed. "I'm fine with being a sheriff. Strap me in."

"There are no straps."

Okawna looked up at the faces of his friends. "I'll see you in the morning." He slid the glasses over his eyes and placed his arms at his sides on the mattress. An instant later, he used one hand to lift the sunglasses off his eyes and looked at Vesta. "Is this position okay?"

"Yes, that's fine, Okawna. Sleep well."

Alex watched the tray slide into the chamber and a transparent hatch slid down to enclose the opening just before the interior light blinked out. "How long before he's in stasis?"

"Three seconds. Who wants to go next?"

David indicated the bed across from Okawna. "I'm not really the law enforcement type, so what about me?"

"Your physics background will be needed as well. I'm sure you'll find something you enjoy doing."

"All right. I'll see you when this is over." He crawled onto the bed, slid on the sunglasses, and placed his arms beside him like Okawna. The lid closed, and the light blinked off.

Jadin did not hesitate to climb onto the next bed to open, which was above Okawna. "I'll see you soon, Alex."

When Jadin was secure, Alex climbed onto the bed above David and stared at Vesta before putting on his glasses. "I understand why you insisted we follow your orders when this all started. If people knew the truth about their shortened lifespans, they'd lose hope and society would have deteriorated into chaos almost immediately."

"I'm just sorry it's happening in the first place, Alex."

"Do you know what caused the burst of radiation?"

"Yes, it was human arrogance. One species thought they could change a brown dwarf star into one radiating light waves visible to the human eye."

"Why would they do something like that?"

"They wanted to illuminate a small planet in a nearby solar system as a new home for their ever-increasing population. Instead, they caused it to collapse to the point of a supernova explosion, which interacted with their experiment. It created the deadly form of radiation, which was ejected in only one direction. Unfortunately, it's spreading across this part of the galaxy like a deadly plague."

"Won't dark matter cause it to diminish over long distances?"

"Yes, but your planet is still close enough for it to kill all the humans."

"Why not the animals?"

"I already told you the radiation only targets a specific human genome."

"You say target like it was designed to be that way."

Vesta heaved a deep sigh of resignation. "No, Alex. It was a freak occurrence five thousand years ago."

Alex decided to let the matter drop and was about to put on his sunglasses when a thought occurred to him. "Was it your people who collapsed the sun?"

Vesta gave him a solemn nod of agreement. "Many generations ago."

"So, this is your penance? Saving humans for what your relatives did."

"Yes. Fortunately, they met the time travelers, and that's why they built this ship. The time travelers send us through time, so we arrive at the affected planet before the radiation hits them, and we save as many humans as we can."

"I see." He slid the glasses over his eyes. "I'll see you when it's over."

Vesta watched Alex slide into the chamber. When the light blinked off, his face was still illuminated by the light in the room, and she stared at him. "No, Alex. You won't see me again. I just hope it works this time."

She walked down the stairs and entered the airlock, closing the doors behind her as she entered her ship. With a final thought, she shut down all the nonessential systems on Alex's ship, and set Melvin on standby mode. Her ship's opening sealed itself behind her, and she continued to her own control room. She climbed into her own stasis chamber next to her team, none of whom wore sunglasses. When she closed her eyes, the light blinked off.

Chapter 23

NORTHERN GREENLAND:

Daniel Broussard was part of a team who were studying the effect of solar radiation passing through the Earth's magnetic field, but the sensors were picking up a different form of radiation. He went over to the cot and shook his friend's shoulder.

"Wake up, Charlie. There's something going on."

Charlie Iverson rolled off the thin mattress and stood as he yawned and stretched out his arms. "What happened?"

"It's some type of radiation I've never seen before. At first, it was weak, but it's been getting stronger over the past hour. Come check it out."

Charlie sat down in front of the monitor and read the information. "It's like nothing I've ever seen before, either. Let's send this data out to some of our friends and tell them what to look for. Maybe one of them is detecting it."

Daniel indicated the monitor. "Look. They're fading. We must be rotating out of alignment, so it's only coming from one direction. Be sure and let them know that."

***

Over the next twenty-seven hours, the replies were separated by hours because of the different time zones, but they were all saying the same thing. They detected the strange radiation, which increased in intensity and faded as the planet rotated away from the source.

Charlie and Daniel sat in front of the monitor as the earth's rotation brought them around to where they had discovered the radiation, but the data indicated it had stopped hitting the Arctic. He had several of his fellow physicists logged in for a conference call. "Are any of you detecting anything?"

"This is Bronson at JPL in California. We're no longer detecting it here. It's as if it suddenly stopped."

They received reports from several renowned physicists from around the world, and they were all saying they could no longer detect the radiation, and then Daniel indicated the data on the monitor. "Something must be blocking it."

Charlie entered a command into the computer. "The sun is now directly between us and the source of the radiation. We won't be able to detect it again for another month. I hope it's like neutrinos, and just passed through everything without doing any damage."

Chapter 24

THREE YEARS LATER

THE COLONY. DAY 1:

Derek opened his eyes and squinted at the woman looking down at him. "Have we arrived already?"

Vesta slowly increased the intensity of the light in the room. "That's correct. The rest of the colonists are on the surface, waiting for you. I saved you for last so I could talk to you before I leave."

Derek slowly sat up on the edge of the mattress. "Why me?"

"Because you're Alex Cave's nephew. Do you know anything about your family history?"

"Not really. Just that we're descended from Vikings on my grandfather's side of the family. Come to think about it, so was my grandmother. Is that important?"

"Yes. Alex has a unique gene marker we can't identify. We don't know its purpose, and I wondered if it has anything to do with your family tree."

"What difference does that make? He's dead."

"He's still alive."

Derek wasn't sure how he felt about the news. "Did he join the colony?"

"No, I'm afraid not."

"That's good to hear. How come he's still alive?"

"Because the comet didn't hit the Earth."

"What about the rest of my family? Are they still alive?"

When Vesta told him the truth about what killed everyone, Derek sat in silence for a moment. "Did my family suffer?"

"I'm sorry, Derek. No one could stop the radiation. I'll take you down to the colony as soon as you can walk without help."

Derek took a few hesitant steps. "I'm good. Let's get out of here."

***

Derek stepped out of the cube and saw Mya staring at him, then looked around and realized he was in the parking lot of a small movie theatre, but when he turned to look at Vesta, the cube was gone.

Mya hurried over to Derek. "I was wondering what happened to you. Are you the last one?"

"Yeah. Where are the rest of the colonists?"

"They're waiting for us at the stadium."

She indicated the electric car. "Get in and I'll take you there."

Derek climbed into the vehicle and it had a brand new aroma. Once Mya was behind the steering wheel, the car began moving and he stared out the windows at the sand accumulated on the streets and sidewalks. It felt like he was passing through a ghost town. "What have I missed so far?"

"From what I've been told, two weeks ago, Vesta brought thirty specialized people down to get some power and water working before the rest of the colony arrived. They opened up some storage facilities, where they found a bunch of electric vehicles and tons of supplies. By the time I got here, almost everyone had already arrived. A dozen people and I were shuttled to the storage complex to gather basic supplies, and then we were taken to the stadium. When I went inside, I expected it to be filled, but there couldn't have been over two-hundred and fifty people sitting at one end. When I couldn't find you, I took one of the cars back here to wait for you."

"Did you see Catori?"

Mya had watched Catori flirting with a crowd of young men who had gathered around her. "Yes, and she's making some new acquaintances."

"Do you mean men?"

"Of course. That's just the way she is. Don't tell me you didn't notice how self-centered she is."

"Yeah, I started getting that feeling when we arrived at the marina."

"If I were you, I'd look for someone else. She's bad news, Derek."

Derek knew Mya was right, then noticed a dome covered stadium in the distance. "Have you seen anyone else you know?"

"Just the council members, who I'm sure I've never met before, but I even know all their names."

"Yeah, me too. It's kind of weird."

"From what I've noticed, some people know each other and have formed into groups like they're old friends, but I don't know any of them. Except you and Catori. And Zane, of course."

Derek looked over at her. "Who's Zane?"

"He's a geneticist I met at my dig site. That was the first time I met Alex and Vesta."

Mya drove them to the storage facility and stopped in front of one of the units. They climbed out, and Derek helped her raise a large roll-up metal door. "Grab one of those tote bags and collect all the toiletries you need. They have water at the stadium, and we'll learn more once we get there."

Derek grabbed one of the bags, and when he looked inside, saw a pen and a printed form tucked into the side compartment. He strolled along the rows of open cardboard boxes, grabbing the usual items. Toothbrush and paste, floss, a disposable razor and shaving cream, toilet paper, and much more. Everything for basic survival, including combs and hairbrushes. When he was finished, he pulled the door back down and climbed into the car with Mya. "I can't believe how organized the colony is on the first day."

Mya drove away from the facility, and a few minutes later, the stadium was rushing toward the windshield as she raced across the parking lot. She parked next to over one hundred matching electric cars and climbed out. When Derek was ready, she led him over to the entrance and indicated for him to go inside. "You must be important, because they're just waiting for us to get here before they begin."

Derek strolled into the structure, past cases of drinking water stacked just inside the entrance, and saw a few people standing in front of the empty food concession stations. One woman noticed him and hurried in his direction, and could sense her outgoing personality from her smile and the sparkle in her brown eyes. When she stopped in front of him, he wasn't sure what to do.

"Hello, Derek. I'm Silvia Burkhart. I'm glad you're finally here. Find a seat and I'll let everyone know we're ready for our first meeting."

When the woman walked away, Derek stared at Mya. "How did she know my name?"

"Beats me. I met her earlier, and I guess she's on the welcoming committee. Let's go find a place to sit down."

Derek noticed the people near the concession were entering, and they followed them into the massive gymnasium. When he stopped to look around, he saw Catori sitting with several men, but didn't see an empty seat beside her. He thought about Kristie's statement that women could have their own haram, and if that's what Catori wanted, he wasn't going to be part of it. When she stood and waved at him, he ignored her, and then picked a location where he didn't have a direct line of sight with her. "I see a couple of seats near the last row."

Mya had seen Catori and her new friends, and had expected Derek to go join them, and felt a sense of relief he had heeded her warning. "Those work for me."

Catori stopped smiling and lowered her arm when Derek walked away with Mya, then sat down with the boys. "What does he see in that ugly old bitch?"

A moment later, a man from the group of council members hurried down the stairs and continued across the floor to the center of the spectators. The man waved his hands in the air to get everyone's attention, and when the room became quiet, he raised his voice to be heard without a public address system. "Hello, everyone. I guess I don't need an introduction. Welcome home."

Derek stood up and applauded with the rest of the people. "He's right about the introduction. His name is Oscar Templeton, and he's a neural surgeon and a member of the council."

Mya wondered how she could remember someone she had never met. When everyone started sitting back down, so did she and Derek.

Oscar waited for the applause to die out before he continued. "Now that we know what really happened here on Earth, let's take a moment to remember all those who died."

When Oscar felt it was a long enough pause, he looked around at all the solemn expressions before continuing. "All of you know the laws, so I won't repeat them. Let's talk about our first habitat. We've routed power from the solar energy farm north of town to the hotel, but the dust covering most of the panels limits the amount of energy we can use until we clean them up. We got the water treatment plant working, but again, it's limited until we get a crew to clean the solar panels. We chose a hotel with a large restaurant, and I hope some of you who like to cook can improve the taste of our canned and dehydrated food supply."

Oscar waited while the chuckles subsided. "It might take some time, but we should be able to connect other parts of the city and suburban areas to the solar power farm, but right now we need to organize teams to manage the tasks ahead of us, so please list your skills and types of committees you'd like to be on when you check into the hotel. You'll find the form in your bag, and for those of you who have working watches, please sync them up with mine." He looked at his windup pocket watch. "It is exactly 3:37 PM. We all know we have a lot of work to do, so tomorrow morning, you need to check the rosters placed at different locations on the main floor of the hotel for your work assignments."

Derek listened as the man laid out the plan to get the new society up and running, including stopping in the deserted stores for clothes and other items that would make their new home more comfortable. He also mentioned a reception later that evening, where everyone could get to know each other. When the meeting was over, he walked outside and saw Catori waiting for him near one of the few remaining cars in the parking lot, then looked at Mya. "Would you mind waiting for me?"

Mya looked across at Catori, standing alone for a change, and wondered if Derek would give in to her seductive behavior. "Sure. Don't forget what we talked about."

When Mya turned and continued over to an empty vehicle, Derek strolled over to Catori and saw there were two people in the back seat of the car. "Hi."

Catori threw her arms around Derek's neck and pulled him close. "I was getting worried when I didn't see you when we arrived. Why didn't you come up and sit with me?"

Derek had not put his arms around her waist and brought his hands up to her shoulders to ease her away. "It looked like you had enough company already."

"Oh, those guys? I can't help it. Men just want to hang out with me. It doesn't mean anything. Come with us. We're going to find some new clothes."

"Don't you think you should check into the hotel first?"

"They'll be plenty of time for that later. I want to find a new dress for the party."

"What's to celebrate? It should be a wake for all those people who died from the radiation."

"I say good riddance. They got what they deserved. Are you coming with us or not?"

Derek just stared at Catori for a moment, realizing what a conceded bitch she was. "You know what? I'll pass on the shopping spree. Knock yourself out."

As Derek turned and headed across the parking lot, Catori's jaw dropped as she stared after him. "I was just kidding," When he climbed into the other car, she waited until it drove away before looking at the two men sitting in the back seat. "It looks like it's just the three of us."

****

Mya and Derek drove to the designated hotel to check in, realizing it would be the beginning of an official record of who made it to the surface. They got in a long line weaving back and forth across the parking area in front of the building, and spent the time getting to know their neighbors, and they all seemed outgoing and friendly while they waited to check in. They were sociable, but already forming into groups.

When Mya reached the front desk, she gave her information form to one of the five people behind the counter. She waited while he wrote a room number on the form, then he gave her an electronic key card to a room. She looked at the card, then over at the young man. "Will these still work?"

"The door locks are battery powered, but if the ones in your door are dead, come back and I'll assign you to a different room."

He gave her a small bag and a sheet of paper. "If your door opens, keep it open until you change out the batteries, because it might not work a second time. Here are some instructions and information to help you."

Mya looked into the bag and saw six batteries and a small screwdriver. "It looks like they thought of everything."

"They tried, but didn't have time to check every room. They're dusty, and some might have been occupied a few years ago. Let us know if yours is too bad to live in and you'll get a different room. You'll have to scrounge for fresh linen, so try the supply closets on each floor or the hotel laundry room in the basement. Oh, and the elevator isn't working yet. I should have it running sometime tomorrow. I just want to do a safety inspection before I turn it on."

"Is that what you did in the old world?"

"No, but I'm a mechanical engineer and it's a simple system."

Derek was standing next to Mya, doing the same thing with a young woman behind the counter. "Could I get a room near her?"

The girl leaned across the counter. "Isn't she a little old for you?"

"We're just friends."

"You should think about pairing up as soon as possible."

Derek slid his form across the counter. "Where's the welcoming party going to take place?"

"There's a banquet room on the first floor." She looked at the form and smiled. "It's nice to meet you, Derek Cave. I'm Amanda Tamura."

Mya had been listening to Derek's conversation and grinned when she saw the look of infatuation in the young girl's eyes, then got Derek's attention. "I'll catch up with you later."

"All Right."

Amanda waited until Derek stopped staring after the woman. "Will I see you there, Derek?"

"I'm sure you will."

Amanda held a key card, a small bag, and a sheet of paper out to Derek. "Here are some instructions to help you get started. I look forward to seeing you again."

***

After climbing five flights of stairs, Mya was relieved when her card worked. She wasn't sure what to expect and slowly eased the door open, then saw the curtains were closed, and the air had a stale odor. She felt around the wall and flipped a switch, and released a sigh of relief when she did not see a skeleton. She set her bag on the floor to hold the door open before stepping into the room.

The bedspread looked gray, fading to pastel colors just above the floor. She continued to the curtains and pulled on the drawstring, allowing dull yellow light into the room. A narrow band of white light filled with sparkling particles appeared to cut the air in half, and she saw it was coming through the only clean area of the glass. She struggled to get the window open, and the rush of fresh air made her skin tingle, and she took several deep breaths, and then turned to study her situation. Other than the dust and cobwebs hanging from the ceiling, the room was in good shape.

Derek noticed the open door across from his room and looked inside, seeing a silhouette in the window. "Is that you, Mya?"

Mya moved into the room. "Yeah, welcome to my new home."

Derek went inside and looked around. "Cozy. No dead body, I see. I'm across from you in number five seventeen."

"While you're here, how about giving me a hand to fold this filthy bedspread out of the way? It's dusty enough in here already, so let's try not to create any more. I'll help you with yours when you're ready."

Derek followed Mya's instructions and helped her toss the bedspread out the window before looking down and seeing the empty parking lot behind the building. "Shouldn't we have put it in the hallway?"

"This isn't a five-star hotel anymore, and there isn't any room service."

Derek grinned. "Right. I guess it's a zero star hotel now."

Mya checked the sheets and pillows and they appeared to be clean, but she wasn't going to take any chances. She found fresh pillows in one drawer and spare towels in the closet. "I'll take everything to the laundry room once I'm finished cleaning this place. I'll grab a bedspread and find some fresh sheets and towels while I'm down there."

Derek looked across at his door. "I just wanted to check my room and change the batteries before I go looking for some clothes."

"I figure I'll have time for shopping later. Right now, I just want to make sure I have a clean bed to come home to."

"I hadn't thought about it, but you're right. I might as well do mine while I'm here."

"Nobody can think of everything, Derek. That's why we need to work as a community. Let's go see what your room looks like."

Derek didn't hesitate to open his door and walk into his new home, and it was a mirror image of Mya's room. Once the bedspread was out the window, he looked at her. "Thanks for the help and advice. I'm sure the clothes I'm wearing will last awhile. I guess I'd better get started cleaning this place."

Mya looked back at her open door. "I'll go grab some new linen for both of us if you'll change out the batteries in my door for me."

"Sure. I'm good at fixing things."

***

Three hours later, Mya finished making up the bed and took one last look around. She had found a vacuum cleaner in the supply closet at the end of the hall and had used it before giving it to Derek. Once satisfied the room was clean, she walked into the bathroom and saw her dirt-smudged naked body in the mirror. She grinned at the fresh towels on the rack above the toilet and turned on the water in the bathtub. After a nice hot shower, she got dressed and left the room, and Derek's door was open, and knocked when she didn't see him.

Derek rolled off the bed and went to the door. "Hey. Come on in."

Mya strode into the room and looked around. She saw Derek had done a decent job of cleaning up, and then noticed there was still a layer of dust on the top edge of the baseboards, but didn't say anything about it. "Have you read the flyer yet?"

"No, I forgot about it."

"The first community meal will be served in the banquet room starting at 6:00 PM."

She looked at her old windup wristwatch. "It started half an hour ago if you want to go down with me."

When Derek turned to look around his room, she noticed a few cobwebs clinging to the back of his hair. "Hold still for a moment." She gently pulled them away and showed them to him. "You might want to take a shower first."

"Good idea. I'll meet you down there in a few minutes."

Mya left the room and went down the stairs to the first floor, then took a few minutes to walk around and check out the rest of the hotel. She found the cocktail lounge, but it was empty, as were the shelves that once held the liquor bottles. When she entered the banquet room, it appeared some people were already forming into ethnic groups, and she wondered if perhaps this new civilization would end up being just as segregated as the society they had replaced. If that were to happen, she would be heartbroken.

She made her way around the people sitting at the tables and understood why they had formed into groups. Many of them were talking in their native languages, so it made sense they would sit together. She saw a few people standing in line at a table with stacks of bowls and a heated serving tray, and went over to stand behind the middle-aged woman who had greeted her and Derek. "Hi, Silvia. Whatever it is they're serving sure smells good."

"Hello again, Mya. Tonight we have two choices of stew. One with beef and one without for the vegetarians."

"You seem to know everyone in the colony. The only people I know are the council members and three others."

"Don't worry about it, dear. You're not alone. I have a photographic memory. Why don't you join a few new friends and me at our table? You need to start somewhere."

"I'd like that. Thank you."

***

A pleasant aroma greeted Derek as he strolled down the hallway on the main floor, and when he entered the banquet room, the air was filled with a soft thrumming sound from all the conversations. He stopped and looked around for a moment, then saw Mya sitting at a table with several older people. He looked for Catori, but didn't see her, but saw Amanda sitting with a small group of young people. When she saw him, she suddenly stood up and waved him over, so he waved back as he headed in her direction.

Amanda remained standing until Derek reached the table. "I was wondering if you would like to join us."

"Sure. Thanks."

"I know you're probably hungry. Go grab a bowl of stew and I'll introduce you to everyone when you get back."

When Derek returned to the table, he noticed the chair next to Amanda was now vacant, so he sat down beside her, and she introduced him to the three girls and two boys before he ate. He listened to them speculating about what will happen in the future, physics, genetics, and parallel universes. Evidently, they were all well-educated, and he wondered if he might be at the wrong table.

***

Catori thought the man behind the check-in counter was joking when he had told her the room would need to be cleaned before she settled in. Now that she was looking into the room, she realized it was worse than she had imagined. She used her foot to slide the two bags of clothes to hold the door open, then spun around and headed toward the stairs.

***

Derek recognized Catori standing in the doorway while she looked around the room. He hoped she wasn't looking for him and turned to look at Amanda. "What kind of work do you enjoy?"

"I'm an astrophysicist. What do you like to do?"

"I'm a firefighter."

"Wow. That sounds exciting. I haven't published a paper in two years."

Derek wondered why publishing a paper could be exciting.

***

Catori looked around and saw Derek sitting next to a young girl, and hurried over to their table, then stood beside him. "What do you think about the rooms they gave us? Mine's a mess. How can they expect me to sleep in that filthy bed tonight?"

Derek could not believe how rude Catori could be and ignored her question. He indicated the girl sitting beside him. "Catori, this is Amanda."

Catori gave Amanda a quick appraisal and then turned her attention back to Derek. "When I went down and asked the guy at the desk for a better one, he said they're all that way."

Derek stood and grabbed Catori's hand, guiding her to a more secluded part of the room. "You knew there was going to be a lot of work before you volunteered. Did you think they would have housekeeping service when you arrived? I warned you about making shopping your priority. I suggest you grab something to eat and start cleaning your room before it gets too late."

"Could you help me?"

"Why don't you get your new boyfriends to do it for you? That's the way you operate, isn't it?"

Catori wasn't about to clean her room tonight and pouted at Derek. "I don't understand why you're acting this way. I thought we were together."

"I guess you and I have different ideas about what together means. Do what you want about your room."

When Derek turned and headed back to join Amanda, Catori stared after him for several long moments, wondering how to seduce him into sharing his bed. When he sat down and talked with Amanda, she looked around the room for the two men she had been shopping with, but didn't see them. She thought perhaps they're cleaning their own rooms right now, and her lips formed into a devilish grin as she headed toward the door.

Chapter 25

THE COLONY. DAY 2:

The next morning, Mya and Derek joined a smaller crowd of people for breakfast in the restaurant, and after eating scrambled eggs and biscuits, went to the lobby to check the roster for work assignments. Derek grabbed the clipboard and saw the assignments were listed by name in alphabetical order, with some of them appearing in different languages, and saw Mya's name. "It looks like you're going to help clean the solar panels out in the desert. It says they'll be picking you up in front of the hotel at 9:30 PM tonight."

"I guess I'll have time to go shopping before I leave. What about you?"

Derek flipped through the pages. "Here I am. I've got kitchen duty from 3:00 PM until midnight."

"Should we go look around?"

"Sure. We might as well get to know our new home."

When they reached the parking lot, there were no cars available, and Mya looked up and down the street to see what was nearby. "It looks like there aren't any shopping malls within walking distance."

Derek noticed a dozen bicycles next to the building. "When was the last time you rode a bike?"

"All the time. It looks like our first stop should be to get some helmets."

When they walked over to check them out, Derek noticed some wrenches lying on the sidewalk next to the building. He handed one to Mya before searching for a bicycle to suit his style of riding, and found a mountain bike and quickly adjusted the seat and handlebar heights, then noticed Mya still finding the right height for her seat. "I'll go grab some water bottles for the trip."

Mya was ready when he came back outside and handed her a bottle, and she clipped it into the bracket on the lower crossbar. "Do you have any idea where we're going?"

"Yeah, I asked the person manning the desk about helmets. The nearest super store is about ten miles further north. We just stay on this street and we'll be fine. At least there won't be a lot of traffic. That should make for a safer ride until we get some helmets."

Mya climbed onto her bike and smiled at Derek. "This should be fun."

They rode side by side in the middle of the road, and what few gas-powered cars they passed along the way were covered in dust and bird droppings. It was an easy ride, but the view of unkempt homes on the outskirts of town only emphasized the fact everyone had died. They passed several small business buildings along the way, but the writing on the signs telling them what type of service they had provided were hidden under a thick layer of dirt, or covered with wild vegetation.

There was two miles of wide-open space between the city and a nearly windowless brick building set back from the road, but there wasn't a sign stating its purpose. The road took them around an abandoned apartment complex and a small housing development into the empty parking lot of a massive indoor mall, and directly ahead was the south entrance.

They stopped and Derek got off his bike, then steered it to the front doors. When he tried opening them, they were locked. He got back on his bike and stopped next to Mya. "I don't really want to break in. Let's continue around the building. Maybe we'll find an entrance that isn't locked."

They rode along the curved wall of the mall until they found the next entrance and saw one electric car parked outside. When Derek tried the doors, one side opened, and he pushed his bike into the dimly illuminated mall before holding the door open for Mya to enter. He looked up at the angled glass panels in the roof, all appearing as if a recent thunderstorm had washed away some of the grime.

Mya stopped at the map of the complex on a stand in the middle of the floor and saw the dirt had been wiped away. "Here we go. It's just up around the corner."

With no one in her way, Mya rode along slowly through the walkway, searching through the store windows for other amenities she might need. When she reached the sporting goods store, she left her bike outside and entered through the shattered glass doorway. The first thing she grabbed was one of the last backpacks and then walked through the aisles, occasionally inspecting an item she might need in the future.

Derek slung a backpack over one shoulder and immediately headed for the guns and ammunition section. He was disappointed when he didn't see a single weapon, plus all the cabinet doors had been pried open and were now empty. He turned when he heard Mya chuckling. "What's so amusing?"

"Here we are, the last population on earth, and you want a gun?"

"I may not be as educated as the rest of those people, but I have a few skills to offer. I figure at some point everyone is going to want fresh meat, and I'm an excellent hunter. It's just a lot easier if I have a rifle or even a pistol."

"Fair enough. As long as you don't shoot people."

***

Catori trudged along the open desert, occasionally looking up to keep sight of the road in the distance. Over the past forty-eight hours, her dream had slowly turned into a nightmare. First, Derek had dumped her just because she had made some new friends, and just when she had needed him the most, he had refused to help her. Even her two new friends had told her they were too busy to help clean her room. She had managed to get the window open in her room and had sat staring at the setting sun, too depressed to clean. She had eventually removed the bedspread and found a blanket in the closet, but mice had chewed the corners away, leaving large holes when she spread it out over the sheets.

And if that wasn't bad enough, her car had died in the parking lot of the mall, and she had to escape from a pack of wild dogs. It seemed nothing was going right for her. After trekking through the sand and brush for the past hour, she stepped onto the asphalt road and it was much easier to walk, as if some weight had been removed from her shoes.

***

When Mya and Derek left the mall, their backpacks were full, making the return trip a little more difficult. In the distance, Derek saw a person with long dark hair and dressed in a jacket and shorts shuffling along the empty stretch of road. He found it odd someone would be out here alone in the middle of nowhere. Especially if it was a woman. As he drew near, he thought he recognized the hair and slowed to a stop beside her, then got off his bike. "Catori?"

Catori flinched when she heard a voice out of nowhere, then spun around and noticed Mya, but stared at the man on a bicycle. "Oh, Derek! You don't know how glad I am to see you!"

"What are you doing out here all alone?"

Catori could no longer hold back her tears and wrapped her arms around Derek's back, burying her face against his chest while she cried.

"Nothing has turned out the way I thought it would. You abandoned me when we were supposed to do this together. Then, when I needed you the most, you refused to let me stay with you and I had to sleep on a filthy bed in a filthy room."

He eased her away. "How did you end up out here?"

"After I ate breakfast alone, I got into one of the cars just to get away and think about things. On the way back, I saw a mall and decided to look around inside. When I came out, the batteries in the car were dead. I thought I saw a shortcut through a housing development, but when I got closer, I heard dogs barking and cut across the desert back to this road. Could I have some of your water?"

Derek pulled the bottle from the bracket and gave it to Catori, then noticed her eyes nervously darting around in search of something while she drank. "What are you looking for?"

"The dogs. The only thing stopping them from getting me was a fence. I'm worried they may have a way to get out."

Mya felt sorry for Catori. The poor girl had spent her entire life living with her tribe and had no idea how to survive in a new environment.

Derek knew there was no way he could take Catori with him on the bicycle, and definitely could not leave her out here on her own, so he turned to look at Mya. "I'm going to make sure Catori gets back to the hotel. I know you'll have to work all night, so you would probably like to take a nap first. Why don't you go ahead and I'll meet up with you later?"

"Are you sure?"

"Yeah, we'll be fine."

When Mya drove away, Catori walked beside Derek and grabbed his hand. "Thank you for staying with me. It's been a scary walk."

"I'm sorry about last night. It's just that you're not taking this seriously enough. Did you look at the roster for your job assignment?"

"Well, no. I need to clean my room, so I'm not doing any other work today."

Derek let go of Catori's hand and stopped. "Do you see what I mean? You only care about yourself. You have a responsibility to the rest of the colony."

Catori suddenly snapped. "Stop saying that word! All my life, everyone hounded me about my responsibility, and I hate it!"

"Hate it or not, that's the reality now, so get over it."

Catori saw Derek suddenly looking past her. "Are you okay?"

Derek didn't hear any barking, but could see a pack of dogs racing in his direction. He let go of the bike and grabbed Catori's hand, dragging her across the dry field to the only shelter: The isolated building set back from the road.

Catori slowed down to look back at the dogs, and he had to drag her arm to keep her running. "Hurry!" He reached the concrete steps, then let go of Catori and ran up to the door, but when he tried to open it, it was locked. There were no windows on the landing, but he remembered seeing one on the side of the building.

Catori had just reached the top of the steps when Derek suddenly spun around and grabbed her hand again. She followed him back down the stairs and around to the side of the building, with a window about eight-feet above the ground. They stopped and he let go, so she stepped back as he dropped onto his knees and dug through the gravel landscaping. "What are you doing?"

Derek didn't answer until he found a large rock, then jumped up and moved away from the building. "Stand back." When he hurled the stone through the window, the shattering glass alerted the dogs, and they started barking. He could tell they were much closer, and moved under the window and put his back against the wall, then waved Catori over to join him. "Take off your jacket. When I hoist you up, use it to clear away any remaining glass, then drape it over the windowsill and climb through. You'll need to grab my jacket and help pull me inside. Can you do that?"

Catori slid out of her coat and wrapped it around her hand. "I can."

Derek held onto Catori's free hand as she stepped onto his knee. When she was balanced against the building, he let go and cupped her other foot in his hands. "Ready? Go!" He stood up with his back against the building. "Can you reach it?"

"Yes, hold on a second."

Catori busted out the few remaining shards of glass and wiped the remaining pieces into the room before draping the coat over the edge. "Okay, go!"

Derek hoisted Catori up and through the opening. When her weight was gone, he moved a few feet away and saw Catori hanging out through the window, waving him to hurry. The dogs were coming around the corner of the building, so he got a running start to gain some momentum, then leapt up and grabbed Catori's hands. The toes of his shoes scraped against the brick wall, desperately searching for some kind of foothold as he dragged himself up to the opening, with the snarling and growling from the dogs beneath him.

He heard Catori grunting under the strain, and then he managed to get one arm draped over the ledge. He suddenly stifled a groan when his pants dug into his crotch because of Catori hauling him up by his belt, then yelled in anguish when one of the dogs bit into his shoe, dragging him down, but the pain was because of the added pressure on his balls. The shoe was suddenly ripped off his foot, and then he managed to drag himself through the opening and dove headfirst onto the floor to curl up in agony.

Catori spun around and knelt beside Derek, who was curled into a fetal position with his hands holding his crotch. "Are you okay?"

Derek slowly rolled into a sitting position and looked into Catori's eyes. "No, but I'll be fine. Just give me a few minutes."

"I'm sorry about your balls, but your belt was the only thing I could grab."

"It's nothing an icepack can't fix, but I could use a hand getting up."

Catori stood and reached down for Derek's hand, then pulled him to his feet. She watched him grimace in pain before he bent over and put his hands on his knees. She could not see his face, but heard him softly groaning. "Just sit down for a minute while I look around this place. Maybe I can find something for us to drink."

"You shouldn't go by yourself. It may not be safe and you might get lost."

"There is no one else in here, Derek. Besides, I'm an Indian. I won't get lost."

Derek eased down onto a padded chair and realized he was in someone's office. "Okay. That feels better. I just need a few more minutes, and then I'll go with you."

"I'll be fine. I bet this place has a break room. I'll be back before you know it."

Derek watched her walk out through the open doorway and noticed a few pictures hanging on the wall of the office. He expected to see family images, but they were of groups of people in white lab coats.

***

Catori saw stairs just outside the office. One set led down to what she assumed was the basement, and the other went up to the next floor, but they were dark and scary. She wandered around the main floor, opening doors and looking into rooms filled with laboratory equipment. In one room, she saw what remained of shattered glass beakers and flasks strewn across the worktable. On the other side was a wall covered with whiteboards, all filled with math formulas and strange symbols. The words 'There is no cure for the radiation', were scrawled in large garish letters in the center of the formulas.

She noticed a massive stainless steel refrigerator in one corner and walked over to look inside. When she opened one of the doors, a black, mold covered liquid drooled out and splattered onto her bare legs and sandals.

"Oh, yuck!"

She stepped back and noticed a sink and hurried over, but when she turned the handles, no water came out. "Shit!" A piece of white cloth protruded from the cabinet next to the sink, so she opened the door, grabbed a towel, and wiped the foul smelling liquid off her legs and shoes.

***

Derek wondered if the dogs were still outside, and slowly stood up. Moving was painful as he shuffled over to the window and looked down, and two dogs were ripping his shoe to shreds while the others growled and bared their teeth at him, then he turned around and made his way to the door. "Catori? Where are you?"

Catori was rounding the corner when she saw Derek calling for her. "I'm right here. The water isn't working and I can't find anything to drink."

They both flinched when they heard gunshots coming from outside, then heard a volley of them, followed by yelps and squealing. A moment later, everything was silent. Derek heard someone yelling his name and smiled at Catori. "Mya must have come back for us."

Derek tried to ignore the pain as he hurried to the main entrance and turned the knob to unlock the front door. When he stepped outside, he saw two cars and four people holding rifles at the bottom of the steps, and one of them was Mya, and smiled at her. "I thought you didn't like guns."

Mya smirked back. "I never said that. I kept thinking about the dogs and thought you could use some help."

"It was close. How did you know we'd be in here?"

"I didn't until I saw the dogs hanging around an abandoned building. Oscar told me they're just getting started with animal control. That's why all the guns were missing in the store." She noticed Derek was missing a shoe. "Do you need a ride?"

"That would be great. I could use an ice pack, if you have one."

Mya waited while Derek and Catori climbed into her vehicle, and when she got in, noticed a foul smell in the car, but didn't mention it.

***

On the drive to the hotel, Catori thought about Derek's comment before they were attacked. For her entire life, the word 'responsibility' had been thrown in her face, and she hated it like poison. Now Derek was demanding the same thing. When Mya parked in front of the hotel, she climbed out and saw a large sign stating everyone needs to check for their job assignment. She knew Derek would demand she look at the roster, so she hurried inside while he was cautiously getting out of the car.

Derek climbed out and didn't see Catori, and waited until Mya joined him, and then slowly strolled beside her into the building. He stopped at the front desk, but didn't recognize the older man. "Excuse me. Where can I get some ice?"

"You can get some in the kitchen prep room. Those are the only two ice makers in operation because of the power consumption."

"Great. Thanks." He looked at Mya. "I might as well see where I'm working tonight."

Mya was curious about his need for ice, but decided not to ask. "Are you going to be all right?"

"I'm okay. I just need some ice."

Mya looked down at Derek's shoeless foot. "Why don't you go on up to your room and I'll bring some ice to you. But that's the last favor I'm doing for you today because I need a nap."

"Fair enough. Thanks."

Derek was grateful the elevator was finally working when he stepped inside and pressed button number five. When the car rose, he thought about Catori and wondered what happened to her, then realized he didn't even know her room number. When the bell chimed, he stepped out on the fifth floor and said hello to one of the people he had met at the party, but couldn't remember his name. His room seemed far away, and he was grateful when he opened the door and saw the bed. He shuffled across the room and nearly lay down when he remembered Mya would stop by with the ice.

He slowly returned to the door and slipped out of his remaining shoe to use as a wedge to keep the door open. When he finally lay down, he released a deep sigh of relief. So far, it had been an interesting, if painful, adventure. Too bad he couldn't tell Alex he was wrong about joining the colony.

Chapter 26

THIRTY DAYS LATER

THE DARK SIDE OF THE MOON:

Alex slowly opened his eyes but could not see anything, then remembered the sunglasses and yanked them off. It took a moment to realize where he was, and then his bed suddenly slid out from the stasis chamber. He heard a soft moan and looked across at Jadin, whose bed was still recessed into the wall, but the cover was open. "Are you okay?"

Jadin removed her glasses and turned her head to look across at Alex. "I think so."

"I was expecting to see Vesta."

"I'm here, Alex."

Alex recognized the voice, and his eyes darted around the room. "I don't see you."

"I'm not physically on your ship. I'm transmitting my thoughts to you through Melvin."

"Is it over?"

"Yes, Alex. It's time to go home."

"What about the rest of the volunteers? Are they still on your ship?"

"No, we took them to the surface thirty days ago, and now we're on our way to another solar system."

Alex's arms and legs felt stiff when he stood and stretched his body, and as his bed slid back inside the chamber, he moved out of the way so Jadin's mattress could slide out. "Why are we the last ones to wake up?"

"We wanted to talk to you about your ship before you go down to the surface. We think it would be best if you didn't let the rest of the colony know about it just yet. Setting up a society is going to be hard enough, and the sudden arrival of a spaceship would only complicate the situation."

"Perhaps you're right. I'll need a secure location to hide my ship. Is there a safe place where I can land within walking distance of the colony? I'm looking forward to seeing my nephew as soon as possible."

"There's a large airfield about ten miles from the town of Palmdale, California, the site of the new colony."

"I'm familiar with it. It's Edwards Air Force Base. They did a lot of aeronautical research at the facilities so I'll be able to hide the ship without any problem. How many people did you end up saving?"

"Only two-hundred and forty-one made it to the departure sites before we were forced to leave."

Jadin was sitting on the edge of her bed, stretching her arms and moving her legs. "That's a lot of people to feed and supply with clean water."

"Several storage facilities were stocked with enough food and basic necessities to last one year. It will probably last longer with only half the number of people using it. The basics of the systems are already in place, and they should have a working infrastructure by now."

Jadin shook her head in amazement. "You've thought of everything."

"This is my eighth time doing this, so we've worked out most of the problems. Each one turned out differently, and I just hope this one works."

Alex noticed the nervous inflection in Vesta's voice. "You don't sound too optimistic about this attempt. Why is that?"

"There is always an unknown factor. Your species has evolved well technologically, but not socially."

"I thought that was why you only accepted people with the GC117 gene. Won't that make a difference?"

"That's what I'm counting on this time."

Alex had the strangest feeling something was not quite right. "Am I missing some of my crew?"

Vesta realized something was wrong. Alex should have a completely new memory without the rest of his team. "What makes you ask that?"

"There are four stasis chambers."

"Alex and Jadin, I must leave you now. Good luck."

"Hold on a minute! You didn't answer my question." He waited for a reply, but she didn't answer. "Vesta? Can you hear me?"

Jadin gave Alex a puzzled expression. "It's always just you and me, unless we have visitors."

"This doesn't feel right."

Jadin scooted off the mattress and stood. "What's gotten into you? You're acting strange, as if you've lost your memory. We came alone, Alex."

He noticed something out of place in the living area. "Did you bring the microwave oven?"

Jadin looked at the black-colored appliance. "I suppose so, but I don't remember."

A knot formed in Alex's stomach. "No, you didn't bring it. It belongs to a close friend of mine named Okawna. I think he's part of our crew."

"If he were part of the crew, I'd remember him. Maybe you invited him to come on one of our missions."

Alex hurried out of the room and up the stairs to the control room, and then slowly approached the four chairs. "This doesn't feel right. I can picture us and two other people sitting in these chairs, and I don't think I'm the one who flies this ship."

Jadin reached up and put her hand on Alex's shoulder as she moved past him. "You're right, you don't." She sat down in front of the control panel and looked up at the holographic monitor. "Melvin?"

"I'm here, Jadin."

"Are you ready to fly?"

"You bet. Where are we going this time?"

"Palmdale, California, USA."

Alex couldn't shake the nagging feeling in his gut, and he had learned a long time ago he's usually right. "Hold on a minute, Melvin. How many people are normally on this ship?"

"You and Jadin are the primary crew, but once in a while, two other people join you."

"Do you know their names?"

"I can't seem to find that information."

"Can you locate Sparrow Valley, Washington State, USA?"

"Yes, I have that location in my database."

"Great. Let's go there first. I want to see what's left of my home."

"I know right where it is, Alex. Buckle up, cause here we go."

Alex had a sense of déjà vu when he heard Melvin's words, and then sat down in the chair next to Jadin, but it just didn't feel right. "Is this where I normally sit?"

"Of course not." She indicated the chair directly behind her. "That's the captain's chair. What's gotten into you, Alex? You act as though you've never been here before."

"I can't quite put my finger on it, but everything just feels wrong to me."

"Well, we were in those stasis chambers for a long time. Maybe you're suffering a side effect."

"What about you? Are you feeling any side effects?"

"My muscles were a little stiff when I first got up, but that's all."

Alex remained standing and stared through the window as the moon's surface slid beneath the ship, then the Earth rose over the horizon, quickly increasing in size. As they drew near, a shimmering halo seemed to surround the planet, and soon Alex realized what was causing the illusion. The Earth was surrounded by the shattered remains of satellites.

Jadin also noticed the halo. "I'm guessing with no one around to correct any change in the orbital paths, they eventually smashed into each other. Melvin, are you going to have any problem getting through that debris field?"

"No, the force field will protect us, but I'll go slowly in case I need to nudge the larger pieces out of my way. I don't want to send them ricocheting back into the atmosphere too fast, or they may not burn up completely."

When they entered the debris field, Alex watched the smaller pieces of metal and plastic move past the side of the ship, while larger pieces, including what appeared to have been the international space station, were further away as they continued toward the Earth.

Jadin smiled. "The atmosphere appears so clear compared to the last time we were going back to the surface."

"I see it too. It must be because there were no humans polluting it over the past three years."

"I wonder why Vesta brought everyone to the United States instead of any other country."

"I hadn't really thought about it until now. I guess we'll never know."

***

SPARROW VALLEY, WASHINGTON.

With no living persons within hundreds of miles, Alex didn't think the cloak would be necessary, until Melvin eased the ship down onto the pasture across from his home. Through the barrier, he watched four appaloosa horses bolt out of the barn, leaping over a collapsed wooden fence before they disappeared into the forest. He was amazed at how much wild vegetation was engulfing all the buildings on the property. Thick tangled blackberry bushes blocked the exterior walls of his house, and the fast-growing alder trees were shading the roof, causing moss to grow on the shingles.

He went down to the cargo hold and over to the airlock, opened the doors, then stepped out of the ship. He looked beyond the white wooden fence at his home and sensed Jadin's presence beside him. "This all seems so surreal to me."

Jadin thought about her home in Oregon. "I wonder what the marina looks like by now. Could we stop there next?"

"Of course. I just wish I had a machete to chop away the berry vines so we can get into the house. Let's look around. Maybe there's another way to get inside"

Alex walked through the knee-high grass, climbed over the wooden railings, then waited for Jadin. They continued over to the back porch of the house and noticed a narrow gap between the berry bushes, and Alex carefully moved a few stray tendrils of barbed vines out of the way, stepped onto the porch, and then stared at the wooden bench swing. It seemed like only a few days ago he was sitting there with his family.

He opened the screen door and tried the doorknob, and when the door opened, they went inside, and everything was covered in a layer of dust and had a musty odor. "Judging from the dirty dishes, I'm guessing they went to a hospital soon after they began feeling sick."

Alex went into the living room and down the hallway, and then stopped to look into Kristie's room, grateful the bed was empty. He continued to Derek's room, which appeared to have never been used again after he had left to join him in Oregon. He continued down the hallway to Robert's room, and it was just as he remembered it. The dressers and nightstands were covered with photographs of his family growing up in Sparrow Valley.

One picture grabbed his attention, and he moved over for a closer look. It appeared to be recent, showing him and a tall blond man with their arms around each other's shoulders, both smiling at whoever was taking the picture. He snatched the photograph off the dresser, slid the picture out of the frame, and read the writing on the back, then closed his eyes, remembering harrowing experiences of him and the person in the photograph. He opened his eyes and handed it to Jadin. "That's Okawna and me. Do you recognize him?"

"No, I've never seen him before."

"That was taken after the Pandora mission while he and I worked together on Mike Tanner's research ship, the Mystic." He felt a lump in his throat as he stared at Okawna's image, then when he closed his eyes, more flashes of memories suddenly cluttered his mind, but he had a hard time fitting the pieces together. "He and I were very close friends."

Jadin noticed Alex appeared to be deep in thought and didn't want to interrupt his concentration, so she stepped out of the room and studied the pictures hanging in the hallway. It was the first time she had seen a picture of Alex's brother, Ken, and she was surprised at the resemblance. The facial features were very similar, but Ken had light brown hair, while Alex's was nearly black. She spun around when she heard Alex swear and hurried back into the room. "What's wrong?"

"Vesta lied to me. Okawna and I were partners in the CIA and he was part of our team on the spaceship."

Jadin thought Alex was losing his mind, like when he couldn't remember who drove the ship. "Hold on a minute. If he was part of our team, why can't I remember him? Maybe you're still feeling the side effects of being in stasis."

"No, I'm positive. It's all coming back to me now. The fourth person on our team was David Conway, a physicist and a good friend."

Jadin recognized the rage building in Alex's eyes. She jumped back when he suddenly grabbed a lamp and hurled it against the far wall."

"Vesta killed them!"

Jadin's jaw dropped. "What do you mean?"

"They were in those two stasis chambers below ours when we first went into hibernation, and now they're empty."

"Then how come I can't remember them?"

"I bet it was the sunglasses. None of Vesta's people were wearing them. Only the volunteers. I think they did something to our memories while we slept, but it didn't work on me. At least, not in the way they expected it would. It might have something to do with a strange genetic marker in my DNA. Zane said he had never seen it in anyone else."

Jadin thought about it for a moment. "What reason would she have to kill your friends?"

"Because both of them had a small amount of Neanderthal DNA. She told me they were allowing a certain percentage of people who were important to the new colony, but it was a lie. She had no intention of letting them be part of the new society."

Jadin noticed the rage building up again in his eyes. "I'm sorry, Alex, but there is nothing you can do about it now. Maybe we should leave this place and head to Oregon. It might take your mind off it for a while."

Alex let his hands relax. "Perhaps you're right, but Vesta had better not return or she'll wish she had never met me."

When Alex stomped out into the hallway, Jadin followed him out of the house and across to the ship, but once they were in the control room, she had a thought. "How come Melvin doesn't remember Okawna or David?"

"Vesta took control of Melvin when we first landed on the moon, so that would not have been a problem. According to Vesta, he's an older model and it would have been simple for her to erase David and Okawna from Melvin's database." He sat down in the chair, and even though it didn't matter, out of habit, he looked up at the holographic monitor. "Melvin, please take us to Humpback Harbor, Oregon, USA."

"I know where it is. Buckle up, cause here we go."

Alex snapped his head around to look at Jadin sitting beside him. "That's what David used to say just before we took off in the ship. Melvin, can you show us a holographic image of yourself?" He waited, but Melvin didn't respond. "Are you still with us?"

"Yes, sorry about that. I have never been given an image to represent me, but I found one in my backup files. Will this one work for you?"

When the image of a young man appeared to float in front of the screen, Alex leapt out of his chair and stood staring at the person. "That's him. That's David Conway, our fourth crew member."

Jadin studied the image. "I don't recognize him."

Alex turned to face her. "You didn't recognize Okawna, either, but the four of us have worked on several classified missions together. I'm telling you, Vesta erased them from your memory."

Jadin knew Alex was usually right about these things, and now she believed him. "It must have been very selective, because I remember going on missions with you, but no one else."

A few moments later, Jadin recognized the shoreline of Humpback Harbor and the floating docks of the marina. They were still far below, so she could not tell what condition they were in, and then her attention was drawn to Melvin's voice.

"Jadin, you need to tell me where to park."

Alex turned back to the monitor, and David's image was still floating in the air. "Why are you asking Jadin?"

"My records indicate this is her hometown."

Alex's jaw dropped slightly when the image appeared to be looking and speaking directly at him. "That's a little disconcerting."

Jadin stared at the floating screen. "What? The hologram?"

"Yeah, the way it looked at me, especially hearing Melvin's voice coming from David's face. Of course, the two of them had a strange relationship. David even brought Melvin a vase of flowers."

"Wow. I rarely get flowers from anyone. Is he gay?"

"No, David was not gay. You even dated him for a few months."

"Really? I mean, he's kind of cute, but I don't know if I would develop a relationship with him." She noticed David's image suddenly smile at her. "You're right. It's kind of creepy."

David's image stopped smiling and spoke with Melvin's voice. "I'm directly over Humpback Harbor. Where would you like me to land?"

"Set us down behind the house with the blue metal roof. That's my home."

"All right."

The log exterior siding of Jadin's home suddenly came into view as the ship set down on a large area of tall grass. Alex followed her down the stairs and out of the ship, and then they strolled over to the front porch. Blackberry tendrils had grown up through the gaps in the steps, blocking their way into the house. Alex carefully grabbed one vine and was about to move it out of the way when he felt Jadin's hand on his arm and let go to turn and look at her. "What's wrong?"

"Don't bother. I'm sure no one has lived here for the past three years. Let's do a low fly-by over the marina to see what's left of it."

When Jadin turned and headed back to the ship, Alex hurried to catch up with her. "Are you sure you don't want to grab a few pictures while we're here?"

"No. It's going to be just like your home on the inside, and I'd rather remember it as being pristine, not covered in dust and smelling of mold."

Neither of them spoke until they were in the control room, and once in the air, Jadin asked Melvin to fly them over the marina. Below them, seals were lounging on the floating docks and there was a thick layer of white seagull droppings covering every horizontal surface, including the shops lining the waterfront, and she heaved a deep sigh of resignation. "I should never have come back here. Now all I'll remember is how ugly it is."

Alex saw the disheartened look in Jadin's eyes. "Are you ready to head for the colony?"

Jadin tried to shake off her sullen mood. "Sure. Lets' get out of here."

Chapter 27

THE COLONY: DAY 31.

Alex recognized Edwards Air Force Base in the distance as Melvin brought the cloaked ship over the city of Palmdale, California. On one side of the valley, an aqueduct carried a small amount of fresh water down from the mountains. On the opposite side, the sun glistened off thousands of solar panels a few miles north of the small city. It was an arid landscape, and the only greenery was cacti and palm trees. There were no lush lawns around the homes, and leafless trees surrounded the swing sets and play equipment in the small parks. He turned to look at Jadin, who was standing beside him. "I don't see any people or moving vehicles."

Jadin pointed to an area up ahead. "I see the hospital. For a moment, I thought I saw movement outside, but I'm not sure. Melvin, take us five degrees left to that three-story structure on the outskirts of the city."

Alex watched the landscape below rush toward him for a second, and then they were flying over a small shopping mall. The parking lot was mostly empty, except for a few dust covered cars, and then he suddenly pointed down at a pickup truck pulling away from one of the stores. "Over there! I can't tell what's piled up in the back of the truck because of the tarp, but it appears to be as much as the truck can carry. Melvin, follow that truck."

The truck pulled onto a four-lane street for a few blocks then took a cross road to a hospital, whereas they flew over the parking lot, and Alex saw people sitting at tables in the shade of the building. "Melvin, drop us off at the mall where we saw the truck, then hover over the hospital. If you see we're in trouble, come and get us. Otherwise, pick us up when we return to the parking lot."

Alex found it a strange sensation, watching the view moving backward as Melvin went into reverse. A moment later, the ship set down on the asphalt parking lot, and then he heard Melvin through their earbuds.

"I've got you covered, my friends."

Jadin exchanged looks with Alex. "Melvin normally doesn't sound so human. I wonder what's going on with him."

Alex hurried down the stairs and over to the personal lockers to grab his backpack. Before opening his own locker, he opened the door on the compartment next to his. His jaw clenched shut in rage as he stared at Okawna's backpack and gear, then he slammed the door closed and opened his own locker.

Jadin noticed Alex's jaw muscles flex when he opened the wrong locker and wondered what made him so angry. "Are you all right?"

"Not at all, but I'll deal with it. You still don't remember Okawna?"

"No. Is that his locker?"

"Yes, and the other one is David's."

Jadin carried her backpack over to a storage container and loaded a variety of dehydrated food packages into the side pockets. "How long do you plan on staying here?"

Alex closed his locker and carried his backpack over to join her. "Not long. I just want to get a feel for how things are going for the colonists. Just bring enough to offer them a gesture of good will."

A few moments later, Alex closed his pack and slung it over his shoulders. When Jadin was ready, he went over to the airlock and opened the doors. With Jadin beside him, he stepped outside and headed toward the hospital.

As they continued along the city streets, they found most of the stores and offices unlocked, but no signs of forced entry. It was as if the owners had just walked away when they became sick from the radiation. When they stepped around the corner of a building, Alex noticed the remains of a large burn pile in the center of a small park, and what appeared to be the top of a small skull protruded through the ashes. He nudged Jadin, and they moved over for a closer look.

Jadin suddenly stopped and stared at the pile. "Is that a baby's skull?"

He bent down, grabbed a short stick, and then stirred the blackened debris, exposing dozens of bones. "Those are animal skulls. It looks like mostly dogs, and a few cats. I guess the colonists had to deal with packs of them roaming the streets."

He tossed the stick onto the pile and they continued along a well-worn dirt trail used as a shortcut to the hospital. They cut across the parking lot toward the shaded side of the building and casually approached the six people sitting at the tables and chairs. Even from a distance, Alex could tell something was wrong. The first person to notice them slowly stood and shuffled in their direction, then stopped and stared up at him. The woman's face was covered with small red sores, and her dull, bloodshot eyes looked sunken into her pale skin. He looked at the other people, who were slowly approaching them, and saw they all had the same red sores. "What happened?"

The woman extended her hand, but pulled it back when Alex held his palms up as a refusal. "I was wondering if you would actually show up, Alex. I'm Silvia. You must be Jadin."

"That's correct."

"Welcome to hell."

Jadin looked at the people gathering around them, and they all looked as sick as Silvia was, or worse. "Should we be wearing masks?"

"It's too late for that now. The virus is airborne, and you were infected as soon as you were within a hundred feet of us. I'm sorry I didn't see you coming or I would have warned you to stay back."

Alex looked past Silvia at the other people now standing around them and didn't recognize anyone. "How do you know us?"

"Derek told us you would come for him."

Alex's heart leapt into his throat. "Is he infected?"

"No, he's inside taking care of the really bad cases. For some reason, Derek and Mya are immune."

Alex heaved a deep sigh of relief. "Are there any others who are immune?"

"Only those two. Zane and a few of his colleagues tried to isolate the specific antibody in Mya and Derek's immune systems, hoping to create a cure, but without the proper lab facilities, they couldn't create one."

Alex had more questions, but put them aside. "Where is Derek right now?"

"It's hard to say. The survivors are on the first two floors, so he'll be in those areas."

Alex turned to Jadin. "I'm going to find him."

"I know. I'll stay here and find out what happened."

Alex slung his backpack to the ground and jogged to the entry doors, shoving them open as he rushed inside while looking around. He didn't see anyone in the reception area, but heard deep coughing and some soft moans coming from both hallways. He turned right and hurried along the corridor, peering into the rooms as he passed by. All he saw were the ravaged bodies of the sick and dying. When he reached the end, he slammed his palms against the door leading to the stairs, running up two steps at a time until he reached the second floor. He kept hollering Derek's name as he jogged past the rooms, and when he reached the opposite end of the building, he leapt down the stairs and rushed along the opposite walkway. He slid to a stop and spun around when he heard his name, and it took a moment to recognize the woman, because it was the first time her smile was trembling.

Mya ran up to him and wrapped her arms around his neck. "Oh, Alex. I can't believe you're really here."

He felt Mya's tears against the side of his neck and wrapped his arms around her waist. "Do you know where Derek is?"

Mya didn't want to let go of him. "I'm so thrilled to see you. It's been horrible."

"I can only imagine. Where is Derek?"

Mya let go and wiped the tears from her eyes with the back of her hand. "I guess you're immune, too."

Alex wasn't sure if he was or not. "I guess so. Now tell me where I can find my nephew."

"He's out back, burying the dead."

"What's the quickest way to get there?"

Mya indicated the door at the end of the hallway behind her, but grabbed his arm when he started to leave. "He's very courageous. When he realized everyone was getting sick, he felt the least he could do was bury the bodies."

Alex turned to face her. "How is he holding up?"

"He stopped hating you, Alex. I think his deep belief you were still alive gave him hope you could save us."

Alex knew for the moment it seemed an impossible task. "Thanks for giving me a heads up about Derek. I'll see you soon."

Alex jogged down the hallway and shoved the door open, then stepped outside and stopped to get his bearings. He didn't see Derek, but the dead lawn was filled with dozens of large mounds of dirt. He noticed a dirt road going past the end of the building and ran to the corner and recognized the pickup truck from the mall. Wisps of fine white dust drifted around the front of the truck, so he walked over to find out where it was coming from. As he rounded the front of the vehicle, he saw freshly opened bags of lime scattered on the ground, and Derek throwing shovelfuls of the powder into a large pit, not noticing his arrival. "Hey, Derek."

Derek looked up and couldn't believe his eyes, then yanked his mask off and stared at the man smiling at him. "Alex? Is that really you?"

A sense of relief washed over Alex as he stared at his nephew, but wondered if Derek still hated him. "In the flesh."

Derek walked over and stopped a few feet from his uncle. "Things didn't turn out the way I thought they would." He stared at the ground and dragged the toe of his white-powder-covered shoe through the dirt. "I guess you were right."

"From what I've seen, it doesn't matter anymore. Let's leave all that behind us, Okay?"

Derek looked at Alex and blinked a few times to clear the tears welling up in his eyes. "I was thinking I'd never see you again."

"It seems we're going to be spending a lot of time together."

Derek rushed forward and wrapped his arms around Alex's back for a hug. "Where have you been?"

Alex could only imagine what horrors Derek had gone through during the past month, so held him close for a moment, but his heart soared, knowing they were friends again. "It's a long story. How did you know I was still alive?"

Derek let go and stepped back to look at Alex. "Vesta told me when I came out of stasis. It's really strange, Alex. I knew we were returning to our own planet as soon as I woke up, and I already knew the names of the council members before I even met them."

Alex smiled. "I'm glad to hear you and Mya are both immune to the virus."

"Mya said it's because we have a special gene. You must be immune, too."

Alex looked down into the pit, and it was like a scene from a horror movie. Several fully clothed bodies lay piled on top of each other, all covered with white powder, then he turned back to Derek. "To be honest, I just arrived, so I don't know if I'm immune or not. I know my best friend was murdered."

Derek stared at his uncle. "Who was that?"

"Okawna."

"I don't remember him."

"You've met him before. The last time was at Jadin's home in Oregon." Derek gave him a blank stare. "Do you know Jadin Avery?"

"Of course. She worked for NASA. We were wondering what happened to her. Is she immune, too?"

"Like I said, we've just arrived."

"So, where have you been for the past thirty days?"

"It's a long story. Right now, I need some answers. How did all this happen?"

"It's my fault, Alex. I let Catori down because I was jealous. She couldn't help it if men were attracted to her, and she tried to tell me they didn't mean anything, but I wasn't listening. All I felt was rage when I saw her with other men."

"Jealousy is a powerful emotion. Wars have been started because of it."

"Just the same, I should have helped her when she needed it. Especially since I'm the one who convinced her to join the colony." He explained everything that had happened up to Catori being splashed with some kind of disease-infested slime. "Later, we found out it was an experiment they thought might cure the radiation sickness causing everyone to die."

Alex noticed the tears forming in Derek's eyes. "You couldn't have known Catori would find the experiment."

"If I would have helped her clean her room on the first day, none of that would have happened."

"Why didn't they isolate her, so she didn't infect the rest of the colony?"

"Because she didn't tell anyone. Not until three days later when she started getting sick, but by then, it was too late. It doesn't matter anymore. The last members of the colony are dying here in the hospital. In a few more days, we'll be the only living people on the planet."

"Can I give you a hand with the lime?"

"No, I'm done for now."

Alex indicated the hospital. "Let's go inside and find Mya and Jadin. There's something you need to know about what really happened while we were in stasis."

Derek gave him a nod of agreement and headed towards the front entrance, with Alex at his side. "I knew you would come to help us."

Alex remained silent, not wanting to disappoint his nephew as they entered the building. He found Mya and Jadin sitting together on a small sofa in the reception area.

Jadin stood when she saw Alex and his nephew. "It's good to see you again, Derek. Mya was just telling me what happened. I'm so sorry to hear about Catori. The way I understand it, it was her fault for not telling anyone she had been infected."

"Thanks. Have you been with Alex the whole time? Where have you been?"

Jadin looked at Alex, who indicated he would tell them. She nodded that she understood, then sat back down next to Mya.

Alex sat in one of the chairs, as did Derek, and told them about his spaceship going into stasis, and his theory about the sunglasses. "Vesta woke us up this morning, and we arrived here in Palmdale half an hour ago. You can imagine our surprise when we found out about the virus."

Mya suddenly sat up straight. "Is Vesta still here?"

"Uh, no. I should have said she left us a message. She's on her way to another solar system."

Mya leapt off the sofa in frustration. "That's just great! If she would have told us the truth, thousands of people could have gone underground to escape the radiation."

Alex gave Mya a moment to calm down. "There was no place deep enough, so it wouldn't have worked."

Mya crossed her arms and stared out the window. "She should have stuck around to make sure we were going to be okay."

Alex stood and went over to stand beside her, then put his arm around Mya's waist. "Vesta couldn't have seen this coming."

Mya leaned her head against Alex's shoulder. "I suppose so. What makes you think she altered our memories?"

"Because it didn't work on me. Didn't the fact you remember people you've never met before give you an indication something was wrong?"

Derek stared at his uncle. "I didn't remember everyone. Just the council members. And all the laws, of course."

Mya stared at the people sitting outside. "It was the same with me. So, now what do we do? Everyone here will be dead soon, and we can't save our race with only two women and two men who are related."

Derek had a thought. "How come you weren't affected when you were parked on the moon?"

"My ship protected us from the radiation."

Derek stared at Alex. "Wow. I can't believe you have your own spaceship. You're taking us with you, right?"

"Of course. I don't know where we'll go, but you're certainly welcome to come along."

Mya turned from the window to look at Alex. "One thing I don't understand. If the time travelers knew enough to send Vesta and her people here to save us, they must have also known about the virus that killed all the colonists. So why bother sending Vesta here in the first place?"

Alex knew she was right. "I guess we'll never know. I'll have Melvin land here at the hospital. We'll stay and help these people as best we can, but after we bury the last body, we're leaving this town."

Chapter 28

THREE DAYS LATER:
Alex siphoned the last of the gasoline from the truck and carried the red plastic container over to the tractor, and glanced up at Derek as he poured the fuel into the tank. "I'm surprised there is any gasoline left."

Derek draped his arms over the steering wheel while he watched Alex. "During our first meeting, we found out Paul had set up warehouses with everything we needed to get started. Basic supplies, like fresh water, soap, toilet paper, and a bunch of other stuff like that."

"You were already having meetings?"

"Yeah, it was like everyone knew what to do and who was in charge. We found a bunch of electric vehicles in one of the warehouses, and we did a lot of scavenging when we first arrived. After everyone started getting sick, we went back to the building where Catori got infected, and saw the CDC sign hidden behind the overgrowth."

Alex screwed the cap on the gas tank. "You're all set."

"Thanks, I'm just glad it's over. Once I cover the grave, I'll feel like my obligation for making them sick has been fulfilled."

Alex noticed the despondency in Derek's voice. "Do you still think it's your fault?"

"In a way, I guess. I'll just be glad to get out of here."

Alex stepped away as the engine roared to life, and then he leaned back against the pickup while Derek deftly used the tractor's bucket to move mounds of dirt into the hole. A few minutes later, the engine shut down and Derek leapt off the tractor, and saw Derek toss the key over his shoulder as he walked over to join him. "I bet you never thought working on a farm would come in handy someday."

"Sure I did. Robert taught me a lot while I was there. He always said if you learn how to do something now, it will come in handy down the road. I miss him and Kristie."

"Yeah, me too."

"What are we going to do now?"

"I was thinking about settling on the west coast."

They strolled around the building to the spaceship parked a short distance away. "I knew you were into some neat stuff, but you blew my mind when your spaceship suddenly appeared in the field. It's awesome. I can hardly wait to go into space."

"That will come later, but for now, you'll just have to settle for a ride back to my secret base. I need to get some extra power crystals before we head to the coast."

"Don't tell me. Area 51?"

Alex gave Derek a sly grin. "That's the one."

"Man, you're the coolest uncle in the world."

***

Mya was staring out the side of the ship and saw Alex and Derek headed in their direction. She turned to Jadin, who was sitting in front of the control console. "It looks like they've finished."

Jadin remained seated. "I wish there was a way to get rid of these memories Vesta put into my brain. It's so weird remembering people that apparently I've never met before."

"I know what you mean. I can live with that, but I wish I could forget about all this misery and death I've had to watch for the past few weeks."

Jadin rolled up her left pant leg. "I guess I'm not immune."

Mya moved from the window and looked down at the dozens of red sores covering Jadin's leg. "How far has it spread?"

Jadin reached out and grabbed Mya's arm. "Up to my lower abdomen, but please don't tell the men about this. Alex has enough to worry about right now. I need for him to do his job without worrying about me."

Mya saw the pleading look in Jadin's eyes. "Personally, I think he should know you're not immune, but I'll abide by your wishes."

Mya saw Jadin quickly pull down her pant leg as Alex and Derek stepped into the control room. "Yes, me too, Jadin. I'll be glad to get out of here."

Alex indicated for his nephew to stand next to him at the window and put his hand on Derek's shoulder. "You're gonna love this. Melvin, take us home."

"Buckle up, 'cause here we go."

Derek spun around to see who was talking and saw Jadin and Mya grinning at him, so he looked at Alex. "Is there someone else in here with us?"

"In a way. That was Melvin. He's the artificial intelligence, and this is really his ship."

Derek stared down at the landscape rushing towards them at an incredible speed, and then the ship soared over the Sierra Nevada Mountains, dividing California and Nevada. "It doesn't feel like we're moving."

"This ship has all kinds of fancy gadgets, including an inertial dampening system."

"Wow, just like in the movies. Does it have beaming technology, too?"

"No, even though it is possible. According to Vesta, it takes a hell of a lot of computing capability and storage capacity, so they don't even use it."

"How did you manage to get your hands on this ship?"

"I found it in a dormant volcano in Alaska."

"No shit? I guess being a geophysicist has its perks."

Derek watched the barren desert racing past beneath him, but it suddenly stopped moving as the ship landed, and looked over and saw Alex's surprised expression. "What's wrong?"

"I'm not sure. Melvin, how come we stopped?"

"I'm sorry, Alex, but I'm almost out of power."

"Why didn't you say something sooner?"

"It just happened. Something on this ship has suddenly drained a massive amount of power."

"Do you know what it is?"

"Not exactly, but the drain comes from the sleeping area."

Alex ran down the stairs, and when he reached the room, he saw neon blue light flickering in two of the ship's power cables, which now hung out of the wall above the counter. He also saw they were still attached to the power supply Okawna had built for his microwave oven, which was now on the floor. He grabbed a blanket off one of the beds and used it as insulation as he grabbed the microwave and yanked it free from the power supply. He sighed with relief when the blue cables stopped flickering, then ran up to the control room. "Melvin, did that stop the drain?"

"Yes, what was causing it?"

"An electrical short. Can we continue to the base?"

"I could try to go further, but if I use up my reserve power, no one will get in or out of the ship."

"How much farther is it to the base?"

"Fifty-two miles."

"Okay. Allowing for rough terrain, I should be able to walk about four miles an hour, so that's a thirteen hour hike. The sun will set in another hour, so the desert temperature should cool down enough to keep me from overheating. I'll load up a backpack and head out now, and I should make it back in two days with new power crystals. Sooner, if I can find a working vehicle."

Derek decided he wasn't going to let his uncle leave his sight. "I'm going with you. I did a lot of hiking at home, and it was all mountains. I can handle the flat desert."

"All right. Let's get packed."

Alex hurried down the stairs, with Derek right behind him. When he reached the lockers, he opened the door next to his, pulled out a small backpack, and then held it out to Derek. "This was Okawna's. I think he'd like the idea of you using it."

Mya had followed Jadin and the men down into the cargo hold, then watched them load up two backpacks with food and several bottles of water. Normally, she would have loved to join them, but after too little sleep from tending to the sick and listening to their moans and coughing, she felt too exhausted for a trek across the desert. Right now, she just wanted to lie down and sleep. Mya watched them sling the packs over their shoulders, then followed them and Jadin over to the airlock. She wrapped her arms around Alex's neck and held him close for a moment, gave him a soft kiss on the lips, then stepped back. "You're the last two men on Earth, so please be very careful."

"We'll be back before you know it."

Mya had grown very fond of Derek over the past month. She held him close, leaning her cheek against his. "I don't know if I could have done what you did in Palmdale, especially if I had been all alone. Thanks for being there for me."

"You sound as if you think we won't make it back here. We will."

"I hope so, but ever since Vesta arrived, nothing has gone like I thought it would. I try to keep a positive attitude, but now we've run out of power, and there is no guarantee either of you will return. I guess it's another one of Vesta's unknown factors."

Derek let go and looked at his uncle. "We have our own unknown factor, and it's Alex Cave."

Jadin noticed Alex's face flush and then looked at Mya. "Derek is right. You have no idea how many times he has saved everyone on the planet from annihilation."

Alex grinned at Mya. "I couldn't have done any of it without a great team. We'd better get going. I just hope there's a full moon tonight."

Alex continued out of the ship into the hot desert air and checked his compass as he stared out across miles of sagebrush and rolling hills. His best landmark was an interesting peak just above the horizon to his left, and he recognized it as part of the Rocky Mountains. It would help him until the sunset, then he would need to rely on only the compass, and hoped he didn't stray too far off course to the base.

Jadin stepped out from the ship and stood next to Alex. "I'll take care of Mya while you're gone." She reached up and put her arms around his neck, and had the strangest sensation they were supposed to be a couple. When she saw Mya walking out from the ship, she felt a twinge of jealousy. On impulse, she leaned back and gave him a soft kiss on the lips. She felt a moment where he started to respond, and then he gently eased her away.

Alex let go of Jadin's arms. "We'd better get going."

Jadin didn't want him to leave, but knew he had to. "I'll see you in a couple of days."

When Jadin turned and hurried over to Derek, Alex realized he cared for her much more than just friendship, something he had never felt until now. Mya was suddenly standing at his side, wrapping her arm around his, but he already knew he and Mya were never meant to be anything more than friends.

Mya had noticed the kiss Jadin had given Alex, but it didn't bother her. She knew if they were the only humans on the planet, she and Jadin would need to share both men.

Derek indicated the vast desert. "I'm ready. Let's go."

Jadin stared after the men as they walked away, and felt a sense of hope when they simultaneously turned, smiled, and gave a final wave goodbye. If Derek was anything like his uncle, he and Alex would be back soon with new power crystals. When she suddenly scratched the itch on her abdomen, she realized she was going to die, and she could only hope she could hold Alex in her arms one last time before it happened.

Mya noticed the sad look in Jadin's eyes and wondered what she was thinking. "I'm going back inside."

Jadin gave Mya a brief smile, and then they both went into the ship. When Mya had her back to her, Jadin reached down to scratch an itch on her left thigh before following her up to the control room and over to the chairs. They sat in comfortable silence, watching the men hurrying across the desert and the sun setting over the low mountains to the west, until they lost sight of them.

Jadin felt an itch on her right shoulder and stood to look at Mya. "I need to check something. I'll be back in a minute."

Mya could see the concern in Jadin's eyes. "Do you need some help?"

"Uh, no. I just need to use the bathroom."

Mya waited until Jadin had disappeared down the stairs and then pulled the handle to lower the back of the chair. She stared up at the first stars, but they appeared to be moving in random patterns, occasionally flashing and changing direction.

"Melvin, why are some of the stars moving so fast?"

"Those are remnants of satellites."

"Oh, right. I forgot about them."

Moonlight spread across the desert, and Mya noticed Jadin had been in the bathroom for a long time. She stood and walked down the stairs to the living area, but didn't see her, so continued over and knocked on the bathroom door. "Are you all right in there?"

Jadin had stripped down to her underwear to study the red sores now covering her body up to her neck. When she heard Mya, she opened the door and stepped out of the small room. "It's spreading faster than I expected."

Mya felt her heart sink when Jadin showed her the sores. "Oh, Jadin. I'm so sorry. I wish there had been a way for me to warn you to stay away."

Jadin moved to the table and sat down, then indicated for Mya to do the same. "I know you and Alex have a relationship, but if I die before he gets back, tell him I love him."

Mya had suspected as much when she saw them kissing. "I know, and I don't mind. He and I are just friends. I'm surprised you and Alex didn't have a relationship."

Jadin thought about it for a moment. "Actually, I don't think he ever thought of me in that way. I didn't either until we came out of stasis. Maybe it was programmed into my head by Vesta's sunglasses. Like the way she wiped away my memory of Okawna and David. I wonder why only Alex can remember them."

"Alex and I have a strange gene no one else has. Well, I guess Derek has it, too. However, Alex also has another gene Zane had never seen before. It's attached to one of the DNA markers that determine eye color. Maybe that's why the memory wipe didn't work on him."

Jadin thought about the Pandora operation. "I suppose you're right." She slowly stood and crawled into one of the sleeping chambers. "I'm not feeling too good. I think I'll lie down for a while."

Mya felt a slight sense of panic as she realized she didn't know how the ship functioned. "What about the Melvin? Who will be in control until Alex gets back?"

Jadin held up one finger to indicate for Mya to be quiet. "Melvin, I want you to add Mya to your list of authorized personnel."

"Of course, Jadin. I'm sorry you're not feeling well."

Mya looked around the room. "Can he hear everything we say?"

"Yes, but he's very discrete."

"What about cameras?"

"He can only see us if we're in the control room."

"That's good to know. I wouldn't want him watching everything I do. Some things can be embarrassing."

"It's an artificial intelligence, and neither male nor female. He couldn't care less about what we look like naked."

"Then how come you keep calling it him, as if he's alive?"

"I don't know. Perhaps because he has a male personality."

"I hope he doesn't get angry."

Jadin stared up at the ceiling of her chamber. *You have no idea.* "You don't need to worry about it with Melvin. According to Vesta, he's an older model."

"Melvin seems like an odd name for a computer."

"I know. He didn't have a name when Alex found him."

"Why would Alex name him Melvin?"

Jadin turned and gave Mya a troubled expression. "I don't know. It's disturbing, knowing my brain's been reprogrammed to remember only certain things."

"I still can't believe how badly things turned out."

"I've learned when you're with Alex, nothing is over until he gives up. That's what I admire about him. He never gives up."

When Jadin closed her eyes, Mya stood from the table. "Can I get you anything before I go back up to the control room?"

Jadin kept her eyes closed. "I'm fine, thanks."

"All right. I'll check on you later."

Mya walked back up the stairs, but didn't sit down. She slowly strolled along the outer wall, staring out over the moonlit desert. A knot formed in her stomach as she realized when Jadin died, she would be the last woman on Earth.

Chapter 29

GROOM LAKE:

The sun was high above the Rocky Mountains when Alex and Derek reached the top of a barren hill and stopped to drink some water. Below them was the infamous Area 51, with its two runways and a variety of structures on the sprawling base, and Alex took several swallows before checking the time on his wristwatch. "It's just past noon. Damn! It took us two hours longer than I thought it would."

Derek screwed the cap on his empty bottle and slid it into his backpack. "At least we made it. I thought everything would be hidden underground."

"Some facilities are, but most of the research being conducted here dealt with aeronautics and the aircraft were kept in those hangars."

"Have you ever traveled to another world in your spaceship?"

"No, not yet, and I don't want to. I have enough to deal with right here on our own world."

"How come we didn't need to climb barbed wire fences to get in?"

"If the base was still operational, we would have been stopped long before we got close. We need to get moving."

They hurried down the side of the hill through tangled brush to the flat area of desert and then headed across the runways. Alex led Derek around the outside of the security checkpoint to the back of the building, hoping to find some kind of transportation. He found two golf carts, slung his backpack to the ground, and climbed into the first one and turned the key. None of the instrument lights came on and knew the battery was dead, and looked at Derek.

Derek reached inside the other cart and turned the key. "Nope. This one is dead, too."

Alex climbed out and checked the power cord for the charger, then saw the thick layer of dust covering the solar panels. He looked around for some kind of cloth, but didn't find one. When Derek raised his arm to use his hand to wipe them clean, he stopped him.

Derek lowered his arm. "What's wrong?"

"Let's check inside the building before you get dirty. You may not be able to wash your hands for a while."

Alex tried the handle on the back door and it opened, but the putrid odor escaping from inside reminded him of the burial pit at the hospital in Palmdale. He held his breath and stepped inside, but immediately stepped back out and closed the door, then stepped away and took several deep breaths through his nose. "We should be able to find something in one of the other buildings."

Derek wrinkled his nose in disgust. "Where was that stink coming from?"

"It appears to be a makeshift church for people waiting to die."

Derek saw a trash dumpster near the corner of the building and went over to look inside. He reached in and brought out an old newspaper, slid a few pages out from inside, then handed the rest to Alex while he wiped away the dust on the solar panels.

Alex noticed the bold letters on the front page. "Hey, listen to this. It says this will be the last newspaper published by the Las Vegas Herald. It's dated thirty-three months ago. That's three months after the radiation hit the planet. According to this article, five point six billion people across the planet died in the first month, and they buried the bodies in mass graves."

"I wonder if Robert and Kristie had to watch everyone dying. Did you see their graves when you stopped at the ranch?"

"No, but I wasn't looking for graves. I just wanted to find you."

Once satisfied with his work, Derek tossed the newspaper to the ground and checked the inside of the golf cart. "This one is charging."

Alex checked the dashboard on the other cart and the charge light was on. "Good job. My office is not too far from here. That's where we'll find the spare crystals."

Alex slung his backpack over his shoulders and they hurried up the road. Derek tried looking into the hangars along one side of the street, but the windows were covered with a reflective film, and all he could see was his distorted image on the dust-covered panes. "You have an office?"

"Not really. It's where all the normal people work. I have an apartment here on base."

"Did you spend most of your time flying in your spaceship?"

"No, we only use it in emergency situations. We didn't want the rest of the world to know we had one."

"So, what else did you do for your job?"

"I helped with other projects all over the base. Most of them dealt with experimental aircraft, so it was a great job."

He stopped at the main building and opened the door, and then they stepped inside and saw the light streaming in through the windows was dulled by a thick layer of dust coating the glass. They continued along the hallway to Holly's office and stepped inside to look around.

Alex saw two plastic bags stuffed with shredded paper, and the lockable file cabinets were open and empty. Evidently, she had made sure no one else had access to her top-secret documents. Another thought occurred to him, and a knot formed in his stomach. If everyone else on the base became that paranoid, they might have secured the vault so no one else could get inside. "Damn! Let's go see if we can get into the vault where we store the power crystals."

Alex hurried down the hallway to the large freight elevator and noticed the cutting torch and the doors were open. When he looked inside, the steel cables had been cut. He brought out his flashlight and aimed it down the shaft, and saw the roofless cab at the bottom, one hundred feet below. He leaned inside and his flashlight illuminated a black steel ladder mounted to the wall on his left.

He leaned back and looked at Derek. "We'll have to climb down, but that's not our biggest problem. That will be getting into the vault to get the crystals."

"Don't you know the combination?"

"I do, but they might have changed it when everyone started dying. I'd hate to have to make two trips, so let's bring the cutting torch down with us, just in case they did."

They had attached a large flashlight to the large steel tanks of oxygen and acetylene gas, so they could watch it descend to the platform at the bottom. Now the bottles hung precariously on the end of a long nylon rope as Alex and Derek lowered them down the elevator shaft.

Alex readjusted his grip on the rope to let a knot go by, and then it became stuck on the edge of the concrete floor. He kicked it free with his foot and let the rope continue sliding through his gloved hands. A few moments later, a dull thud sound echoed up the shaft, and the rope became slack.

Derek grabbed the rest of the rope and leaned around the corner to the ladder. He was going to tie it to one of the rungs, but could not quite reach it, so he changed hands, swung his leg around, and stepped onto the ladder. When he grabbed the rung with his free hand, he felt a greasy substance, then his feet suddenly slid off the rung and he screamed as he fell through the air. "ALEX!"

Alex was slinging the coiled hose with the regulator and cutting torch over his shoulder when he heard Derek's scream and spun around, but Derek was gone. He tossed the hose to the floor and stared down into the shaft, then saw Derek's crumpled body illuminated by the flashlight at the bottom. "DEREK!"

When Derek didn't move, Alex swung his leg and arm around the corner to the ladder. When he tried to put his weight on the rung, his shoe slid off and he nearly toppled over the edge. He managed to get back onto the concrete floor and then stared at the black grease coating his glove. "Damn!"

He slid his hand out and grabbed the flashlight from his pocket, then aimed it at the ladder, and saw the black grease was nearly invisible on the black rungs, but it glistened in the light. He aimed the flashlight further down the ladder and spotted randomly scattered blotches of grease as far as he could see, and realized when they had cut the cable, it must have whipped around the inside of the shaft, spattering globules of grease as it fell.

He knew there was still a chance Derek was alive, so he slid the glove back on, and then carefully stepped back onto the ladder, slowly making his way down. It seemed to take forever to reach the bottom, then he tossed the gloves off and felt Derek's neck for a pulse. When he couldn't find one, tears clouded his vision as his body jerked with his deep, silent sobs, and then he sucked in a deep gasp of air and roared up the shaft. "NOOOO!"

After several moments, he reined in his emotions and stared at Derek's body without really seeing it, lost in thought about all the good times they had spent together when he was young. He felt drained of energy, both physically and emotionally, so he turned off the light and leaned back against the wall.

Chapter 30

MELVIN:

Mya slowly opened her eyes and realized she had fallen asleep in one of the control room chairs again. She knew Alex and Derek should have already begun their trek back to the ship, and with a little luck, would arrive before sunset. She brought the backrest up and stood, then stretched her arms and looked around. When she did not see Jadin, she hurried down the stairs and found her still in the chamber and knelt beside the bed. All day long she had kept returning to check on her, always wiping away the blood seeping from the corners of her mouth, but now the red sores covered Jadin's ash-colored face, and her closed eyes appeared to be sunken into her skull. She placed her fingers on Jadin's neck to be sure, and then gently placed her palm over Jadin's heart. "Be at peace, my friend."

She thought she had left all that misery and death behind her, but now she was forced to see it again. She gently spread the blanket over Jadin's face, then stood and saw the three empty sleep chambers and thought about Alex's friend, Okawna. She had no memory of him, and decided perhaps if she checked out some of his personal possessions, she might remember him.

She walked down into the cargo hold and over to the lockers, but found no nametags, so started with the first one. She opened the door and recognized the aroma wafting from inside, and knew it belonged to Alex. She opened the second door and saw some clothes and a sports jersey hanging from a rod, and a stack of microwavable popcorn on the top shelf, but couldn't form an image of the person in her mind. She opened the third locker and could tell it was Jadin's by the folded female clothing on the shelf. Three sets of jeans and four blouses hung on a rack above a spare pair of shoes.

She opened the fourth door and one of the shirts had the name David embroidered above the pocket and according to Alex, she had never met him before. She spread the hanging clothes apart and saw a square cardboard box, and out of curiosity, she grabbed it and opened the lid, and inside were four flat crystals, each three inches in diameter and three quarters of an inch thick. She remembered Alex talking about needing crystals to power the ship and carried the box up the stairs to the control room. She looked around, but had no idea where the cameras were located, so she stood in front of the control console. "Melvin?"

The holographic monitor came on, and David's image appeared. "I'm here, Mya."

She opened the lid and held the box out toward the image. "Can you see inside this box?"

"No, I cannot."

Mya grabbed one of the crystals from inside and held it out toward the screen. "Are these the crystals Alex went to find?"

"Yes. Go to the front of the control panel and I'll tell you how to replace them."

Mya followed Melvin's instructions, and after placing the fourth crystal in an empty slot, she looked over at the monitor. "How's that?"

"Excellent. Buckle up, 'cause here we go."

***

AREA 51:

Alex opened his eyes, but it was as if they were still closed. It took a moment to realize where he was, and then he grabbed the flashlight and turned it on. Derek's body was the first thing he saw, and a lump formed in his throat as he realized it wasn't part of his dream. He wasn't sure how long he had been asleep, but remembered Jadin and Mya still needed his help, and he swore he would not let them down. He stood and pried the elevator doors open, then grabbed the flashlight and stepped into the large hallway. He hurried down to a vault door built into the concrete wall and carefully entered the combination, and when he pulled on the handle, the thick steel door swung open.

He stepped into the vault and went over to a large metal locker, and when he opened the doors, saw dozens of sealed cardboard boxes. He pulled one off the shelf and ripped the top flaps open, then grabbed the four crystals and shoved them into his pockets. He hurried out of the vault, not bothering to close the door, as he ran down the hallway to the elevator.

When his flashlight illuminated Derek's body next to the gas bottles, he realized they had wasted time by getting the cutting torch, and if Derek hadn't been holding onto the rope with one hand, he might have been able to hang on to the ladder. He shoved the thought out of his mind. There were two people depending on him, so he needed to focus on his mission. He knew when he returned with Jadin and Mya, they could help him haul Derek's body up the shaft and give him a proper burial. After that, he would fly to the Pacific Coast to live out the rest of his life.

He untied the end of the rope from the gas cylinders and tied it around Derek's chest. When it was securely under Derek's armpits, he grabbed the other end and tied it around his waist, then put on the greasy gloves and carefully ascended up the shaft. When he reached the top, his gloves and shoes were slathered with grease, and he was barely managing to hang on. He hooked his right forearm over the rung, pulled the glove from his left hand, and untied the rope from his waist and tied it off to the ladder, then grabbed the edge of the opening and dragged himself back onto solid footing.

Moonlight was trying to make its way through the filthy windows, but his eyes quickly adjusted. He tossed the last glove to the side, then knelt down and used Derek's backpack to wipe away most of the grease from his shoes, then transferred the unused water bottles from Derek's pack into his own and slung it over his shoulders. He looked down the elevator shaft one last time, surprised the flashlight was illuminating Derek's body at the bottom. "I'll be back to get you."

He turned and ran to the exit, burst through the doors, then jogged back to the golf carts. He looked at the dashboard of the first one and saw the charging indicator light was now green, and tossed his pack into the back and climbed in behind the steering wheel. When he stepped on the accelerator pedal, the cart lurched forward and he drove around to the front of the building.

He was thinking the wheels on the cart were wide enough to drive across the sand and dirt without being stuck, and would at least make it partway back to the ship before he would need to get out and walk. He was just about to drive across the first runway when a massive reflection of the moon suddenly appeared above the nearest hill. He couldn't believe his eyes and stopped the cart, then leapt out and waved his arms at his ship. A moment later, it dropped onto the runway in front of him. The door to the airlock opened, and Mya stepped outside, so he ran up and hugged her. "How did you convince Melvin to use the rest of his reserve power to bring you here?"

"I didn't. I found four crystals in David's locker."

Alex could tell she was holding something back. "Where's Jadin?"

Mya's vision was suddenly blurry and tears ran down her cheeks. "She's dead."

Alex stared at her in numbed surprise. "What happened?"

"She wasn't immune to the virus. While you and Derek were burying the bodies, she showed me the sores on her legs, but she didn't want me to tell you about it. She said you had enough to worry about without needing to worry about her, too. I'm so sorry, Alex."

Alex stared at the ground and slowly shuffled away from the ship, then dropped to his knees and stared out across the moonlit desert. "Everyone I love is dead, and it's my fault."

It took Mya a moment to realize Derek wasn't with Alex and had a sinking feeling in her heart as she slowly moved over and knelt down beside Alex. She reached over and gently grabbed his hand, but didn't say anything as she, too, stared out across the desert.

Alex did not turn to look at Mya for fear he might lose control of his emotions. "Derek is dead."

"What happened?"

"When we were going down an elevator shaft to get spare crystals, I didn't realize the ladder bolted to the wall was covered with grease. If I had just looked, I could have prevented Derek from falling. But now he's gone, and it's my fault."

"No, Alex. It's fate, that's all. I think there was never any chance for our race to survive. Only a brave attempt."

Alex thought about it for a moment. "I believe we make our own fate by what we do or don't do. Right now, I don't feel like doing anything."

Mya let go of his hand and wrapped one arm around his waist, then leaned against his shoulder. "I'll stay with you as long as you need me."

"When the sun comes up, will you help me bury them?"

"Of course. Until then, maybe we should go inside and get some rest. Have you eaten anything since you left us?"

"No, and I appreciate your concern, but I can't eat anything right now."

They sat in silence for several minutes, and then Mya reached over and grabbed Alex's hand. "I hope you realize we're the last two people on Earth. We can start over, like Adam and Eve."

"You know that won't work. Besides, Vesta was right. Our race of humans was too immature. The news announcement about only a select group of people would be chosen to leave this planet proved her point. We'll probably do horrific things to each other for our own survival."

Mya thought about it for a moment. "Actually, I don't think we did that badly. Out of eight-billion people on the planet, only a small percentage became violent."

"Well, it's a moot point now."

Mya sat thinking about what she would like to do with the rest of her life. She turned her head to look at Alex's profile against the stars, grateful she had a decent man to live with, and leaned her cheek against his shoulder. "Of all the men in the world, I'm glad I ended up with you."

Alex felt the comforting warmth of Mya's body against his as he rested his cheek against the top of her head. He stared at the row of hangars and imagined seeing his team standing in front of the ship. In his mind, Okawna was staring back at him with a mischievous grin.

Mya heard Alex's soft chuckle. "Would you care to share?"

"I was just thinking about Okawna."

"I wish I could remember him. Was he some kind of athlete?"

"He kept himself in good shape, but he wasn't fanatical about it. He was there for me when I needed him and saved my life in more ways than one."

Mya was glad Alex was over his initial mourning. "Listen, we can't do anything until the sun rises. Since you and I are the last people on Earth, it would be nice to sleep beside you tonight, but there isn't enough room in one of those beds for two people."

Alex leaned back away from Mya to look into her eyes. "I think I can take care of the problem."

When he stood and reached down to take her hand, Mya let Alex pull her onto her feet. "What have you got in mind?"

"I'll move the mattresses up to the control room and we can sleep on the floor."

Alex held her hand as they went back inside the ship, then let go as they climbed the narrow steps to the living area. He stepped inside and knelt down beside Jadin's body, then eased the blanket off, but was shocked by the clusters of red sores covering her face.

"Rest easy, my friend." He eased the blanket back over her face, then stood and turned to Mya standing in the doorway. "Thanks for taking care of her."

"I liked Jadin, too."

Mya waited while Alex grabbed two mattresses and left the room, then grabbed some blankets and pillows and followed him up to the control room. She watched him place the twin pads on the floor and step aside while she made up the bed.

Alex dropped onto one of the chairs and removed his shoes and sox. "Melvin, how's your power holding up?"

"I'm good for now, Alex. Thanks for asking."

"That's good to hear. I have some new ones for you when you're ready."

Alex stared at Mya as she bent over spreading out the blanket and realized she was right about them being the last people on Earth. When she slipped out of her clothes down to her underwear and crawled inside the makeshift bed, he took off his shirt and pants, and then crawled in beside her. "Melvin, turn off the lights."

Mya was enjoying the view through the ceiling, but her eyelids seemed to be made of lead. She rolled over and draped her arm across Alex's chest, and when he responded by moving his arm up out of the way, she snuggled against him, consuming his aroma.

"Mya, I feel the same way you do about ending up with the right person to spend the rest of your life with. I'm glad it is you."

Mya smiled to herself and let the dream state take her away from reality. Alex was staring at the star formations when his eyelids slowly closed.

Chapter 31

AREA 51:

A vision of his team sitting around the control room was unspooling in Alex's dream, and Okawna suddenly gave him that mischievous grin. He had received that same grin the first time he had showed him the spaceship, when it was inside a dormant volcano during the Cold Energy operation, but now Okawna was shaking his head no. He was suddenly yanked from his dream and opened his eyes, and saw the stars blinking out as the sun crept toward the eastern horizon, and knew what he needed to do. He felt Mya stirring beside him. "Are you awake?"

Mya rolled onto her back and opened her eyes. "I am now."

"I have an idea. There's a chance we can change this outcome."

Mya was disappointed, thinking he had a more pleasurable idea in mind. "That's not what I was expecting, but what's your plan?"

Alex knew what she was thinking, but now he had a mission. "There's plenty of time for that later. Vesta isn't the only person with time travel friends. I know one named Paladin, but the problem will be contacting him." Alex swung off the thin pad, stood up, and then began getting dressed. "We need to find a tow truck."

Mya swung around and dragged her pants on. "All right. Can we eat something first?"

"Sure. We'll grab a few power bars to take with us."

Alex grabbed his shoes and sat on one of the chairs to put them on. "Melvin, I need to gather the four weather devices into one place. I'll meet you outside our hangar when I'm done."

"Is that wise, Alex? The reason they are stored separately is they interact with each other when they're turned on, and they nearly started a new ice age."

"I don't plan on turning them on. During the Red Energy mission, Paladin told me he would return to collect the devices when we had all four of them together in one place. I'll bring them all to the hangar and wait for him to arrive."

Mya wasn't sure about any of this. "Weather devices? What kind of job did you do for the government?"

"It's a long story. Let's go and I'll tell you on the way."

When Alex moved past her, Mya grabbed his arm. "Are you sure he'll come? How long will we have to wait?"

Alex realized what she was getting at. "I don't know. At least we'll have power, food, and water. We'll just have to wait and see what happens."

Mya slid her hand along his arm and grabbed his hand. "All your friends had a lot of faith in you, and that's good enough for me. Just tell me what to do."

Alex pulled her close, wrapping his arms around her waist. "Have you ever broken into a vault?"

***

It was a short ride back to the main paved road, running between a row of hangars and research buildings. They continued past the barracks and mess hall until Alex stopped the golf cart in front of the motor pool and climbed out. "We should be able to find everything we need in here, and we'll use the tow truck to get the devices." Mya followed him into the building. "Let's just hope it has fuel."

Alex saw the tow truck through the dusty windows on the other side of the roll-up doors. "I'll check the office for the key so I won't have to hot wire it. See if you can find a set of jumper cables."

Mya gave him a puzzled expression. "Jumper cables? What do they look like?"

Alex stared at her in stunned silence. "They're two long pieces of electrical wire." He stopped speaking when she smirked at him, then he smiled. "It's nice to see you have a sense of humor."

"I had you going for a minute, didn't I?"

"Yeah, good one."

He hurried over to the office and checked the walls until he found a key rack, then studied the nameplates above each hook. He grabbed the set for the tow truck and went back into the truck bay, where Mya was waiting with the cables hanging from one hand and took them. "Drive the golf cart around to the back and I'll meet you there."

Alex went out through the back door and then dropped the cables near the front tire of the tow truck before climbing in and inserting the key. When he turned it to start the engine, it was just as he had expected. The battery was dead. He climbed out and opened the hood, and discovered mice had built a large nest around the battery and tossed several handfuls of the mixed soft fibers and shredded cardboard away from the truck, then waited as Mya arrived.

Mya drove around the corner of the building and over to Alex, then backed up to the front of the truck. While Alex was attaching one end of the cable clamps to the truck battery, she knelt down, opened the rear cover of the cart. She attached the other ends onto the battery clamps, then stood and turned to Alex. "I'm all set."

"Let's find out if it will start."

Mya opened the driver's side door and climbed up into the cab, leaving it open so she could talk to Alex. When she turned the key, the starter motor cranked the engine over several times without starting and looked at the fuel gauge. "It shows it has half a tank of gas. I'll try it again."

Alex waited while the engine turned over and realized what was wrong. "Hold on a second."

He brought a pocketknife out from his pocket and sliced through the thick rubber tube from the air filter, then tossed it to the side and leaned out to see Mya. "Okay. Try it again."

When Mya turned the key, the engine roared to life, and she left it idling as she climbed out. "What was the problem?"

"The mice were using the air intake tube for a home."

Alex removed the jumper cables from the batteries, then tossed them to the ground and closed the hood. He went around to the back of the truck and climbed up into the truck bed, then moved forward to the cutting torch and gas bottles bolted to a frame behind the cab. He opened the valves to check the pressures, and the bottles were nearly full, then he leapt over the side to the ground and climbed into the cab, checking the gauges on the dashboard one last time, while Mya climbed in beside him.

Alex drove away from the garage, and a few moments later, he turned onto a long graveled road toward the base of a small mountain behind the complex. When he came to a dead end, he turned the truck around and backed up to a fifteen-foot square concrete opening with two heavy steel doors, then climbed out and went around to the back of the truck and stood next to Mya. "This is where they keep the weather devices."

"Are you talking about alien technology?"

"That's right."

Alex grabbed the cutting torch and uncoiled the hoses, then searched the side compartments until he found a set of dark-colored goggles and a pair of gloves. A moment later, the hiss of gas through the nozzle was replaced by the roar of a flame from the tip of the torch. Alex held it against the first of four industrial grade hinges, melting them one by one, and when he was finished with the last hinge, he slid his goggles up onto his forehead. Satisfied with his handiwork, he shut off the torch and set it in the back of the truck.

He grabbed a long pry bar and moved back to the door, and saw Mya studying the melted metal. "You should move over to the side. I'm going to pry this door out of the way, and that should also knock the other door out of the frame and allow us to drive inside."

Alex inserted the pry bar between the door and the frame and heaved against the rod. The squeal of tortured metal pierced the air as the doors toppled back from the opening and slammed onto the ground, sending a billowing cloud of dust into the air. He stared into the large tunnel, but the light quickly faded into darkness, and he indicated for Mya to get into the truck. He climbed in and turned on the rear facing halogen lamps, then put the transmission into reverse and looked over the backrest as he slowly backed over the doors.

As he drove the truck backwards through the tunnel, he saw the individual steel doors on both sides and glanced over at Mya, who was also looking back over her shoulder. "The first device is in vault seventy-six on your side. The doors are spaced twenty-feet apart, so let me know when we're getting close to number seventy-four."

The doors were slightly recessed into the concrete wall, and Mya only had a second to read the white numbers as they swept past the window. "We're at seventy-two, so start slowing down."

When he was alongside the next door, Alex stopped and climbed out. "Could you grab that flashlight?"

Mya grabbed the plastic handle of the lantern and turned it on to make sure it still worked. A bright light burst from the lens, so she climbed out and went around to the rear of the truck to join Alex. He used the torch to cut away the lock, and when he opened the door, Mya aimed the light into the chamber at a twenty-foot long by twelve-inch diameter cylinder on a four-wheeled trailer.

Mya followed Alex into the room and recognized the pewter coloring of the device. "This looks like the same material as Vesta's landing craft."

"It is. That's what had me so concerned about when it appeared above your dig site. I need you to help me get this one out of this room. You pull on the tow bar and steer while I push. We'll leave it against the far wall and pick it up on the way back."

Thankfully, the trailer had large pneumatic tires, allowing Mya to easily guide it across the tunnel and parallel to the opposite wall. They climbed back into the truck, and then Alex backed further down the tunnel, where they repeated the process three more times. When the fourth device was out of the chamber, Alex hooked the tow bar to the back of the truck and dragged it toward the entrance. He stopped when the back of the trailer was even with the tow bar on the next one and stopped to attach it to the end of the first trailer. He continued the process until all four trailers were attached one behind the other, creating an eighty foot long train behind the tow truck.

Having to creep along at five miles an hour to keep the trailers from veering from side to side, the return trip took much longer. He towed them out onto the tarmac in front of Hangar 5, where the ship was parked outside the massive doors. He shut off the engine and climbed out, and then he and Mya went over to the ship. Alex ran up the stairs to the living area and grabbed bottles of water from the refrigerator, and then carried them back outside.

Mya accepted the water and sat in a plastic chair, then stared out through the open hangar doors at the line of pewter-colored devices. "What's next?"

"Now we wait for Paladin to show up."

"That's it? We just hang around until he makes an appearance?"

Alex knew telling Mya Paladin might not come, or might show up but refuse to help him, would serve no useful purpose, so decided to just wait and see what happened. His only other option was to leave the base and move to some small harbor town along the Pacific Coast, and spend the rest of his life with the only woman on earth. "That's it. Paladin said when the devices are together, he'd come back to get them."

Chapter 32

SEVENTEEN DAYS LATER:

AREA 51:

Alex climbed the tall ladder welded to one of four legs supporting the massive water tank while listening to the soft roar of the large portable generator he had hooked up to the well pump. When he reached the top, he crawled onto the curved surface and opened the lid, then aimed the beam of light from his flashlight down inside. When he saw the current of water swirling around in the bottom of the nearly empty tank, he closed the lid and climbed back down.

He sat behind the steering wheel of the golf cart and grabbed a towel off the seat to wipe the sweat off his face, beard, and hair. He had parked in the shade, so he stretched out on the seat while he thought about his situation. Until he had needed it to refill the water tank, he used the propane generator to power the electrical panel for the hangar, which allowed them to heat the canned goods Mya had scrounged from the main cafeteria, but as each day passed without Paladin showing up, Mya was becoming more anxious to leave.

He was also bored out of his mind, just hanging around the base, and Mya had her quirks, but so did he, and knowing they were the last people on the planet made it easier to overlook her little idiosyncrasies. Too bad she wasn't as forgiving about his.

The first three nights, he had slept on a recliner outside the ship to make sure he didn't miss Paladin's arrival. It was only after Mya's less than gentle persuasion he realized Melvin would let him know if anything changed and started sleeping next to her in the ship.

He heard water splattering onto the ground and sat up, and it was flowing out of the top of the tank. He got out and spent a moment under the cool liquid before shutting down the generator and towing it back to the hangar. When he arrived, he found Mya in her usual position, lying naked on a reclined lawn chair outside the ship, so he parked and climbed out. "We have water pressure again."

Mya sat up and stood facing Alex with her hands on her hips. "I've had it. As you finally told me, there's no guarantee he will even show up, and I can't stand looking at nothing but desert and eating canned food every day. I say we leave and find a place on the west coast."

Alex knew his only chance of changing their current situation was with Paladin's help, and he wasn't about to give up. "We just need to give it a couple more days."

When Mya stomped into the hangar, Alex knew better than to follow her inside. He walked into the cargo hold of the ship, continued up to the control room, then sat down on one of the chairs facing out across the desert while waiting for Mya to calm down. His thoughts were interrupted when he heard the crashing of metal, and when he heard another crash, he ran to the opposite side of the ship and saw Mya leveraging a long metal rod under the third cart, tilting it over and dumping the device onto the ground. He had a moment of panic before realizing they couldn't be damaged anyway, and decided to let her get rid of her frustration.

He waited until she was done, then went down the stairs and out from the ship. He had forgotten about the slight downslope of the tarmac for water runoff until he saw all four devices rolling away and piling on top of each other in the drainage ditch. He casually strolled over to Mya and smiled as he wrapped his arms around her waist. "Two days. We'll leave on the third morning." He felt her body suddenly stiffen, then she pushed him away. "I promise."

Mya pointed behind Alex. "A giant ball just appeared near the ship, and a bald man in a silver suit just stepped out."

Alex spun around and smiled, then ran over to the man with no ears. "You finally got my message! I've been waiting for twelve days."

Paladin gave Alex a quizzical stare. "I don't know what you're talking about. I received the signal an instant ago."

Alex glanced over at the pile of devices. "That's when they piled up together."

"I told you they needed to be together to send a signal."

"I thought you meant. Well, never mind. I'm just glad you're here now. I need your help."

Paladin noticed the naked woman running into the hangar. "Is that one your new mate?"

"Yes, her name is Mya."

"Does she know who I am?"

"Yes, we've had plenty of time to share our experiences. In case you didn't know, we're the last two people on earth."

"No, I did not know that. What happened?"

"Are you and your people the only time travelers in this galaxy?" He saw the frustrated expression on Paladin's face. "I take that as a no."

"That's correct. There is another group. A splinter group from our race who disagreed with our strict noninterference policy."

"I would have thought you would have agreed with them. I mean, you helped me out."

"I was the one who started the new group, but they thought I was still too restrictive for what they wanted to do."

"Well, they sent a woman named Vesta to save our race of humans." He told Paladin everything that had happened up to this point. "That's why I need your help. I want to go back in time and stop Vesta's people from collapsing the sun in the first place. That way, none of this will be necessary."

"I know about Vesta. She works with the group to help certain species of humans in their technological advancement."

"That's all very interesting, but you didn't answer my question. What about it? Can you send me back?"

"I won't do that, Alex."

Alex's hands clinched into fists at his sides. "But that means you're condemning our species to extinction. You wouldn't allow it to happen the last time, so why won't you help me now?"

"You misunderstand me, Alex. To do what you ask will affect too many timelines. The ramifications are unfathomable."

Alex realized Paladin was correct and relaxed his hands while he thought about it. "All right. I have another idea. I was thinking I could go back in time and block the radiation with my ship before it reaches this planet."

"Your ship is too small, Alex. You would need a mass the size of Earth's moon to block enough radiation to make a difference."

Alex turned when Mya moved up beside him, now wearing a two-piece swimsuit she had found in the women's barracks. "Mya, this is Paladin."

Mya could tell he was human, but without any hair, and the cartilage around his ear canal was missing. "Hello. Welcome to Earth."

Paladin held his hand out to her. "I believe this is one of your customs. Thank you."

Mya shook Paladin's hand. "I hope you don't mind me asking, but I've been wondering about this a lot since I learned of your existence. If you're a time traveler, are you from the past or the future?"

"It depends on where I am when asked. In this time period, I'd be from the future. On another world in this universe, I might be from the past. It's all relevant."

"Okay, but if you can see the future, how come you didn't know about the plague that killed all the colonists?"

"We can't see what we're not looking for. Even Vesta and her people cannot foresee the unknown factors."

Alex smirked at Paladin. "I'm an unknown factor. You said I need a bigger mass. What about the comet? It's big and its water will block the radiation."

"As you well know, comets are not entirely made of water. Once it gets close to your sun, the dark rocks will absorb the heat and melt the ice. It will start out-gassing as water vapor, but when it refreezes, it will only be ice crystals. Even if you managed to get it into the exact location needed to protect your planet, the crystals will be too dispersed to provide enough protection."

Alex wasn't ready to give up and stepped away to gather his thoughts. He saw the four devices lying in the drainage ditch and got an idea, then grinned as he turned back to Paladin. "I can use the devices. Send me back and my team and I will haul them to the comet, attach them to the surface, and turn them on. We already know how cold they can become. We'll use them to freeze the water vapor into a solid mass before it floats away. It will be like an umbrella to block the radiation."

"Even if I allow you to keep the devices, which I'm not authorized to do without prior approval, you still need the comet to be at a specific location at a specific time to make it work."

"I can move it with my ship. Melvin moved a solid gold asteroid, and the comet should be much lighter."

Paladin stared at him. "Who's Melvin?"

"Do you remember David Conway? Well, he named the artificial intelligence on the ship Melvin. Anyway, back to my original idea. If you tell me the exact coordinates and time for where the comet needs to be, I'll get it there."

"I can give you the numbers, but your odds of success are less than one in a million. There are too many variables."

"I never care about the odds of success. At least let me try to save my race of humans."

Paladin just stared at Alex. "I would break too many time travel laws."

Alex threw his hands in the air in frustration. "Oh, come on, it's not like you haven't done it before. This is the only way to save our species. Vesta told us there aren't that many intelligent humans, so how can you stand by and let ours go extinct?" He was about to continue when Paladin held his palm up to stop him. "What now?"

"You didn't let me finish, Alex. As I said, I would break too many laws, but I'll help you."

Alex watched Paladin turn around and step back into the six-foot silver sphere. When he stepped back out, he was holding another silver suit. Alex had done this before and immediately took off his clothes.

After everything she had been through since she first met Vesta, Mya accepted the time travel issue as if it were an everyday occurrence. She grinned as Alex stripped naked and watched him climb into the strange silver material. She couldn't stop herself and chuckled. "I wish I had a camera. Both of you look like you should be on a movie set, especially with that Christmas ornament and a spaceship in the background."

Alex grinned at her. "I need to be wearing this suit to get inside the time capsule."

Paladin looked over at Mya. "It's a time ship, not a capsule. Even if you took a picture, the changes Alex will make to the timeline means this moment will never happen."

Mya rolled her eyes at Paladin. "I know that. It's just a figure of speech." She turned to Alex as he closed the front of the suit, and the seam vanished. "Will I still meet you in the new future?"

Alex reached out and wrapped his arms around her waist. "I'll make sure of it."

Paladin waited until they parted. "We still need to determine a time and destination for your arrival in the past. A marker of some type where you had a life altering moment."

Mya had an idea. "Vesta's arrival at my dig site changed my life."

Alex grabbed Mya's hand and looked into her eyes. "You're right. It certainly changed my future. That's the perfect moment. I'll tell Vesta about my plan and maybe she can help me."

"Do you know the exact time she arrived?"

"Yes, my watch stopped at 5:27 PM, so send me back to 5:00 PM. That will give me time to get into position to meet Mya."

"Alex, we've been through this before. I can get you close, but it could be thirty minutes on either side."

"Fine, I'll make it work." He turned to Mya. "I guess I'll see you soon."

Paladin indicated the surface of the sphere. "I'll give you the coordinates for where you need to be to block the radiation once we're inside."

Alex gave Mya a smile and stepped into the sphere. Mya watched Paladin step in behind Alex, then it vanished, and so did she.

Chapter 33

THREE YEARS EARLIER. THE DIG SITE:
Alex followed Mya into an eight-foot wide room and looked at the paintings. On one side was a drawing of a square block with two human figures standing in front of it, and he studied the symbols on the wall. "Do you know what these smaller pictures represent?"

"Yes, they tell the story of the vanishing stone magically appearing above this cave. According to stories passed down through generations of Native Americans living near this cave, the stone should appear sometime this year."

"On the plane, you said you found more of these drawings."

"That's right, but only in European countries. This is the first one found here in North America."

***

Zane remained in the pit when Mya and Alex left, then knelt close to study the jawbone and upper palate of the female skeleton. "You must have known about oral hygiene."

He looked up when he heard a drone flying overhead, then climbed out of the pit and ran back to the meadow. The drone suddenly died and crashed, and when the man near the tent pointed up at the side of the mountain, he ran to the entrance of the cave and cupped his hands around his mouth to holler inside. "Mya! There's something going on above you!"

***

Mya turned when she heard Zane's voice and froze in place. The Alex Cave standing before her was wearing a silver jumpsuit and had a beard. She blinked her eyes a few times, but the image remained the same. "Alex?"

"Hello, Mya. It's a long story and I'll explain later, but right now, we need to join Zane."

Mya did not move as Alex rushed out of the room, and then hurried to catch up with him. "This has something to do with the vanishing stone, right?"

"Correct. It just landed above us."

***

Zane jogged up a trail along the side of the rock and abruptly stopped in front of a massive twenty-foot square cube. He slowly reached out and placed his finger against the pewter-colored surface, and it was cool and smooth. He pressed his palm against the side and it felt solid, then he tapped his knuckles against it to confirm it was not hollow. He smiled and spun around when he heard footsteps, but his smile vanished when he saw Alex. "What happened to you?"

"It's a long story, and I don't have time to explain it to you right now."

Mya could not believe her eyes and ignored Alex's strange appearance. She slowly moved over to the block and placed her hand on the surface, then jumped back when the area beneath her fingers vanished and an opening appeared. She took another step back and bumped into Alex when a woman in a black jumpsuit stepped out.

Alex moved Mya out of the way and stepped in front of Vesta, but knowing she had killed Okawna and David, the only way he was keeping his emotions in check was by remembering this is a new timeline, and she had done nothing wrong. At least, not yet. He looked into the opening, but didn't see her companion. "Hello, Vesta. Did you come alone this time?"

Vesta stared at the stranger, wondering how he knew her name. "Who are you?"

He leaned closer to whisper. "I'm Alex Cave. I've come back in time to do the same thing you are. Save my species from extinction. I need to talk to you in private, so take me up to your ship."

Vesta was curious about how Alex knew so much about her and stepped back inside, staring at the stunned expressions of the other two humans as she indicated for Alex to enter.

Mya watched Alex step into the opening, then the entrance closed and the stone vanished, and she turned and stared at Zane. "What just happened?"

Zane closed his mouth. "I have no idea, but at least now we know your vanishing stone legend was true. What about Alex? How did he change like that?"

"I don't understand what happened to him. I was showing him the pictures, and when I turned around, he looked like that."

"Maybe he brought his twin brother with him."

Mya scoffed at the idea. "Yeah, right."

"Do you have a better explanation, Miss Archeologist?"

"Well, I guess not. I just hope it comes back. I didn't even get a picture."

Zane turned and headed down the trail. "Come on. We need to document everything about our discovery while it's still fresh in our memories."

Mya was disheartened she didn't have visual proof of the vanishing stone, but turned to follow Zane, and smiled when she saw a pickup truck racing away from the dig site. At least she had witnesses that it had actually happened, picture or not.

***

Once Alex was inside, Vesta activated the cloak, but there was no way she was going to take him up to her ship. "All right, Alex. I recognize your time travel suit, but I don't remember meeting you. Why don't you start by telling me how you got it?"

"Have you heard of a time traveler named Paladin?" He saw Vesta's vacant expression and knew she was connecting with her team members. "Tell Paul I said hello."

Vesta ended her connection. "I know about Paladin. Continue."

"He's the one who sent me back to this point in time. I know you're going to lie about the comet hitting us, and I understand why, but there's a good chance I can stop your mission from being necessary. I'm going to use the comet as a shield to block the radiation." He told her what he wanted to do. "Can you help me accomplish my mission?"

"I appreciate your optimism, Alex, but there are too many variables."

"I know, but the odds will be increased significantly if you help me."

"Have you even calculated how long it will take you to reach the comet? Or how long it will take you to move it into place to block the radiation? Those are all factors that will determine the outcome."

Alex knew she was right, but that wasn't going to stop him from trying. "Listen, I have a great team, but we don't know all those variables. If you know the answers to those questions, I'd appreciate it if you told me."

"I'm afraid I can't without knowing the capabilities of your ship."

"I know you can interface with its artificial intelligence, so you and Melvin can work out the details for me."

Vesta gave him a questioning stare. "Who is Melvin?"

"That's the name we gave the AI. What about it? Can you at least do that much for me?"

"Perhaps, but the odds will still be against you accomplishing your mission."

"As I said, I have a great team."

Vesta considered it for a moment. "All right, but my mission is to save as many of your species as I can."

"I know you need thirteen days to gather anyone with the GC117 gene who meets your criteria. I also know you won't get as many as you think you will, and your unknown factor will kill everyone in the new colony a short time after they arrive. I know, because I was there after it happened."

"If you know how it happens, tell me so I can make sure it does not."

Alex knew she was right. If he failed to block the radiation, at least the colony would survive. "Of course." He told her about what happened at the CDC building. "I know you alter everyone's memories, so perhaps you can add a warning while you're at it. Just in case my plan doesn't work."

"If I help you, I'll be breaking at least one law."

Alex smirked at her. "Paladin said your time traveler friends are already breaking the law. Why is this any different?" He saw Vesta's eyes looking at nothing again, and he had difficulty accepting the idea a race of humans could have telepathic abilities, and then wondered how long it would take for his race to have such a gift.

Vesta contacted her team and looked over at Alex. "All right. I'll do what I can to help you, but I need a favor in return. I must get started in three days, so I'll need to contact your world leaders today. I'll also need Zane Kinkaid's help."

Alex smiled at her. "I can take care of that, but I'd appreciate it if you would have them hold off making the announcement to the public until I have a chance to move the comet."

"I'll let you know once I estimate the odds of your success. Where do you keep your ship?"

"The same place where I'll introduce you to Holly Blake. She knows all the right people you'll need to work with. We call it Area 51, but geographically, it's at Groom Lake, Nevada." Alex realized they couldn't just land inside a top-secret facility without causing a panic. "Can we leave your ship while it's cloaked?"

"No. Is that a problem?"

"Yeah, a big one. Can you land inside a specific structure?"

"Yes, if the area is large enough and you can give me an exact location."

"Well, that's a little difficult." He looked around at the solid walls. "Does this thing have a window?" The opening where he had entered was suddenly transparent, as was the floor beneath him. "Great. Once we get close, I'll point out which building to land in."

Without warning, the ground beneath his feet was suddenly shrinking away below him, and he placed his hands against the wall to steady himself, even though he didn't feel any movement. A moment later, he was looking down at the Rocky Mountains, and then looked out over the desert and pointed to a familiar sight. "Do you see that city to the southwest? We call it Las Vegas, and the base is just north of there."

Out of habit, Alex put more pressure against the walls when the mountains were suddenly replaced by desert, then the city was rushing toward him. The direction abruptly changed, and they were soaring over the low mountains north of Las Vegas. He let go of the side of the ship and pointed through the opening. "Over there. Do you see that dry lakebed? That's the base."

It seemed only an instant later he was floating above the mountain behind the lake. "You need to land inside that last hangar. Oh, my ship is in the center of the room, but there's still plenty of room for you to land beside it."

When the cube descended over the hangar, Alex braced himself for a collision, and then had the strangest sensation of watching the roof slide along the side of the opening and his ship rising into view. When Vesta's craft landed ten feet away from his ship, he dropped his hands to his sides in relief. "That was incredible. I wish my ship could do that. Can we pass through the opening?"

"Yes, the door is open."

Alex stepped out of the craft and led Vesta around the outside of his ship to the airlock. "As you can see, it's a much older version, but I know the coordinates and the exact time where the comet needs to be to block the radiation."

***

David had his head buried inside the engine room when he heard Alex's voice, but when he turned around, his jaw dropped. "Who the hell are you and where's Alex Cave?"

Alex walked into the cargo hold and straight over to his young friend and then gave him a hug. "You don't know how glad I am to see you again."

David studied Alex's appearance. "That's an interesting suit, but I don't understand the beard. You just left early this morning, so how could you have grown so much hair in a day?"

"I'll tell you later." He turned around to introduce Vesta, but she was deep in thought again. This time, he didn't interrupt. From her closed eyes and slightly contorted expression, Alex thought she was having difficulty concentrating, and then her features relaxed as she opened her eyes and looked at him. "Well? How did it go?"

"Your ship's operating system is an antique compared to mine. I was surprised it has remained operational until I learned it had been buried for millions of years."

"I know. So was I. This is my good friend and a member of my team, David Conway."

"Hello, David. I'm Vesta."

Alex saw David's questioning expression, but right now, he needed to know if his plan could work and turned to Vesta. "Did you find the answers to those questions?"

"Yes, I did."

Alex stared at her, waiting for her to continue, and from her silence, he knew the news wasn't good. "Will I be able to reach the comet in time to move it into the correct position?"

"You will get there in time, but there is only a marginal chance you could get it to the right place in time to block all the radiation. If it's even slightly out of alignment, it won't be enough to stop some of it from hitting your planet, and the damage will still be horrific."

Alex straightened his shoulders. "Then there's still a chance I can make it work. How much time do I have?"

"It will take your ship eight hours to reach the comet, and another six hours to get it into place. I'll give you three days to make it work before I implement my plan."

David stared at Alex. "What's going on?"

"We need to move a comet." He turned to Vesta. "Why such a short time frame? The radiation won't hit the planet for another thirteen days."

"It's doubtful your ship's artificial gravity system can handle the load without burning up, so there is little chance of success. If you leave now, you will only need to make a small change in the comet's trajectory, but the longer it takes you to leave, the less chance it will work."

David stared up at Alex. "How do you know about all this stuff?"

"I'll explain everything once the rest of the team is here, including Holly. For now, I'll just say I've come back from the future. Again."

Now Vesta's curiosity was peaked. "Are you saying Paladin helped you once before?"

"Yes."

"That is not the same traveler I heard about. He would never break the law."

"I don't know why he helped me, and I don't care." He reached out to David. "Let me borrow your phone. I need to call Holly and have her send a plane to pick up Jadin and Okawna right away."

"I'm right here, Alex."

Alex spun around to the airlock and saw Holly standing just outside his ship. "Great. Listen, I need to send the jet." He stopped when Holly held her palm out towards him. "Director?"

"I heard that part. Would you mind telling me why this cube is in the hangar?"

Alex indicated for Holly to come inside. "This is Vesta, and it's her transport ship."

"Hello, Holly. This was Alex's idea, so I'll let him explain it to you."

Holly turned to Alex. "Did you say transport ship?'

Alex told Holly about the approaching comet, the radiation, Vesta's mission, and his plan. "I've only returned to this timeline a few minutes ago. As you can tell, time is of the essence, no pun intended."

Holly looked up at Vesta. "Do you think he can pull it off?"

Vesta shook her head no. "There are too many variables. The odds are against him succeeding."

Holly turned back to Alex and saw the pleading expression in his eyes. "How soon will you need to leave?"

"The sooner we get out of here, the better the odds of success."

Holly turned to David and watched him straighten his shoulders as a sign he was willing to go with Alex, and turned back and gave Alex a nod of approval. "All right. Since the cloak is working, I don't see any reason to send the jet to pick up Jadin and Okawna. I can have them meet you at secluded areas near their locations."

Alex felt a great sense of relief. "Before we leave, we need to load the weather control devices into the cargo hold, because we need to fasten them to the comet."

Holly's eyes went wide. "You left out that part of your plan. That means you need to leave the ship and work on a moving object. That lessens your odds of success even more."

Alex saw the skepticism in Holly's eyes. "That's the easy part. We've done it before. We can do this, Holly."

Holly remembered what she had read about Alex's other missions, and the odds were always against him, but somehow, he was successful. "I read it was a bad idea to have all the devices in one place."

"You're right, but this time they're part of *our* plan, not some industrialist. I know what I'm doing this time."

"All right. You have a go."

"Thanks, Holly. I'll let you and Vesta to work out her details while I collect the devices."

Holly stepped back and gave Alex a head to foot appraisal. "You might want to change clothes first, but the beard looks good on you."

Alex looked down at the silver suit covering his body. "Right. David? Make sure we have at least one set of spare power crystals on the ship. In fact, from now on, we should keep two extra sets on board at all times."

David shrugged his shoulders. "I've told the research and development department that for a long time, but they refuse to let me have more than what I need for each mission."

Alex turned to Holly. "Can you take care of the problem?"

"I'm new here, so I didn't realize there *was* a problem. I'll take care of it."

"Great. I'll go to my apartment to change clothes and shave, then I'll get some help to get the devices here. I'll check in with you when we're ready to leave."

Holly stared after Alex as he ran out of the cargo hold, then turned to Vesta. "What's your contingency plan, and what do you need from me?"

"I don't want to explain it more than once, so I'll need to contact all of your world leaders at one time. I won't start the evacuation unless I have their full cooperation."

"That could take some time to set up."

"You have three days. That's the time Alex and his team has to attempt their plan, which will undoubtedly fail."

"I can set up a video conference call here at my base. How do I get in contact with you?"

"You can't. I'll return to this structure in three days."

"All right. I'll be waiting for you."

When Vesta and Holly abruptly walked out of the cargo hold, David followed them over to Vesta's transport ship. "This is amazing. Can I go inside?"

Vesta stepped into the opening and turned to face Holly and David. "I'm sorry, but no. I must leave now."

David stared at Vesta with an imploring expression, but suddenly the entrance became solid and the ship vanished, so he turned to look at Holly. "Wow. When I woke up this morning, I never expected something like this would happen. I'd better go get some spare crystals."

Holly indicated the exit from the hangar and headed in that direction. "I'll go with you to make sure they don't give you any hassles before I contact a friend in Colorado. I need to do some damage control with Zane, Mya, and the local tribe members."

***

Holly stared at Donner's image on her desk monitor as she explained her meeting with Vesta. When she told him what was going to happen and what Alex and his team was going to do with the comet, she saw his jaw drop open. "Martin, I also know it may not work."

Donner thought about it for a moment. "How long until we know if Alex is successful?"

"If all goes as planned, the comet will start moving in three days. We know it's a long shot, but it's our only chance of blocking the radiation."

"All right. Do you think Vesta is telling the truth?"

"Yes, I think she wants to help us. According to her, they've helped other civilizations avoid extinction."

"Good grief, several? How many civilizations are out there?"

"She didn't say."

"Keep me posted. I'll let the President know what's going on."

When Donner's image vanished from the screen, Holly leaned back in her chair and stared out the window, hoping Alex's reputation was true. Her only other concern at the moment was a chance the president might over rule her decision.

Chapter 34

EN ROUTE TO THE COMET.

While David had loaded the last of the supplies and topped off the water tank, Alex searched the base and found what he needed to anchor the devices to the comet. Alex pressed the button on the hangar wall to open the massive doors, then hurried into the spacecraft and closed the outside door to the airlock.

David was waiting in the cargo hold when Alex closed the outside airlock door. "We're all set. I asked Holly to let Jadin and Okawna know we're running late."

Alex looked over at the devices on their carts, which were now strapped to the floor. "Good idea. Let's go get them."

They headed up the stairs to the control room, but when they reached the living area, David stopped and pointed into the room. "Why did you have me secure Okawna's microwave to the countertop? We have an inertial dampening system."

"It's just a precaution."

David was about to ask why when Alex turned and headed up to the control room. He followed him up and continued past Alex, who was staring out the window, and sat behind the control console. He engaged the cloak, then eased the ship out of the hangar and gained altitude as they headed away from the base.

A few minutes later, they landed in the desert east of Pasadena, California, and Alex's heart raced when he saw Jadin alive and well. He ran down the stairs and opened the airlock doors, then ran over to greet her. He bent over and wrapped his arms around her shoulders, and held her tightly against his body. "You can't imagine how good it is to see you again."

Jadin put her arms around Alex's neck for a moment and then stepped back. "What are you talking about? I just saw you yesterday afternoon."

Alex grabbed her arm and guided her onto the ship. "It's a long story, but it will have to wait until we pick up Okawna."

Jadin slid her backpack from her shoulders to the floor in front of her locker. "Holly didn't go into any details. She just said it was urgent I meet you out here in the desert. The taxi driver thought I was crazy being dropped off out here in the middle of nowhere, which, by the way, was over an hour ago."

"I'm sorry about that. Holly was supposed to call you about our delay."

Jadin looked at the four devices on their carts, now secured by straps to the floor. "I didn't have phone reception out here. Anyway, where are we going?"

Alex grinned at her. "To hitch a ride on a comet. I'll tell you the rest once Okawna is on board."

Through the intercom, they heard David tell them they had arrived at their next destination, and Alex opened the airlock door and gave Okawna a warm hug. "It's good to see you, my friend."

Okawna looked over Alex's shoulder and gave Jadin a quizzical expression, but she just shrugged her shoulders at him, then when he stepped back, he saw the urgency in Alex's eyes. "Are you going to tell us what's so urgent? I had a date lined up for tonight."

Alex pressed the button to close the airlock and headed towards the stairs. "We don't have a lot of time, so I'll tell you on the way."

By the time Alex reached the control room, he saw the Earth getting smaller through the window and indicated the chairs to his friends while he stood in front of them and David. "I've been sent back in time again." He told them everything that had happened since he had left that morning for Colorado. "That's when David and I gathered everything we need to accomplish the mission and went to get you."

Okawna grinned at Alex. "How come you always get all the beautiful alien women?"

"Just my bad luck, I guess. We're on our own this time, and the odds of success are not in our favor."

Okawna chuckled. "They never are. So, what's your plan?"

Alex told them what needed to be done and looked at his watch. "It will take eight hours to reach the comet, leaving us only ten hours to attach the devices, and another six to get the comet into position."

Jadin's eyes went wide. "What are we supposed to do until we get there?"

Alex had shown David Melvin's mute button before he went to get the devices, and had an idea. "Melvin, are you in control of the stasis chambers?"

"Yes, Alex."

Okawna glanced at Jadin, and then stared at Alex. "Who was that?"

Alex grinned. "That's the name of the artificial intelligence running this ship."

Jadin closed her mouth. "It can speak?"

"Yes, and he's interactive to an exceptional degree. He runs everything on this ship." Alex saw both Jadin and Okawna's postures stiffen. "No, no, no, he's nothing like Pandora. In fact, he has a great personality. I spent a lot of time with Melvin before Paladin sent me back in time."

Okawna stared at him. "You named it Melvin? You couldn't think of a cooler name?"

"David is the one who named him."

Jadin got Alex's attention. "Hold on a minute. Did you say stasis chambers?"

"Yes, that's why the beds are so narrow." He looked up at the holographic monitor and expected to see David's image, but there was only data on the screen. "Melvin, can you put us into stasis until we reach the comet?"

"No, Alex. It would be too detrimental to your physiology. The minimum duration is three months."

Alex looked at his friends. "I guess we'll have to entertain ourselves."

Okawna got up from his chair to look at David. "Did you grab my box before you left?"

"Yes, I brought your digital move collection and popcorn."

Okawna smiled at his team. "We're all set."

***

EIGHT HOURS LATER:

Everyone stared out the window while Melvin approached the dark mass against the star-filled background. As they moved closer, they saw small geysers of white ice crystals erupting from the gray surface and Jadin was the first to notice some eruptions shutting down as that section on the comet moved into the shadow. "It's just as we thought. It's rotating. Now we need to calculate how much time we have to anchor the devices to the surface. We don't want to be exposed to the sun any longer than necessary. Melvin, can you determine the comet's gravity?"

"Yes, it is 1.522 m/s squared."

Jadin noticed her friend's questioning expressions. "It's almost the same as the gravity of our moon, so we'll be able to walk around.

Melvin, using the data we gave you for what we need to do, can you locate the optimal locations on the surface for us to anchor each device?"

"Yes, but they are approximately one hundred miles apart."

"All right. Calculate the time it will take to move from one location to another."

"Jadin, I understand what you are trying to determine. Each stop will have variables that will change at each location."

"Such as?"

"The time it will take to find an adequate spot once we land, how long to remove the device from inside the ship, how long it will take to anchor each device, and how long it will take for each of you to get back inside and decontaminate after each attempt."

Okawna was getting frustrated. "Oh, come on. Just give us a ballpark figure."

"Forty-four minutes at each location."

Alex knew anyone who steps outside and back in again would bring surface dust with them, which would contaminate the ship. "That's cutting it close. All right. To save time, only Okawna and I will leave the ship. Melvin, are you positive it will take six hours to move the comet into the correct alignment?"

"I would not state it unless I was certain."

"Good. Take us to the first location."

The surface appeared to zoom toward them, and then the ship slowed down as it moved into the dark side of the comet. An instant later, all motion stopped as the ship set down. Alex could not distinguish the rock from the ice, which was going to make his task much harder, so he turned to Jadin. "Is it supposed to look like coal dust?"

"Yes, it's the dust particles pulled from space by the comet's gravity. Unfortunately, there is no way of telling how deep it is until we go outside."

Okawna led the way down the stairs and over to the spacesuits, then glanced up at Jadin while he began putting on the inner suit with the liquid circulation system. "I know this works to keep us cool in the sun, but how about in the shade? Will they keep us warm as well?"

"Don't worry about the temperature. You may get a little cold, but if we spend too much time in the sun, the exposure to the radiation will kill us. Then there are the micro asteroids that could punch through our suits. We could be hit by a gamma-ray burst from the opposite direction, and also the possibility . . ."

"Okay. I get the point. I'm better off not knowing about all the horrible ways I can die in space. Let's just go have fun."

Knowing he had such great people to work with, Alex felt more confident about the success of the mission. "All right. Let's get started."

When Alex had his outer suit and helmet on, he checked the progress of his team. David was ready, as was Okawna, who was locking Jadin's helmet in place. "Let's do a radio check." His team all confirmed theirs were working, but he needed one more reply. "Melvin, how do you read?"

"Loud and clear, Alex."

"Great. We're ready down here. Remove the atmosphere."

Alex and his team moved over to the airlock, and then a moment later, the red light near the exit came on. He opened the doors and entered the small room, but stopped before stepping out onto the surface. Starlight illuminated the surreal landscape as he stared out across the vast expanse of dark gray hills and valleys.

Alex turned on the high-powered lights on either side of his helmet and then accepted one of the five-foot long fiberglass rods from David. He held it outside the ship and poked it down on the surface, feeling a solid thud an inch beneath the dust. When he stepped outside, dust blossomed into a swirling gray cloud filled with sparkling ice crystals around his shoes. He felt someone's hand on his shoulder and turned to look, and saw Okawna's grinning face behind the face shield. "What do you think?"

"Can you believe this is really happening, Alex?"

"I hear ya, buddy. I keep wondering if I'm still in stasis and this is all a bad dream."

Okawna gave Alex a friendly punch on his arm. "Well, let's get started, so it has a happy ending before you wake up."

Alex slowly moved forward, testing the surface in an arched pattern and occasionally glancing over at Okawna, who was testing the surface six-feet to his left. When he was thirty-feet away from the ship, he stopped and turned to Okawna. "Any problems on your side?"

"Yeah, a small gully, about two-feet across and ten-inches deep."

"My side is fairly level, so we'll roll the first device out to this area."

Alex walked back to the ship, where Jadin and David had moved one device partway into the airlock. "Roll the first one out to us."

Jadin and David shoved the cart further into the airlock, and with Okawna's help, Alex dragged it out of the ship. He watched the front tires sink half an inch into the dust as he pulled it out of the airlock, and once the rear wheels were on the surface away from Melvin's artificial gravity, it became lightweight and he had no problem dragging it by himself.

Okawna took the straps and anchor gun from David, then went over to join Alex. He tossed the ends of the straps across the bottom rails of the cart, placed the end of the gun against the end on his side, and then held it in place with both hands. When he pulled the trigger, he felt the explosion from the charge as the gun was nearly ripped from his hands, but the metal spike was through the strap into the rock.

A billowing cloud of dust blocked his vision for several long moments, and when it cleared, he did the same with the second strap, ready for what would happen. Once finished, he moved around to the other side and repeated the process, then looked at Alex. "That wasn't so hard. One down, three to go."

Alex led them back inside the airlock, where Jadin and David were smiling at them through the window of the closed inside door. "Melvin? How long did it take?"

"Thirty-two minutes, Alex."

Alex knew the other three might take longer, but at least they had a cushion for their time frame. "Let's just hope you can find similar locations for the other three."

When they stopped at the next location, Alex and Okawna stepped back outside. They had to wait while the airlock was purged of any contaminates before Jadin and David could open the inside door and roll the next device out onto the surface.

The second device went as smoothly as the first, but it took six attempts and wasted over an hour to find a smooth enough surface for the third device. It had also taken forty-eight minutes to attach it, because on several attempts, the anchors did not hold.

Jadin and David rolled the last device out to Alex and Okawna. Once it was clear of the ship, they closed the inside door and pressurized the cargo hold as they stared through the window.

Okawna knelt down and tossed the ends of the two straps over the rails to Alex, then shoved the end of the gun against the first anchor. When he pulled the trigger, the bolt ricocheted off some hard material and hit his leg, and then a warning buzzer sounded in his headset as he toppled onto his side, grimacing in pain, but gritted his teeth to keep from crying out. "I need a little help over here."

Alex hurried around the device and knelt beside his friend, then saw the crystalized red blotch on Okawna's leg. "You're injured and losing atmosphere." Alex grabbed the strap and wrapped it around the injury, cinching it tight to seal the tear in the suit. "Can you walk on it?"

Okawna reached out for Alex's hand. "Help me up and I'll find out." Okawna got up from the surface and wobbled for a second before gaining his balance. Having low gravity helped, and he kept one hand on Alex's shoulder as he put all his weight on the leg and gritted his teeth against the pain. "Yeah. I can make it back inside, but the bolt bounced off something really hard, so we need to find a different location."

Alex grabbed Okawna's arm and helped him back to the airlock. "We don't have enough time and you're losing air. While you decontaminate, I'll drag the device further away and try it again."

David was staring out at Okawna, hobbling back to the airlock. "I'm still in my suit, Alex. I'll come out and help you."

"No, that will take two decontamination cycles, and we can't afford to waste that much time. I can do it alone."

Okawna made it into the airlock and closed the door to start the cycle, then stared out the window at Alex, who was trying to drag the device away from the ship. Through his headset, he heard Alex grunting under the strain and realized that compared to the last three locations, this time it had been much more difficult to roll this device across this surface.

Alex had barely managed to drag the device two-feet further away from the ship, and knew he was wasting valuable time. "Melvin, why am I having so much difficulty?"

"This piece of the comet is a remnant from a supernova, which exploded approximately 4.7 billion years ago. It has sufficient gravity to hold this device in place."

Alex stopped pulling. "Why didn't you find a better location?"

"Because this is the only area that will work. The outside edge of this piece of material is fifty-three miles away, and that's not suitable for our needs."

Alex dropped the tow bar and headed back to the airlock, then saw the line between the shadow and sunlight on the surface of the comet quickly moving toward the ship. He knew Okawna's decontamination cycle would not be complete before he was exposed to the sun's radiation, but didn't mention it to his friends.

Okawna stared through the window at Alex as he waited for the ship's artificial gravity to pull all the dust particles from his suit. His brows bunched together in curiosity when he saw Alex close the gold-colored shield over his visor, then a moment later, both Alex and the device were bathed in brilliant sunlight.

Jadin watched Okawna wobble for a moment, indicating he was running out of air, and possibly blood. She had David remove her helmet before removing her suit. She then helped David remove his equipment before running back to the door. The airlock would not pressurize until all the contaminants had been removed, and it seemed to take forever. "Melvin, how much longer?"

"Twenty-three seconds to equalization."

Okawna felt light-headed and leaned back against the wall, and then slowly collapsed onto the floor. When Jadin watched him slide out of sight, she pressed her face against the window so she could see him, and when she looked up, she saw Alex's helmet through the window in the outside door. "I can't tell if he's still breathing."

Alex could not get his face close enough to look down at his friend, and slammed his fist against the window. "Don't you dare die on me again, Okawna! Do you hear me? Okawna!"

When Jadin heard Melvin tell her to proceed, she opened the inner door and knelt down to open the face shield on Okawna's helmet. His skin was pale blue, so she placed her fingers over his open mouth, and then leapt up and turned to David. "He's not breathing! Help me get him out of here!"

David moved to Jadin's side and helped her drag Okawna into the cargo hold, then he jabbed his finger against the button to close the door and knelt down to help remove Okawna's helmet. "He doesn't look good."

Jadin felt for a pulse on Okawna's neck, but it was weak, so she bent over and began breathing for him, then glared at David. "Don't just sit there! Start taking his suit off!"

David reached under Okawna's body and tried removing the life support system on the back of the suit, but the clips holding it in place seemed to be jammed. He grabbed the zipper and dragged it down to the crotch, then tried the clips for the life support system, but it remained stuck.

The outside airlock door opened and Alex hurried inside, closing it before rushing to the inside window and sliding his sun shield up to see how Okawna was doing. He saw Jadin breathing into Okawna's mouth and David struggling with the awkward support backpack.

David noticed the crimson stain growing larger on Okawna's leg and knew his friend could bleed to death before they got the suit off. He knew the suit was ruined anyway, so he jumped up to run to his locker, grabbing his pocketknife as he ran back. He knelt beside Okawna's leg and removed the strap Alex had tied around the tear, then tried cutting through the suit, but the blade barely sliced the outer layer.

Alex watched David sawing the knife blade across the suit. "It won't work. You'll need to roll him onto his side to get the support system off. Melvin, how much longer?"

"Three minutes, Alex."

Okawna's breath was suddenly forced into Jadin's mouth as he coughed, so she leaned back. When she looked at his face, the color was returning and she smiled and looked over at David. "He's breathing on his own. He's going to be okay."

Alex stared through the window as Jadin and David managed to get Okawna onto his side. When David released the clips, the support system fell off Okawna's suit, and he dragged it out of the way. When Jadin let Okawna roll onto his back, Alex could not see his face. "How's he doing?"

Jadin didn't reply as she listened to Okawna's breathing, and then looked up at Alex. "He's going to be okay."

David helped Jadin pull Okawna's suit off and saw blood oozing from the small wound in Okawna's leg. He pressed his palm against the spot, and the oozing stopped.

Okawna slowly opened his eyes and stared up at Jadin. "I dreamed you were kissing me."

"Only in your dreams, Okawna. How are you feeling?"

"My leg stings a little, but I'm fine."

Jadin got up and ran to one locker, yanked open the door, and grabbed an orange plastic case. She hurried back to David and knelt down beside him, then reached inside the first aid kit and handed him some surgical scissors. She brought out pads and gauze and then bound the quarter inch gouge in Okawna's leg.

Alex caught a flash of green light in his peripheral vision and opened the inner door. He took off his helmet as he stepped into the room and then stared down at Okawna. "How are you doing, buddy?"

Okawna still felt lightheaded, but managed to smile up at Alex. "Fine. Are you okay?"

"Yeah."

Okawna gave Alex a smirk. "I finally got Jadin to kiss me."

Jadin playfully slapped Okawna's hand. "That was saving your life, you idiot."

Inside the airlock, the vacuum cycle stopped and Alex removed his suit. "I guess we're ready to go. Melvin, how are we doing for time?"

"We are thirty-two minutes past our failsafe range. I'll be able to make up the difference, but I'll require several new power crystals along the way."

David looked up and saw Alex staring back with a questioning expression. "We only have twelve spares. That's all Holly could get for me without a lot of red tape and delaying our departure by another day."

"All right. Melvin, will that be enough?"

"Possibly. I'll know more after the first hour."

"Okay, let's get moving."

***

SIX HOURS LATER:

While Melvin maneuvered the comet into position, it was deathly quiet in the control room as Alex watched the Earth slowly vanishing behind the massive chunk of ice and rock. From his viewpoint, the devices looked like the tiny for spokes of a propeller on the edge of the comet.

Melvin's voice broke the silence. "We are in alignment."

"All right. Let's see if these things still work."

Jadin was standing next to a separate control console for the devices and tapped a glowing blue touchpad. When it turned red, she turned to see what would happen. All four devices appeared to be shimmering, and as each one rotated into the sunlight, the billowing clouds of gas bursting from the comet quickly froze, creating thick white wings rising from the surface. With each rotation, the wings slowly merged into an ever-expanding umbrella of ice around the comet.

A thought suddenly occurred to Alex. "Melvin, how are we doing with the power supply?"

"Getting the comet here drained the crystals much faster than I had expected."

Okawna was laid back in his chair with his injured leg propped on the control panel in front of him. "Okay, Mel. Will we have enough power to move the comet out of the way once this part is over?"

"It will be close, OK."

"Hey, I'm just asking a question. You don't need to get all snippety about it."

"What is snippety? You called me Mel, so I called you OK, for Okawna."

"That's too confusing. I won't abbreviate yours, and you don't abbreviate mine, all right?"

"Okay. That was my answer, not a joke."

Okawna turned to look at David. "Can you put him on mute?"

David grinned and shook his head no. "He's working and needs to keep us updated. Maybe once the mission is over."

When Okawna turned back to the view, David stopped grinning and stared at the expanding umbrella of ice. He suddenly realized they had no way of knowing if it worked. If Alex was correct about a pandemic, they would know in a few days.

***

GROOM LAKE:

Holly grabbed the remote control for her television and sat back in her chair. She was worried about Alex's plan, since he never mentioned the comet could still hit the Earth, but on the screen was the image of a news announcer, with a comet in the background. She knew the change in the comet's trajectory was already baffling every scientist on the planet, and now it had settled onto a course that would smash into the Earth at a nearly perpendicular angle.

She turned up the volume when the picture behind the announcer changed, showing a simulated trajectory of the comet and the shock wave spreading across the planet. The picture changed, showing glimpses of groups of people praying in the streets, then the images changed again, showing scenes of chaos at various locations around the world.

***

THE COMET. TWENTY-NINE HOURS LATER:

David was watching the diminishing numbers as the power was quickly being drained from the last of their crystals. For the past two hours, they had been trying to drag the comet onto a new course so it would miss the Earth, but it wasn't working. According to Melvin, the comet was in a tug of war with the Earth, the moon, and the planet

Venus, and the combined gravitational pull was making it extremely difficult to change the comet's trajectory.

As one of the two remaining crystals turned black, David replaced it with his last fully charged one. "That's it. If the power consumption stays the same, we'll smash into the planet with the comet."

Alex had an idea. "Melvin, could we move the comet if we had four new crystals?"

"It would be close, but yes, I could do it."

"How much time do we have before it's too late to make a difference?"

"Sixty-three minutes."

"How long will it take to get us back to Earth so we can get some new ones?"

"Eighteen minutes each way."

"That leaves us twenty-seven minutes to get the crystals. All right. This isn't working, anyway, so take us home."

Chapter 35

GROOM LAKE:

It was near noon as the ship set down on the tarmac outside Hangar 5 and Holly had promised to meet him inside the hangar with the new crystals. Alex turned from the view and looked at his friends. "This shouldn't take more than a few minutes. I'll be right back."

He hurried down the stairs and into the airlock, then when he stepped outside, the heat was like a slap in the face. He jogged toward the side of the hangar and yanked the door open, then ran inside, but abruptly stopped. In front of him were four men wearing SWAT gear, and one man dressed in a suit and tie. When two members of the SWAT team ran past him and out through the doorway, Alex stared at the man in the suit. "What's going on? Where's Holly Blake?"

***

Okawna was standing near the inside wall with Jadin and David, watching Alex entering the building, but his posture stiffened when two men in SWAT gear ran out from the same door. "Melvin, cloak the ship and hover at thirty-feet above the hangar." He watched the men stop running and look around. "There's some kind of shit going on down there. Melvin, connect me with Holly so I can find out what's going on. Put it on speaker."

***

Holly stared at the flashing button on her phone console and then looked up at the female Secret Service agent sitting on the other side of her desk. A moment later, the flashing button went dark. "Listen, agent Yen. You need to let my people do their job and stop the comet from hitting us."

"That's not my call, Miss Blake. Hold on a minute." She looked away and touched a button on her wrist device. When a text message appeared on the tiny screen, she turned to look down at Holly. "Your people have stolen the ship. The guards said it disappeared."

Holly leaned back in her chair and grinned. When the agents had entered her office, she had slid the four new crystals into her pants pockets. Now all she had to do was contact Alex and arrange a location to meet him.

Yen tapped OK in the reply and stared at Holly. "We captured one of your team members. His name is Alex Cave."

Holly's stomach tightened into a knot. "I suppose you plan on using him as leverage to get the ship back."

"That's right. The President will be arriving in thirty minutes, and my boss isn't very tactful when he wants something for our Commander-in-Chief. Get up. We're going to the hangar where they're keeping your friend."

Holly stood and went out through the doorway with Yen a step behind her. If it were under different circumstances, she knew she could take away Yen's weapon and go rescue Alex. Unfortunately, there were two more Secret Service agents waiting in the hallway to accompany them to the hangar, and knew she would just have to wait and see how things progressed.

***

HANGAR 5:
When the suited man suddenly ran to the window in the large hangar door, Alex pretended to scratch his ear as he removed his earbud and cupped it in his hand. He could not take the chance they would take it from him. He waited until the man came back and stopped in front of him and then stared him in the eyes. "Who the hell are you?"

"I'm Secret Service Deputy Director Brickner, and I'm here on behalf of the President. He, three of his staff members, and his wife and daughter will be arriving in thirty minutes, and you and your team will take them off this planet in your spaceship. Now get it back here."

Alex straightened his shoulders and glared at Brickner. "I don't have time for this. Let me get what I need and I can stop the comet from hitting us."

"We know all about your heroic effort to stop this from happening, but it didn't work, did it? I don't trust you, Mister Cave. You'll do as ordered by your Commander In Chief."

"I don't give a damn about your orders! Don't you understand? Let me complete my mission or the comet *will* hit us."

"I'm under orders. You'll do as you're told or I'll have you arrested."

"Let me speak with Blake about this, damn it!"

Brickner grew frustrated with Cave's defiance. He reached inside his coat and brought out his 38. Caliber pistol, aiming it at Cave's head.

Alex was not about to be intimidated. When Brickner aimed it at his forehead, Alex crossed his arms and glared back at him.

Brickner clinched his teeth together and lowered the gun. "Get that ship back to this hangar or I'll hurt your new boss. They're bringing her here as we speak. You can wait for her in the break room."

***

SPACESHIP:

Okawna pointed down at a black SUV stopping on the other side of the hangar. "That's not one of ours." He recognized the woman climbing out from the back seat. "That's Holly. Maybe she's going inside to talk to Alex."

Jadin studied the people entering the hangar. "Maybe. Those two guys getting out of the car look like they're taking orders from the woman in the suit and tie. I bet she's a Federal Agent." She noticed Holly acting strange. "She's acting as if she's under arrest. See the way she keeps looking up at the sky? Maybe she knows we're watching, and she's giving us a clue what's going on."

David pointed out the window. "Did you see that? She just looked up and shook her head no, as if she doesn't want us to come to her rescue."

Okawna turned to David. "Are you sure?"

"Absolutely. She wants us to stand by."

Jadin had also seen the movement. "I think David is correct. We can't match that much firepower."

Okawna heaved a deep sigh of resignation. "Yeah, I know. Melvin, how much time do we have to get the crystals and leave?"

"Twelve minutes."

Okawna slammed his fist against the transparent barrier. "Damn! Wait until I get my hands on whoever is responsible for stopping us. They'll wish they had never pissed me off."

***

BREAK ROOM:

Alex paced back and forth behind a table, occasionally glancing at the two men in SWAT gear standing just inside the doorway. He looked at his wristwatch and the minute hand seemed to be racing across the dial. He was about to miss his deadline, but still held out hope he could move the comet if he could just get out of here. He stopped pacing when Holly stepped into the room. "We can still fix this. You have to let us go."

Holly sat down at the table. "I tried everything I could think of and called in as many favors as I could to stop this from happening. You must believe me."

Alex sat down across from her. "I do, Holly. I'm frustrated, is all. What did Donner have to say about it?"

"He tried to convince the President taking your ship was a major mistake, but the President's advisors convinced him it was his only option. You know how it is with most new presidents. They're a rookie, so they depend on their advisors to keep them out of trouble."

Alex realized his battle was lost and slumped down into his chair. He couldn't believe after everything he had already been through, he was going to lose his family and friends again. "Those sniveling advisors of his just want to save their own butts. I'm not taking them anywhere. They can die like the rest of us."

***

SPACESHIP:

Okawna caught a flash of white in his peripheral vision and turned to see what had caused it. "We have company."

The trio watched the unmarked white passenger jet taxi to the front of Hangar 5 and stop. The side door opened, and two men dressed in suits looked around for a moment before walking down the stairs to join a man at the bottom.

When Okawna recognized the next man who stepped out from the plane, his hands clenched into fists at his sides. "Damn! It's President Autry. I bet he wants to take our ship to save his own butt."

Jadin also recognized the next person to step out as the President's chief of Staff, Helen Rathbone, followed by two more people she didn't recognize, then the President's wife and daughter. The Secret Service agents led everyone into the hangar, with one man remaining outside. "I wonder if the President realizes what he's done."

Okawna continued to stare out the side of the ship. "I'm sure Alex will get in his face about it."

David looked up at Okawna. "I wish I could be there to see it. Alex must have removed his ear bud, so I guess he'll contact us when he can."

***

BREAK ROOM:

Alex stared at Brickner when he suddenly walked into the room with President Autry and his Chief of Staff right behind him. At this moment, he couldn't care less about showing fake respect to the leader of our country, and remained seated with his arms across his chest.

When Alex didn't stand up at attention, Brickner's jaw clenched shut for a moment, and then he leaned across the table and glared at him. "Get your butt out of that chair for the President!"

Alex just stared at him. "Or what? Are you going to arrest me? Go ahead. It won't be the first time."

The President stepped forward and put his hand on Brickner's shoulder. "That's okay, Ellis. I understand I'm asking a lot of these people."

When Brickner straightened up and stepped back, Alex slowly stood and looked the President in the eyes. "Do you realize what you've done? I could have stopped this from happening if you would have let me do my job."

The President turned to look at Rathbone, giving her a scathing stare for a moment before turning back to Alex. "I was told there was no chance you could stop the comet from hitting us."

"Why didn't you trust Director Donner when he told you about me and my team?"

"As you know, I'm new to this job and I'm still learning who I can trust. My experts tell me not everyone will die."

"Not right away, but life as you know it will be over. When the comet hits, not only will the shock wave destroy everything in its path, volcanoes around the world will erupt and the sun's rays will be blocked by a blanket of dust and ash for a long time. Nothing will grow naturally, and the acid rain will poison the streams. Those who survive will kill each other over food and clean water, and won't give a damn about anyone's status, including you."

"I know, and that's why I want to leave in your spaceship."

Alex could not believe the audacity of the President. "And go where? You'll still end up having to come back here, anyway."

"From what I've been told, there are other worlds with people living on them. You can take me to one of those."

"I have no idea where they are, and even if I did, I wouldn't take you or your cronies. I don't want my species to be represented by a bunch of cowards."

Brickner had enough of Cave's insolence and put his face close to Alex's. "You're talking to your Commander In Chief and I demand you show him some respect!"

Alex moved his face an inch closer to Brickner's. "Back off!"

When neither man backed down, the President grabbed Brickner's shoulder and eased him away from Alex. "I apologize for Ellis's behavior, Mister Cave. He can get a little overzealous."

Alex sat down and looked up at the President. "Leaving in my ship now won't make any difference. After that comet hits, there are going to be a lot of scared and desperate people needing help from FEMA and other government agencies. You should get back on Air Force One and do your job, Mister President."

The President gave Alex a solemn nod of agreement. "For what it's worth, I'm sorry, Mister Cave."

"Save your apologies for the people, Mister President. We're done here. Let us go so we can be with our loved ones while there's still time."

"Of course. You're free to go."

Holly remained behind when the President and his people left the room. "If you like, you can use the ship to take all of you to your families."

"What about you? Don't you want to see your family before it's too late?"

"My parents are dead and I'm an only child. I don't have anyone to say goodbye to, so for what it's worth, I'll stay here and make sure everything is secured."

"You're welcome to come with us."

"I appreciate your offer, but I'll stay here."

"I'll let my team know what happened. I'm sure they will appreciate you letting us use the ship to go home."

"Then I guess this is goodbye."

"Just so you know, it's been a pleasure working with you, Holly. Good luck." He looked past Holly when he saw a familiar face in the doorway. "Hello, Vesta. It almost worked."

Vesta stepped into the room and over to the table. "Yes, it did. I would never have thought the first part was possible."

"Yeah, well, I lost anyway, didn't I?"

"That's where you're wrong, Alex. I could not let your valiant effort be wasted, so my ship is trying to move the comet, but it's not changing fast enough. Even with both our ships, it might be too late to move the comet onto a new trajectory to miss the planet."

Alex leapt out of his chair and stared at Holly. "I need more crystals."

Holly stood and reached into her pockets. "Here are four new ones."

Alex smiled and inserted his ear bud. "Come and get me. We have a mission to finish."

Alex hurried out of the break room and down the hall, with Vesta and Holly close behind him, then stopped while Vesta stepped into her transport ship. "What's the plan?"

"I'm already pushing, so you pull. I'll talk to you from my spaceship."

Alex held out his hand to Vesta and realized it was the first time since they had met. "All right. Thanks for helping us."

Vesta stared at Alex's open hand for a moment with the realization he finally trusted her, then she grabbed it. "Let's just hope this works. I'll meet you up there."

While Alex ran to the side door, Holly smiled at Vesta. "Good luck."

"Thanks."

When Vesta's ship vanished, Holly hurried to the window in the hangar door and saw Alex entering the airlock of his ship, and then the spacecraft disappeared. She turned and headed back along the hallway, hoping there would be some kind of vehicle she could use to get back to her office. She stepped outside and saw a golf cart and climbed in, then stomped the foot pedal to the floor. She could only hope one of the news stations was still broadcasting.

***

SPACECRAFT:

When Alex stepped into the control room, his friends waited to find out what was going on. "Vesta is trying to move the comet, but she needs our help." He reached into his pocket and handed David the new crystals. "These are from Holly."

While David inserted the new power supplies, Alex explained what had happened in the cafeteria. "Now we need to drag the comet again."

Vesta's voice came through the intercom. "I'm here, Alex. I gave Melvin the information on which direction he should pull. He's just waiting for your command."

"Melvin, are you ready?"

"I am, Alex. Let's do this."

Alex stared out the window as the base appeared to shrink below him. It only took a few moments to reach the comet, and he realized how much closer it was to Earth. The ship stopped at one-hundred-feet from the rotating surface, but he could still see the planet through the window, which appeared to be growing at an incredible rate.

For no necessary reason, Alex looked at the holographic monitor. "Melvin, are we moving the comet?"

"Just barely, Alex. The gravity from the Earth, the moon, and Venus are pulling in the wrong direction. I don't think it will be far enough and it will still graze the planet."

Alex suddenly had an idea. "David, shut down the devices. Maybe the umbrella will break away and make the comet smaller."

David ran over to the other control console. "I can do better than that. They can also create a lot of heat. Watch this."

A few moments later, Alex watched the ice umbrella fracture into four pieces and drift away, leaving the four devices on the surface. He turned back to the view of the Earth, which still filled his field of vision. The edge of the planet slowly came into view, and then the entire world rushed past his ship. He spun around to his friends as he held one fist in the air. "Yes! Well done, everybody. Good job, Melvin. Vesta? Are you still with us?"

"I'm here, Alex. I still find it difficult to believe your plan actually worked. Congratulations."

"Well, it all would have been for nothing if you hadn't helped at the last minute."

"My help would not have mattered if you had not gotten rid of the ice. That was a brilliant idea."

Okawna was a little jealous Alex always got the hot alien women. "Hey, Vesta. Are you going to stick around and celebrate with us?"

"I'm afraid not, Okawna. I've already affected the time line by helping you. I have another race of humans to save from the radiation, and they don't have an unknown factor like Mister Cave. Alex? Perhaps someday you and your team can return the favor by helping me with a serious situation."

"Any time. No pun intended. Could you do me one last favor? Tell Paladin it all worked out for us?"

"I will, and it was interesting meeting all of you. Good bye, crew of the Melvin."

Alex strolled over and plopped down on one of the chairs. "I've had enough excitement to last me a while. Melvin, take us home."

***

GROOM LAKE, NEVADA. HANGAR 5:

After receiving a message from Alex they were coming home, Holly had returned to the hangar and opened the massive doors. Now she was standing to one side, waiting for the ship to arrive. It was still daylight, so the ship would be cloaked, and she would not know if it was inside until it appeared. As if by magic, she suddenly saw her reflection in the mirrored surface. The airlock door opened, and she strolled over as Alex stepped out. On impulse, she reached up and wrapped her arms around his neck as he bent over, then gave him a warm hug. "You did it."

Alex patted her on the back, then let go and stood up straight. "Was it on the news?"

"Yes. One station in Las Vegas stayed on the air and reported the comet broke up in the atmosphere, and didn't cause any damage."

Jadin had moved next to Alex. "It wasn't the comet, just massive chunks of ice that broke off from the surface. The comet is on its way out of the solar system. If there is anyone still working at JPL, they're probably tracking it right now."

Okawna hobbled out of the airlock. "Hey, Holly. Do you have a golf cart nearby?"

"Yes, it's parked out front. What happened to your leg?"

"I shot myself, but it's a long story. Right now, I just need a ride home so I can get a decent meal and a real bed to lie down on."

David joined the group. "If the jet is still available, I'd like to go home and see my parents."

Jadin smiled at the thought she had helped save her family. "So would I."

Alex smiled at his friends. "After what I've been through over the past few weeks, a trip home would be nice."

Holly indicated the hallway leading out of the hangar. "All right. Take the next two weeks off. I'll call you sooner if I need you to save us again. By the way, Alex. What happened to Vesta?"

"She left to save another race of humans. I don't think we'll see her again."

Holly smirked at him. "What about Mya? Do you plan to see her again?"

An image of Mya lying naked on the chair outside the hangar appeared in Alex's mind, and then he looked over at Jadin. "I don't think so. I want to spend a few days with my family and apologize to my nephew. After that, I'm thinking of taking a trip to Humpback Harbor, Oregon."

Jadin's lips parted in surprise. "Yeah, sure. Just let me know when and I'll show you around." She headed for the exit and smiled to herself, wondering what had suddenly gotten into him, and then decided it didn't matter. Perhaps he was getting over thinking of her as just a member of his team.

The end.

Movie script available from the author.

I hope you enjoyed DNA and I'd appreciate it if you would take a moment to write a short review.
Thank you.
James M. Corkill

Here is a preview of the next exciting Alex Cave Adventure.

PARALLEL
The Alex Cave Series book 7

Chapter 1

GROOM LAKE, NEVADA:
The special jet stopped in front of the security checkpoint, and Alex looked out the window as an unmarked vehicle drove up and stopped next to the plane. A knot formed in his stomach as he released his seatbelt and stood to grab his backpack, but the attendant indicated for him to leave it on the plane, and then she opened the exit door and lowered the stairs. He slowly descended the steps and stopped in front of two armed men dressed in suits and ties. "What's going on?"

"I'm Secret Service Agent Garcia, and we have orders to escort you to Director Blake's office. Get in, please."

Alex did as instructed and climbed into the back seat, and they drove past the security check terminal. They stopped in front of the admin building, and everyone climbed out, then Alex led the way inside and down the hallway to Holly's office. The door was open, so he stepped into the room, noticing the two agents remained in the hallway. He saw Holly sitting in a chair behind her desk, and a tall, masculine looking woman dressed in a US Air Force Captain's uniform standing beside her. His heart raced when he saw Jadin Avery standing to one side of the room. She was part of his team, and he hoped she was not in trouble as he turned to Holly. "What's going on, Director?"

"This is Captain Sharon Fargo. It seems our new President wants the military to take over operation of your spacecraft, and she's in charge of the first training program."

Alex stared at Fargo. "That ship belongs to me, and the government can't just take it."

Fargo moved around the desk and locked stares with Alex, looking down slightly because of her height. "It's done. Live with it."

Alex's hands clenched into fists as he turned to look at Holly. "You can't let them get away with this." The look in Holly's eyes told him she had no choice, so he turned back to Fargo. "On whose authority?"

Fargo grabbed a folder on the desk and held it out to Alex. "This is from the Attorney General, granting me the authority to claim the ship under the law of Eminent Domain. Meaning, if it's for the good of the country, the government can take your spaceship."

Alex didn't take the folder and stared up into Fargo's eyes. "Over my dead body!"

"I hope it doesn't come to that, Mister Cave."

"What about my team?"

"Since Jadin officially works for NASA, she will teach us how to operate the spacecraft. I'm sure we can get by without you, so I revoke your security clearance and my people will escort you back to the plane. Your belongings in your apartment will be shipped to your designated location."

Jadin saw the rage in Alex's expression and his clenched fists, and wanted him to shut up before he got into more trouble, so she grabbed Fargo's arm to get her attention away from him. "I think I can work with you on this, Captain Fargo. How about I start the training on Monday morning? That gives me three days to shut down my research project at the Jet Propulsion Laboratory in Pasadena."

Fargo tossed the folder onto the desk. "That's fine."

When Jadin saw Fargo indicate for her men to get Alex back to the jet, she reached up to wrap her arms around his neck, pulling him close for a hug. "Call me later, okay?"

Alex put his cheek against hers so he could whisper into her ear. "This isn't over."

Jadin noticed Fargo staring at them and slowly raised her hands up to Alex's face. She cupped them over his ears to pull him close, covertly inserting a communication device into his right ear. "I have an idea, so don't do anything rash. I'll explain later."

When Jadin gave him a soft kiss on his lips and stepped back, Alex reached across the desk to shake Holly's hand. "It's been nice working with you, Director."

Holly didn't accept, and walked around the desk to give him a hug. When he bent down, she turned to him so Fargo could not see her face, and whispered in his ear. "I'll keep you updated on what happens here."

"Don't get in trouble over me."

Holly let go and stepped back. "Stay safe."

Fargo saw the moisture building up in Jadin's eyes. "Am I going to have any problems with you, Ms. Avery?"

Jadin wanted to tell her where to shove her problems, but her self-restraint won. "No, Captain. I'll meet with your astronauts at Hangar 5 first thing Monday morning."

Fargo indicated the doorway to Alex. "After you, Mister Cave."

Alex reluctantly left with the two men for the flight back to Las Vegas. "I'll miss both of you."

Jadin stepped into the hallway and stared after Alex, finding it hard to believe he was leaving for good. She felt Fargo's hand on her shoulder and moved back into the room, then folded her arms across her chest and stared at the Captain. "What about David? He can help."

"Mister Conway no longer works here and left four days ago."

Jadin's jaw hung open as her arms dropped to her sides. "That's ridiculous. He's the only person who knows how the engine works and needs to be here, too."

Holly locked stares with Fargo. "She's correct. If you have any problems, you'll need his help."

"Don't worry. I'll call him in as an advisor if necessary. I'll expect daily reports on the program's progress, Ms. Blake." She spun around and headed out of the room toward the exit.

Jadin gave Holly a troubled expression. "I don't think this will work. Even if I show Fargo's people how to use the ship, Melvin, the ship's AI, won't follow their commands."

"Will he follow yours?"

Jadin thought about it for a moment. "I have no idea."

Holly moved around the desk to sit in her chair. "I'm worried about David. Fargo was less than subtle when she fired him, and he took it hard, and I haven't been able to contact him since he left the base."

"I'll try to locate him."

"All right. When will you leave for JPL?"

Jadin suddenly realized she could ride with Alex to Las Vegas. "Right now. I don't need to pack anything, so I'll ride with Alex. I'd better hurry, so I'll see you on Sunday afternoon."

"Wait a minute. I know how you feel about Alex, but you need to let him go. At least for now. Fargo will be on that flight and we don't want her thinking there is a conspiracy between you two. The plane will be back in an hour, so take care of things here before you leave."

Jadin realized Holly was correct. "All right. What do you know about my feelings for Alex?"

"That he thinks you two can't be lovers and work together."

"Is it that obvious?"

"To me, yes, but I can't speak for anyone else."

"At least that won't be a problem anymore. I'll start packing Alex's personal items in his room while I wait. I'll see you when I get back."

Holly leaned back in her chair and stared after Jadin. "This should get interesting."

Award-winning author James M. Corkill is a Veteran, and retired Federal Firefighter from Washington State, USA. He was an electronic technician and studied mechanical engineering in his spare time before eventually becoming a firefighter for 32-years and retiring. He has since settled into the Smokey Mountains of western North Carolina and has a fantastic view from his writing desk.

He began writing in 1997, and was fortunate to meet a famous horror writer named Hugh B. Cave, who became his mentor. In 2002, he rushed to self-published a dozen copies of Dead Energy so his wife could see his book published before she was taken by cancer. When his soul mate was gone, he stopped writing and began drinking heavily.

His favorite quote. "When you wake up in the morning, you never know where the day will take you."

In 2013, he met a stranger who recognized his name and had enjoyed an old copy of Dead Energy, except for the ending. When she encouraged him to start writing again, he realized this chance meeting was just what he needed to hear at the right moment. He quit drinking and began the rewrite of Dead Energy into The Alex Cave Series, and thankful for that fateful encounter.

Other books by James M. Corkill
Dead Energy. The Alex Cave Series Book 1.
Cold Energy. The Alex Cave Series Book 2.
Red Energy. The Alex Cave Series Book 3.
Gravity. The Alex Cave Series Book 4.
Pandora's Eyes. The Alex Cave Series Book 5.
Parallel. The Alex Cave Series Book 7.
Impact Yellowstone

Movie scripts available from the author.
You can contact him at. Jamesmcorkill@gmail.com

 www.ingramcontent.com/pod-product-compliance
Lightning Source LLC
Chambersburg PA
CBHW071524110726
47908CB00003B/944